TO CROWN A KING

ALSO BY RAEDENE JEANNETTE MELIN

Las Hermanas

TO CROWN A KING

RAEDENE JEANNETTE MELIN

SKJALDMAER PUBLISHING

Illustrations by Joel Feenstra

ISBN 978-1-9992532-0-2 (Paperback)
ISBN 978-1-9992532-2-6 (Hardcover)
ISBN 978-1-9992532-1-9 (eBook)

Our books may be purchased in bulk for promotional, educational, or business use. For information, please email Skjaldmaer Publishing at info@skjaldmaer.ca.

www.skjaldmaer.ca

———————

*"One life is all we have and we live it as
we believe in living it. But to sacrifice what
you are and to live without belief, that
is a fate more terrible than dying."*

—Joan of Arc

TO CROWN A KING

LOCHMABEN CASTLE

CHAPTER ONE

PALM PRESSED AGAINST cold earth, winter's lingering hold numbed Christina's fingers. Out in the field, far from the shelter of the trees, blustery winds swelled around her as she waited – hoped – for warmth in the dirt beneath her skin. But she felt nothing. The land was frozen. Winter was not finished with them yet.

"Another fortnight, at least."

Christina glanced up at the man beside her. Short in stature, his grey hair curled as it came to rest against his shoulders. In service to her father and her grandfather before him, his stooped frame was as familiar as the ground she crouched upon now, never one without the other. Watching his sharp eyes roam the sky, as if appealing to the billowing clouds for leniency, she pulled her hand back under the snug comfort of her cloak and stood.

A sudden gale threw off her hood. Strands of auburn hair swept across her face. Brushing them aside, she spotted the men waiting for her at the edge of the clearing.

The daughter of a nobleman, she was never alone. Watchful eyes followed her every move. Most days, at least one brother hovered nearby, but this time was different. Her grandfather had sent her and her alone to check on the land. No one else was there to tell her what she could and could not do. Turning away from the lingering men, she walked farther into the field.

Flat and fertile, the land of Annan extended a few miles south to the Firth of Solway, the channel of water that began the western border between the land of the Scots and the Kingdom of England. Annandale belonged to her father. He ruled as lord. By now, the fields should have been ploughed and the seeds prepared for sowing. But spring's warmth had not come. Ever since the death of her mother, the soil seemed reluctant to begin anew.

Reaching the edge of the clearing, Christina glanced behind her. The men in the field remained where they were. No one moved to follow. Lifting the hem of her cloak, she headed towards the river.

Thickets of pine swayed gently overhead as she passed through the trees. Sheltered from the open air, the wind no longer filled her ears or felt sharp against her face. She strolled, enjoying the sound of leaves rustling around her as she wandered past fallen logs and prickly shrubs. Light streamed through an opening up ahead. She heard the river in the distance. Reaching out to touch the blue-green needles protruding from the branch, she emerged from cover and approached the water.

The River Annan carved through the Scottish Lowlands, its wide girth twisting back and forth over the landscape before emptying into the Irish Sea. Christina had played along the muddy, grass-filled shore often as a child. Choosing her path carefully, she stepped across the bank. Frost-covered tussocks sagged beneath her weight. Crouching at the edge, she dangled her fingers into the channel. The water felt cold against her skin. She watched the current flow steadily past for a few moments and then glanced up. Darkened clouds met her gaze. She would be expected in the village before night fell. Taking a drink, she stood and shook the water from her hand. She turned to find a man staring at her from inside the trees.

Her feet stilling, she watched with guarded apprehension as he took a step towards her. He looked like a farmer, his clothes filthy and worn, but he was not of Annandale. She did not know him. Catching sight of the long knife looped in his belt, her concern increased as he came closer. She waited for him to explain his presence but he offered her none. Looking upon her with an unabashed smirk, he stopped an arm's length away. She was trapped between him and the river. Her stomach twisting in knots, Christina opened her mouth to shout.

A hand slammed down over her lips before she could make a sound. It felt like she had been slapped, the man's grip on her face tight and unrelenting. She tasted blood. The sharp stench of him filled her nostrils. With her heart pounding in her ears, she struggled against the arms that held her in place. She reached down for the knife hidden inside her cloak. Fingertips straining, sudden relief washed away her fear as her palm wrapped around the carved, wooden handle. She did not hesitate to wrench the blade from its sheath. Turning it upwards, she drove the knife into his throat.

His arms fell down and away. Dropping to his knees, he clutched at the hilt beneath his jaw, failing to pull the steel out. Blood trickled from his mouth as he choked. Reaching forward, he grabbed the skirt of her dress. Christina pushed his hand off. Desperation looked up at her before he stilled and toppled into the mud.

Her breath felt ragged against her throat as she looked at the body before her. His eyes were open, but there was no life left. Kneeling before him, she pulled the knife from the man's neck, the handle slick and warm. The ground around him grew dark. Red hues crept like pointed fingers through the soggy grass towards her. Wiping the blood off the blade, her hands trembling, she tucked the knife back into her cloak.

Bewilderment kept her there. She tried to make sense of what had happened, but could not. He should not have been watching her in the woods. He should not have grabbed her that way. Her gaze unable to leave the lifeless form, she knew, in the end, it would not matter. She had wandered off alone, unprotected, and now a man was dead. Her father would not care if her actions were justified. Consequences would follow.

She shoved the man's shoulder in frustration. He flopped over onto his back. She thought about dragging him into the river but quickly abandoned the idea. He was a head taller than her and twice as wide. She would never move him on her own.

Bracing herself to stand back up, her eyes fell once more to the knife at his side. It looked well-made, as if a blacksmith had taken his time to properly shape and balance the steel. An intricate design adorned the top of the handle. The longer she stared at it, the more it seemed out of place. Like him sneaking up behind her, it did not make sense. Before she could convince herself not to, she leaned forward and ripped open his cloak.

Hands urgently running through the fabric, Christina searched the man's clothes. Besides a small bag of coin, his coat was empty, as was his tunic. Pushing her arm down his undershirt, her fingers grazed curly, moist chest hair. She gagged. But the moment she touched parchment, she forgot about the bile in her throat.

Clumsy fingers unrolled the small piece of paper. She shivered, suddenly cold. The note trembled in her hands as her eyes fell over the faded marks. She read it in its entirety and then went over it again. The man in the mud before her was not just out of place. He was a spy, collecting information on the castles along the border. He was English, and he was dead on Scottish soil.

Sliding the note up her sleeve, Christina pushed herself to her feet. She could not leave him there now. Tensions between King Edward of England and John, King of Scots, were already at a breaking point. Ten years earlier, the two kingdoms had been close, family and decades of friendship uniting them. But now King John refused to send Scottish knights to fight in England's war against the French and English soldiers were being slaughtered in the Lowlands. No, the news of another Englishman's death would not bode well for Scotland or Annandale. Thinking of how her family would be the ones charged with finding the person responsible, Christina grabbed the dead man's hands and pulled him towards the river.

He did not budge. Mud sucking him down, the Englishman remained firmly planted in the grass. Dark skies indicated someone would come looking for her soon. Desperately searching the shore, she spotted a large branch a few feet downriver. She hurried towards it. Sludge clung to her feet as she carried the log over to the body. Jabbing the branch beneath his torso, she brushed a lock of hair away from her face before placing her hands on the other end of the stick. Movement near the bushes made her pause. She scanned the treeline. Her heart sank when Christopher Seton emerged from cover.

He hesitated. Like a hunter, his eyes cautiously examined

the riverbank before he stepped forward, his feet silent despite the solid frame they carried. His gaze dropped to the Englishman in the reeds. Concern creased his brow. It disappeared just as quickly. He stopped beside her.

Christina waited for him to speak. The scent of oak and earth drifted towards her. She felt conflicted by his presence. Loyal to her house, he had been sent with the other men to accompany her to Annan. His family had served hers for generations. Whether in England or Scotland, crusading to the Holy Land or battling Norwegian invaders, the men in his family always stood next to hers. Close in age, he had been raised under the guidance of her grandfather at Lochmaben Castle alongside her brothers. Christina had known him for most of her life, but he was a still a stranger. He would help her now – of that there was no doubt – but it was who he would tell after that concerned her most.

"Are you hurt?" he asked.

Like a perfectly sharpened knife, his voice cut through the thick, murky bog of despair that pulled her under. She shook her head.

An unreadable expression stared back at her, his green eyes obscure. His gaze dropped to the log in her hands. Christina glanced down.

Her cloak was smeared with mud and her arms were caked. The hem of her dress was filthy, no longer blue. Looking back up, she explained. "He's English."

His jaw clenching told her he understood. Seton looked away for a moment before he reached out and took the branch from her hands. Christina moved back.

Seton levered the body out of the mud. Tossing the stick aside, he grabbed the man's ankles and pulled him towards the river. The corpse had stiffened, creating lines in the grass as it went. A large, blackened divot marked where the dead man used to lay.

Watching Seton push the body out into the water, Christina shivered. She tightened her cloak around her. If she was lucky, the man would float the short distance to the sea unhindered. If she was not, her crime would be discovered and someone would be held responsible. Either way, there was nothing she could do about it now. The only problem she needed to be concerned about was the tall figure walking towards her. Not waiting for Seton to tell her to go, she turned and set out for the village.

Night had descended, the last remnants of daylight melting away. She could see the burgh in the distance as they strode through the fields. A dark fortress loomed in the woods up ahead.

Perched on a mound of earth along the river, Annan Castle towered above the landscape. It had been built more than a hundred years ago by her ancestor, the first Lord of Annandale, to guard the road north and rule over the land. But their residence there was short-lived. Only twenty years later, the fortress was abandoned for good. A curse had been cast upon their kindred. Despite her grandfather's acts of penance, it haunted them still.

She shuddered unwillingly, the movement wracking her torso and making her muscles clench in pain. They were not far from the tavern. She could almost see it. Thinking of the warm, soft bed waiting for her inside, she increased her pace. She stepped from the trees. Seton's voice stopped her.

"Wait."

Reluctantly, she turned.

Untying the strings around his neck, Seton handed her his cloak. She looked at him in confusion. He explained. "You are covered in blood."

Glancing down, she saw nothing. Running her hand lightly against the front of her cloak, the wool crusty and hard, she noticed the discoloured stains splattered across the dress she wore underneath. She took the cloak from his hand. Throwing it around her shoulders, she walked towards the inn.

The village was quiet. The cold kept everyone inside, huddled around fires or wrapped in warm blankets. Christina took a deep breath to prepare for the man she knew would be waiting for her just outside the tavern door. Every word she spoke, each twitch in her face would be scrutinized. She turned the corner. Cailean emerged from the shadows the moment she came into view.

His glare was piercing. Eyes quickly assessing her, his forehead scrunched into a scowl. "You have been gone too long."

Though the Gaelic words were spoken softly, he spit them out like an accusation. He looked that way ever since she could remember, the frown a permanent feature in her childhood memories, dark irritation constantly clouding his eyes. Perhaps the only thing that had changed over the years was his beard. While still full and untamed as ever, if she stood close enough, as she did now, she could see tiny hints of grey peeking out from beneath the red.

"Where were you?" he asked.

Determined not to break beneath the stare that cut into her, she answered without hesitation. "By the river."

He matched her pace. "What happened?"

"Nothing." She refused to tell him about the Englishman. Though Cailean did not serve her father, escaping his watchful gaze was stressful enough. There was no need to make it impossible. If Seton decided to tell her family, she would deal with the consequences then. She was not going to cut short what freedom she had left.

Cailean smirked. He moved even closer. "Then why is there blood on your lip?"

Christina lifted her fingers to her mouth. Her bottom lip was swollen and tender to the touch. Finding the cut, she ran her tongue across it and tasted metal. Cailean waited for her answer. "I fell," she said.

His smirk widened for a moment before it disappeared, as if he found her words amusing. Keeping his eyes on her all the while, he waited for her to relent and tell him the truth. She remained silent.

"Lady Christina."

The sound of her name rescued her from her predicament. Breaking away from Cailean's stare, she turned to find her father's men waiting with the horses ready. One of them stepped forward.

"A messenger arrived," he said. "We are to take you back to Lochmaben tonight."

Uncertainty bloomed to life in her chest. She did not ride in the dark often. It was perilous and prolonged the journey. Wanting an explanation for such a request, she looked at the men expectantly. They stood there awaiting her reply. She knew she did not have a choice. Nodding, she followed the men to her horse.

❧

Lochmaben Castle was an intimidating fortress, especially in the dark. Built of stone in the year 1162, it was difficult to attack and easy to defend. A deep canal encircled the stronghold's approach. Riding across the bridge in the dead of night, Christina urged her horse through the open gate and the thick walls that surrounded the bailey. It should have felt like coming home. Lochmaben was her favourite place to be. Spotting her eldest brother's horses near the stable, the unease she felt in Annan grew. She did not know what his arrival meant. Pulling to a stop in front of the keep, she dismounted and entered the tower.

The sound of laughter greeted her. Moving to the staircase, the noise increased as she climbed, candle-lit sconces lining the walls. Stepping out onto the second floor, she straightened her shoulders. A few months had passed since she had last seen her brother. Upon her grandfather's request for her to live with him at Lochmaben, Christina had left her siblings behind. Her brother had not been pleased. But the former Lord of Annandale was not a man often told no. Reaching the doors of the grand hall, she hoped her brother had not come to take her back.

The room was full. Her brother's arrival always drew a crowd and the hall brimmed with people eager to lay eyes on the young Mormaer of Carrick. He had not come alone. Familiar faces sat around the long table, her grandfather at the head. No one noticed her at first, but as the elderly man's sharp gaze spotted her by the door, he pushed himself to his feet. The room quieted. Christina walked forward.

Her grandfather left the table, his long strides making short work of the room. Slowing as he reached her, he took her hand and squeezed it as he passed. It was not until he let go that she felt the note in her palm. Closing her hand, she slipped it into her pocket before she glanced back to watch him leave. Conversations began around the hall once more. Christina turned to face the man who had come.

To say Rob Bruce was an admired son of Scots would be an understatement. Over six feet tall, he was a force to be reckoned with, sword or no sword. Knighted at sixteen, their father bequeathed him their mother's land of Carrick only two years later, making him a mormaer. It was a significant gesture. The acquisition gave him not only wealth but power. Not that he needed it. Even the English king favoured him. Looking across the table, Rob staring back, she saw the side of her twenty-one-year-old brother those outside the family rarely did – distant, demanding, and cold.

"Did you enjoy your time in Annan?" he asked.

Christina smiled sarcastically. The bitterness of his question was impossible to miss. Of course he was annoyed she had been sent to Annan. As the firstborn son, Rob expected to be handed everything, but it was more than that. Following the death of their mother, their father had taken their eldest sister Isabel to Norway, leaving Rob as acting head of the family. Isabel did not disappoint. Married within a year of her arrival, she became Queen of Norway. Three years had passed, and still, their father did not return. Despite Rob's titles and his authority, their grandfather continued to do what he wanted. He refused to apprise Rob of his plans, including Christina instead. Rob had more than most, and yet, it was not enough. Staring into his hardened, light-brown eyes, Christina walked to the head of the table and took her grandfather's seat.

He glared at her as she sat in the chair reserved for lords. The muscles in his jaw clenched, and his hand tightened around his cup. She waited for him to lecture her on obedience and knowing one's place, but it did not come. Instead, he drained the ale in front of him and stalked out of the room.

Her gaze followed him as he went. He was more miserable than usual, his temperament sour and his patience gone. Not long ago, he would have just told her what was wrong. But they were not children anymore. Distracted by a soft chuckle, she turned and looked to the man sitting next to Rob's empty chair. She relaxed as soon as she saw her favourite brother's face.

At nineteen, Neil was two years older than her. There were nine Bruce children altogether – five boys and four girls. Rob was the oldest, then Isabel, followed by Neil, Christina, and Edward, who was barely sixteen. Mary came three years later; then Thomas and Alexander, the two boys born in quick succession. By the time Matilda arrived, her shrill cries echoing off the castle walls, Rob was already thirteen and well on his way to becoming a knight.

"Are you certain you're not a Comyn?"

Smirking at Neil's jest, Christina leaned back into the chair. He looked like Isabel, except he was prettier, green eyes highlighting a perfect face. His slender frame made him light on his feet and prone to mischief. While he did not have the following Rob did – especially at tournaments – he received more than his fair share of attention, particularly of the female variety. He took advantage of it every chance he got.

"You torture him more than you should."

Christina smiled at the light-hearted expression on Neil's face. It was the reason why she cherished him the most. Unlike Rob, he never took himself too seriously. Reaching for the pitcher of ale, she poured herself a drink.

"I heard you dismissed your ladies-in-waiting." He

smirked. "You have even been riding unescorted into Selkirk Forest." He shook his head in amusement. "No wonder Rob has been unbearable these last few months. I thought I was supposed to be the difficult one."

His words carried a cautious undertone. Despite his care-free nature, he was still a Bruce, dedicated first and foremost to protecting the family. Their father's emotional flight to Norway had not gone unnoticed. It made them look weak, and the Bruce children did not have to be told to under-stand that it fell to them to restore the formidable reputation of their house. It was the reason why her brothers trained harder and longer than anyone else; why her sisters excelled in every task given to them, mastering the intricate societal relationships that governed the kingdom. They often fought amongst themselves, but whatever they did outside the family, the Bruce children were a united, unbreakable force. Perhaps that explained Rob's misery. He was afraid her actions would cause the family harm.

"Whose cloak is that?"

The question snapped Christina to the present. She suddenly remembered that underneath the fabric, she was covered in blood. Trying her best to look unconcerned, she took a drink and shrugged. "I do not know. I came across it in the forest."

A slow grin pulled at Neil's lips. "And you just put it on?"

She stared back at him with determination. If she showed any sign of weakness or fear, he would pounce like a hunter on injured prey. Ignoring his question, she pretended to be irritated. "Why have you come, Neil?"

The smile faded. Looking down at the cup in his hand, he placed it on the table. When he met her gaze again, there was no denying his concern. "You cannot keep doing this, Christina."

It did not sound like him.

"You have responsibilities," he said. "You cannot come here and do whatever you want. It is reckless."

She nearly scoffed. It was ironic that this lecture was coming from him – the brother caught most often skirting the rules. His face remained serious. Looking away for a moment, she asked, "Why not?"

He smiled sadly. "Why are you wearing someone else's cloak?"

Her face hardened. She should have known he would see right through her. She had learned how to lie and get away with it from him. She did not bother answering.

"You are not a girl anymore." He leaned towards her, eyes never leaving hers. "You have not been for a while."

She pressed her back firmly into the chair. It felt like she was trapped on the riverbank again, all alone as a stranger strode towards her. Her heart pounded in apprehension. Neil's eyes filled with pain. Her face hot, she waited for her brother to say the words she feared the most.

"Rob needs you. We all do. That is why we are here. We have come to take you to Mar."

CHAPTER TWO

"GET UP."

She barely heard the words, the sound faint as she slept. A hand touched her shoulder. She blinked her eyes open.

Her grandfather's face stared down at her. Even in the dark she could see the deep lines etched across his forehead. He tossed her cloak onto the bed.

Reluctantly leaving the warmth behind, Mary and Matilda fast asleep beside her, she lowered her feet onto the floor. Her toes curled in protest. She shivered against the cold. Taking her coat from the bed, she dashed to the smoldering fire, pulling on socks and boots as quickly as she could. A stream of light burst into the room. Her grandfather stood in the doorway. Hurrying to catch up, she ran out the door.

Glimpsing the back of his grey head, she descended the stairs. The tail end of his coat flapped as he stepped from the keep. Shoes slapping loudly against the floor, she rushed out into the grounds. She reached him as he came to a stop before the wall.

They waited in silence for the men to lift the gate.

Wearing nothing but her nightdress underneath her cloak, Christina tried to stop her teeth from chattering. She glanced at the older man beside her. He wore no more than her. The gate groaned as it lifted. Wrapping the cloth tighter around herself, she followed her grandfather out of the castle.

The land slept as they walked. Her breath turned white in the air. They did this often, travelling across Annandale on foot or horseback, with the earth open and full of life. Her grandfather's gait did not slow as the terrain sloped upwards. Forgetting she was cold, Christina bunched the skirt in her hands and matched her strides to his.

Pre-dawn light cast away the fog as they crested the hill. It was one of her favourite spots. The elevation allowed her to see for miles. The loch shone in the distance. Standing next to her grandfather in contented silence, looking out over the trees that carpeted the landscape, she forgot about what happened by the river and the reason why Rob had come. The sun peeked out from behind the mountains. Feeling the warmth against her skin, she closed her eyes.

"The road ahead will be difficult. But it must be travelled."

Her peaceful reverie shattered. She looked at her grandfather beside her. His deep brown gaze stared back.

Robert Bruce, the fifth of his name, was an intimidating man. At eighty-five years old, many expected him to be afflicted with ailments or be a subdued version of his younger self. But besides the skin beginning to sag and the white in his beard, he was unchanged. He lived his life with a stubborn ferocity unmatched by anyone else. No person throughout Christendom wondered why he was called Robert the Competitor.

"We are not what we once were. We are weak and

vulnerable." He crouched down, his eyes suddenly on a tiny purple wildflower that had managed to bloom despite the frost. He plucked it from the ground. Twirling the flower between his fingers, the colour danced in the glory of the rising sun. "You must not yield, Christina." He looked over to her again. "You must not obey the commands of lesser men."

She stared in silence at her grandfather. When he had been denied the crown three years prior – John Balliol becoming King of Scots instead – he withdrew entirely from public life. In protest, he resigned his lands, titles, and claim to the throne, giving it all to her father. To this day, he had never sworn fealty to the new king.

"The letter. What does it mean?"

Her thoughts interrupted, she focused on the question. The note her grandfather had pressed into her palm the previous night consisted of nine words written in French. He had already read the contents; he knew what it said. But that was not what he was asking. He wanted her to tell him what it meant for them, for the Kingdom of Scots.

"War." Her eyes focused on his. "John has signed the Treaty of Paris. King Edward and his army will come."

When he said nothing, looking away from her and out at the view before him, Christina knew she was right. She followed his gaze. The land looked different, as if she could see what was to come. The alliance between Scotland and France would be ratified, and King Edward would march north with thousands of men. The Lowlands would suffer the most – Lothian, March, Annandale, Galloway, and Carrick. All of them would feel the heavy presence of the English king. She could not help but wonder if her grandfather knew this was coming all those years ago when the crown was given to John. Glancing over, she found him looking at her.

"There will come a time when all of Scotland will look for a leader." His eyes gleamed with ferocity in the sunlight. "One uninhibited by fear, indecision, and lack of conviction. A *true* king." Reaching out, he placed his hands on her shoulders. "Remember when you are in Mar. It is far worse to follow a foolish man and live without consequence than it is to disobey and face his wrath." He brought his face closer to hers. "Not all men deserve loyalty. You must decide what you are willing to sacrifice in the name of righteousness." His fingers pressed into her skin. "Trust, Christina. Trust what you know to be true."

She waited for him to continue, but he did not. Letting go, he turned and left her standing there, contemplating the meaning of his convoluted words. It was not like him to hide what he meant – not from her. His mood had changed in recent months. He spent more time alone, often staring at the fire in silence, his brow knit tightly together. Perhaps her father's prolonged absence was the cause, but as she watched his figure growing smaller in the distance, she knew it had to do with Scotland and King John. No man could be denied the crown and remain the same, no matter how noble. Filling her lungs with the crisp, morning air, she descended the hill.

Rob was waiting for her in the bailey as she stepped through the gate. The men mounted on their horses, Neil, Edward, Mary, Thomas, Alexander, and Matilda all sat in their saddles. Their sullen faces looked back at her expectantly. There was no joy in this for any of them. Her grandfather had not stayed to watch her leave. Spotting Cailean next to her mare, her things already tied to the saddle, she glared at Rob. She may have no choice in going to Mar, but no one could force her to like it. If she was going to be this miserable for the rest of her life, then so was everyone else.

⁊

"We received a letter from Norway."

Christina glanced over at Neil. Riding beside her, they followed the king's road north. It would take at least another day to reach Stirling. As soon as they crossed the bridge into the Highlands, the easy part of their journey would be over. Not that Christina cared. In fact, she hoped it was difficult. Maybe then Rob would not make her do this.

"Father said now was the time."

She continued to ignore him. He was trying to make her feel better, to lessen her misery, but nothing he said would.

A long sigh pushed through his lips. "You have been engaged to Gartnait for most of your life, Christina. You had to know this day would come."

She hated how foolish his words made her feel. She had been betrothed to Gartnait of Mar since she was eight. As time went on, she thought less and less about it. When her fifteenth birthday came and went, not a word said about their engagement, she thought perhaps it had just been a formality. Maybe it was only meant to show the rest of Scotland that their kinship with Mar, their northernmost ally, was strong and firmly in hand.

But that was not what had blindsided her. Even if her betrothal had been made with the sincerest of intentions, she never thought she would be married without her father present. As long as he was in Norway, she was safe. Looking at the road ahead, small patches of snow on the ground passing by, she was sobered by the weight of her miscalculation.

A whistle cut through the air. Urging his horse forward, Neil joined Rob at the front. Cailean moved into the space beside her. He said nothing as he looked at her, his body swaying in time with the beast between his legs. She wished she knew what he was thinking. Ever since their return to Lochmaben, he had been conspicuously absent from her side. Deciding his opinion did not matter, she let her mind drift to where it always did when his eyes held her like that – to her mother.

Marjorie, daughter of Niall, had been just thirteen-years-old when she became Countess of Carrick. Niall sired only girls, but he did not care, obtaining permission from the King of Scots to give his lands and title to his eldest daughter. Anyone in his kindred could have contested the decision – the right of inheritance favouring a male descendent – but they did not. As Christina would see first-hand throughout her childhood, the Gaelic people of southwest Scotland loved her mother. Marjorie was everything they wanted in a leader – bold, charismatic, and just. When Cailean met the young countess not long after her father's death, his body beaten and bloodied, his hands tied as he fell to his knees, she saved him with a single word.

Cailean was not of Carrick. He was a Gallovidian and had been caught raiding Marjorie's lands with other men from Galloway, the lordship bordering Carrick to the south. When Cailean's captors brought him before their leader, informing her of his crimes, she did not give them what they wanted. Instead, she set him free.

Christina looked back over to the man beside her. Her

mother's mercy had not gone overlooked. Rather than return to the land of his birth, Cailean took a blood oath, binding himself to Marjorie until he repaid her in kind. But no one, not even Cailean, could save the Countess of Carrick from the fever that took hold. She died three nights before her family was denied the crown. A fortnight later, her husband left for Norway. Cailean remained.

Christina did not know why he stayed or why he chose her. But wherever she went, there he was, his stern expression and brooding silence a constant at her side. Some days she wished he had gone. Her eyes on him now, his presence gave her comfort. When the wedding was over, and her family returned home, he would be the only one who would not leave her. He would be the only one who stayed.

His horse slammed into hers. Taking hold of her reins, Cailean pulled her off the path as two soldiers fled past, their horses kicking dirt up around them. Christina caught sight of their banners as they galloped urgently south, three golden lions of the English king bright against the red fabric. Knowing the burgh of Lanark lay just ahead, Christina snatched the reins out of Cailean's hands and dug her heels into her mare.

She heard Rob call her name as she sprinted past. He was still waiting on the side of the road with his men, their horses stagnant. Confident he would not be able to catch her, she leaned into her horse and headed for the village.

Lanark sat along the banks of the River Clyde fifty miles north of Lochmaben. Though not as large as other royal burghs, it was a designated market town and an important centre for trade in the Lowlands. The presence of English soldiers in Lanark was nothing out of the ordinary. Many castles and towns throughout Scotland were garrisoned with them. Spotting the smoke as she emerged from the trees, her mare's hooves sinking into the shallow mud, Christina hurried through the open gate.

The town bell clanged frantically as she rode into the square. More than one roof was on fire, people hurrying back and forth with buckets of water, desperate to stop the flames. A black haze filled the air. The fumes made her eyes water. Lifting her cloak over her nose, she moved farther down the road to get out of the smoke.

She did not have to go far. The street sloped upwards towards the castle, leading her past the homes and shops that lined the street. Urging her horse up the hill, she blinked to rid the tears from her eyes. Her vision cleared as she turned a corner. She pulled back hard on the reins.

Death surrounded her. Bodies covered the ground, their lifeless forms contorted in unfamiliar ways. The air was eerily still, and it felt weighty on her tongue. Hearing her horse whinny softly, she walked the mare forward.

She had just missed the slaughter. Blood still drained from the dead, darkening the earth beneath them. Stepping carefully around each corpse, she realized what they all had in common. Every man dead on the ground wore the mark of three lions. They were English. She pulled her horse to a stop.

The sound of a rider approaching on the road ahead grabbed her attention. She wanted to move to the side, but could not, the dead blocking her path. The sound of hooves grew louder. Her horse twitched nervously. She had begun to step back when the rider rounded the corner.

An English soldier advanced. He seemed panicked, urging his horse forward recklessly through the carnage. The animal tried its best to avoid the obstacles beneath its feet. There was blood smeared across his tunic. Christina could not look away. As soon as their eyes connected, his face changed in an instant.

Withdrawing his blade, he charged towards her. It felt as if she was someone else watching in the distance. She knew what was about to happen, but could not move, her hands frozen on her reins. Lifting the sword above his head, he bore down upon her. Christina heard nothing but the sound of her breathing. Wondering what steel would feel like entering her flesh, the soldier suddenly went rigid. His face filled with horror. Staring at her in confusion, he fell from his saddle.

The horse did not stop. It fled down the road, winding through the bodies with precision, its rider a crumpled heap on the ground. The soldier twitched only once before he stilled. Christina stared at the axe lodged in his back. Her mouth dry, she looked up to see where the hatchet had come from. Her heart quickened when she saw the Scotsman walking towards her.

His feet made no sound. Blonde, almost white hair covered his shoulders, the longsword visible against his back. His nose was crooked, as if it had been broken one too many times. Dried blood caked his fingernails. Stopping beside the soldier, he bent down and pulled the axe out. Then he turned to her.

He placed his hand on the nose of her horse. Still clutching the reins, Christina watched as he gently stroked the mare's face. Despite his thick, burly beard, he was not much older than Neil. He lifted his gaze to meet hers. His eyes were a peculiar shade of blue. Finding her courage, she opened her mouth to speak.

A shout shattered the silence. Turning to look back down the road from where she came, she watched a plume of ash burst into the air. Rob and the others would be nearby. They would have stopped to help. Knowing she did not have much time, she returned to the man before her.

The Scotsman was gone. She searched for him, her eyes drifting over the various nooks and alleys that jutted away from the street, but there was nothing to be found. He had vanished. Unwilling to remain amongst the dead, she swung her horse around.

The sight of Christopher Seton made her stop. He was off his horse, stepping carefully through the slaughter towards her, his gaze on the ground. Her body tensed. She wondered how long he had been there and what he had seen. She unclenched her fists.

He had been sent by her grandfather to accompany them to Mar. When they left Lochmaben, she had not noticed he was with them. Her anger towards Rob blinded her to everything else. It was not until the second day that she caught sight of him riding up ahead. She almost fell off her horse. The moment he told Rob about the Englishman by the river, her last few days as an unmarried woman would be unbearable. Rob would make sure of it.

Seton climbed back onto his horse. Even now, amongst the bloodshed, Christina found it difficult to read him. She was usually good at assessing others, but Seton was impossible. He had no tells. He could be enraged or delighted, she had not a clue.

She flinched as a long, sharp whistle split the air. Cailean emerged from the smoke moments later. It did not take long for the others to arrive. Covered in soot, they took in what lay before them, their faces grim. A few of the men moved in front of Matilda to shield her from it. Thomas and Alexander looked horrified. Rob stopped beside her.

"Did you see it happen?"

Watching Neil advance, carefully stepping through the wreckage to scout out the road, she shook her head. It could not have been a coincidence, the fire and the dead men. They occurred within moments of each other. She doubted the townspeople had anything to do with it. While they might hate the English presiding over them, such an act was not the work of farmers and tradesmen. It took a certain boldness to do what had been done. A single name came to mind.

Neil gave the signal. The road was clear. Leaving Lanark, they continued to Glasgow. It was well after dark by the time they arrived at the inn. Sliding down from her horse, her legs aching, Matilda took her hand as they stepped through the door. Travellers filled the establishment. Christina hesitated when she saw a group of men near the back of the room.

They were strangers. She had never met them. Staring at the emblem displayed on their cloaks, the banner of House Moray proudly displayed, she could not stop the memory of the first time she saw Andrew from overwhelming her.

She had been thirteen, travelling to Norham Castle to watch her grandfather bring forth his claim to be the next King of Scots. All the noble houses were present. Kin to the Comyns and John Balliol, House Moray stood opposite hers. She took no notice of Andrew as their families faced one another. But when she spotted him sneaking out of the castle later that afternoon, his black hair brilliant beneath the moonlight, he had her attention. The next day as she walked along the river with Isabel, she caught a glimpse of him moving through the trees. She had followed.

"It is impolite to sneak up on someone."

She had almost jumped at the sound of his voice as he stepped from cover. She lost sight of him for only a moment, but it was enough to get caught.

He moved closer, standing just inches away as he stared into her face.

He would not dare harm her. Not even the Comyns could save him from her family if he did. Taking a moment to collect herself, she asked, "Are you accusing me of something?"

He smirked. "So, you deny it?"

Straightening her shoulders, she lifted her head higher. "Deny what?"

He smiled then, his sharp face transforming under a boyish grin. Light-hearted and full of mischief, he was nothing like her brothers. Perhaps that was why she was drawn to him so quickly. All she knew was that she would never forget the way his eyes held her captive.

Thomas Randolph's hand on her elbow broke her out of her daze. The same age as Rob, Randolph was her nephew through a half-sister she had never met. Though her father told them repeatedly that he was not part of their family, the Bruce children thought otherwise. They took him in as one of their own. He rarely left Rob's side.

Following him to the table in the corner where the others waited, she ignored their quizzical stares and sat down. In the chaos of the past few days, Andrew had slipped her mind. It felt like a betrayal. An ache built up in her chest. Feeling too warm under her cloak, she unclasped it and focused on the conversations around her.

"Are you not hungry?"

The Gaelic broke through the sea of voices in the tavern. Looking down at the gruel before her, she lifted a spoonful before she set it back down. She had no appetite. Shoving the bowl over to Cailean, he dug into it.

"It is difficult to see men in such a state." Rob's voice drew her attention. He sat across from her, a cup of mead in his hand. "There is no honour in killing that way."

Honour or not, it was smart. Drawing English soldiers out of a castle in broad daylight was not an easy task. The sight was shocking, but Christina understood the rage of the men responsible. Scotland did not belong to King Edward, and yet his sheriffs ruled as if it was their personal fiefdom. They occupied castles, charged taxes and controlled the churches not for the benefit of the Scots, but for England. And King John did nothing. Perhaps that was what her grandfather meant when he said they needed a true king. One willing to stand up to Edward, no matter the cost.

She took a long drink. The ale warmed her empty stomach. The bloodshed was not what troubled her, but she did not bother correcting her brother. Rob could think what he wanted.

"Perhaps it is a blessing, that you are going to Mar now." He paused. "The trouble near the border will only grow. You will be safe in the north." He held her gaze. "You will not have to witness the acts of violence that will come."

Though she kept quiet, inside, she screamed. She wanted to hit him, grab his throat between her hands and squeeze. It was not that she was marrying someone other than Andrew. She was no fool. Even as she remembered those too few times of his lips on hers, the way his fingers moved across her skin, she knew they would never be together. The rivalry between their kindreds was too great to overcome. Sitting at the table, the men and her siblings watching her closely, she fought to keep the despair from her face. Her torment had nothing to do with Andrew. It was entirely caused by Gartnait of Mar.

She had known her betrothed her entire life. They were the same age, and as children, they often played together in the woods near Kildrummy Castle. The first time she had seen Gartnait drunk, she thought it was funny. He staggered around, stumbling into things as he mumbled incomprehensible sentences. When the rumours reached her at Lochmaben, she dismissed them without a thought. He was the next Mormaer of Mar. He would not be so reckless. But when she saw him at a wedding less than a year later, she could no longer deny the truth. He drank incessantly. His words slurred and slow, he tottered around the room as if he had been kicked in the head. It was all his men could do to keep him upright. Rob's hand on her arm interrupted the memory.

"Whatever faults Gartnait has-" His voice trailed off.

Lifting her head, she stared back at the man responsible for delivering her to her misery. He did not decide this for her, she knew that, but he did not stop it either. It hurt the same.

He cleared his throat. "You are a Bruce," he said. He spoke with conviction. "You will be revered."

She almost laughed. Rob could not possibly believe what he said. She would be revered until her family was gone, leaving her alone and legally bound to a failure of a man. She would be revered until she was not. Until her husband no longer cared who she used to be. Pulling away from his grasp, she stood and left the hall.

KILDRUMMY CASTLE

I T TOOK SIX more days to reach Mar. Though the road north of Stirling had opened for the spring, it was not a comfortable journey, their travels prolonged by snowstorms, hail and unrelenting rain. The weather made everyone miserable and silent, which suited Christina well. Thomas and Alexander slumped down low in their saddles. Mary was bundled in so many layers her face was barely visible. Even Edward looked like he wished he had stayed in the south. Riding into Inverurie, their familial estate east of Mar, Christina's gloomy disposition lightened ever so slightly.

The Bass of Inverurie rose up into the heart of Garioch. South of the village, perched upon a natural mound, the castle huddled against the rivers Ury and Don. It was not grand by any means. The keep and grounds were small. Christina loved it here, especially in the summer. When the snow melted, the soil able to breathe once more, the land turned a vibrant green. Beneath sun-filled skies, she'd wander the hills to her heart's content.

She dropped from her horse. Frozen feet hit the ground as the riders dismounted, their numbers filling the bailey. She moved to untie the pack from the back of her horse. Her fingers were too stiff and sore to loosen the knots. A pair of gloved hands reached over to help.

"Here."

She stiffened at the sight of Gilbert Hay beside her. From Carrick, Hay had joined them in Glasgow with the additional men Rob requested. His family bound to hers, she could not remember a time without him. Whether it was exploring the wilds of her mother's land or venturing out into the Irish Sea, Hay was always at her side. But that was before he betrayed her to her father. Fourteen years of unquestioned loyalty had melted away like snow.

"Remove your hands." She said the words slowly, her tone firm.

He stopped.

Glaring, she watched as he took a step back before walking away, his frustration clear. She had never forgiven him. Not even when he tried to explain those years ago, offering her a handful of excuses, did she relent. If it were up to her, he would not be here at all. But they needed men loyal to their kindred. It was not Mar they were worried about. It was the territory that surrounded it – the land of the Comyns.

The conflict between House Bruce and House Comyn had existed for generations. Their rivalry threatened to split Scotland in two. While Christina's family owned more land, Bruce estates spanning Scotland, England, and Ireland, the Comyns had the most power. They controlled the Highlands. Most importantly, they seized control of the throne when John was crowned. It was why so many knights accompanied them to Mar. They were there to make sure the Comyns did not try anything foolish.

Eager to get out of the cold, Rob and the others hurried

up the slope and into the keep. Christina remained outside. As tired as she was, she did not want to sit. The thought of a particular small house made her smile. Turning on her heel, she walked from the castle towards the village.

She did not have far to go. Snow-covered fields lined the road to Inverurie. The clouds above cast a grey shadow over the land. Reaching the farmhouse on the outskirts of the town, smoke rising out of the hole in the roof, Christina stamped the mud from her boots and knocked on the door.

A face full of freckles greeted her. Ena was a sight to behold. Her dark hair was piled messily on top of her head and her hands were covered in blood. Christina grinned. Ena pulled her into her embrace.

"You're here," she said. She smiled back at Christina before her brow scrunched in confusion.

Christina nodded, answering her friend's silent question. They often came to Garioch in the summer, when the roads were clear and the air was warm. But it was still winter, and Ena knew what that meant. Something had happened; something had changed. Stepping past her friend, Christina entered the house and dropped into the chair in front of the hearth.

Saying nothing, Ena returned to the table. She began skinning the hare once more. Christina watched her work. Her skilled hands pulled back the fur. A deep sigh left Christina's lips.

"The time has come."

Ena did not respond.

"I'm to marry Gartnait."

Her eyebrows lifted in surprise. Placing the fur onto the table, she drove a rod through the length of the rabbit and hung it over the fire. The pot beneath caught drops of grease as it cooked. Wiping her hands on the apron draped across her waist, she sat down beside Christina. "Does he know?"

Christina did not have to ask who. Ena was the only person who knew about Andrew. Residing at Avoch Castle in Moray with his father, he lived just two days ride away. Each time Christina came to Garioch, she felt the pull to see him. They encountered each other often enough. As nobility, the Morays attended the same events her family did. But it had been over a year since they had spoken. Shaking her head as she leaned back into the chair, she dreaded telling him. She did not want their first conversation to be about Gartnait.

Ena leaned forward, bracing her arms against her knees. The flames reflected in her eyes. "So," she said. "What are we going to do?"

Christina could not help but smile at her brazen response. Ena's parents had died when she was young, both falling ill to the same disease. Her uncle had raised her in this very house. When he too passed away just shy of her fourteenth birthday, the village insisted that she be sent south to be brought up by the Kirk.

To say that Ena did not like the idea was an understatement. She refused to leave her home, even barricading herself inside when the nuns came to collect her. Later that month, when Christina's grandfather held court in the grounds of the Bass, Ena appeared, bow over her shoulder, sword tied to her hip. Christina had never seen such determination from someone her own age. Watching her grandfather's smile grow as he listened to Ena make her claim to the farm her uncle left behind, Christina knew Ena's bravery would be rewarded.

"How long do you have?"

Christina shrugged. "I do not know."

Ena nodded and then stood, carefully turning the hare over on the spit. She was silent for some time. When she met Christina's gaze again, she said, "Delay it if you can. I will find Andrew."

Christina tried not to be cynical. She wanted desperately to believe that Andrew could help her. But it seemed unlikely. Andrew could be anywhere in the Highlands, not just in Moray. Her eyes drifted down to watch the fire. As the warmth seeped through her bones, she hoped it was possible. She hoped Ena could find him in time.

They rode for Mar the next morning. They would arrive before midday, but the short journey did nothing to improve Christina's mood. Her dress was rigid and uncomfortable. She had barely slept the night before. If she thought she could have gotten away with it, she would have worn black to mark the occasion. She would marry Gartnait and Andrew would be her neighbour. She would not just be without him. She would have to watch as Andrew married someone else, had children and lived an entire life just a short distance away. She could not think of anything worse.

Pulling at the tight sleeve around her wrist, she felt Mary's gaze as she rode beside her. Christina stopped fidgeting. She had done what she could to protest her impending marriage, but the time for that was over. Her younger siblings were watching. The men of her house took note of every move she made. No matter how devastated she felt, she would ride into Mar with her dignity intact. She straightened in her saddle as the fortress came into view.

Shaped like a shield and just as strong, Kildrummy Castle was the seat of power in the earldom of Mar. Following her brothers through the open entranceway, Christina saw the guards watching from atop the two circular towers that formed the gatehouse. She remembered standing there as a child. The height of the stone structure allowed her to see for miles. She loved how tall it made her feel. But when she had looked down, her eyes moving along the wall and then into the ravine that surrounded the castle, she could not help but squeeze her father's hand a little bit tighter.

Remembering her father's smiling face, she pulled her horse to a stop. He was the reason she was here now and in this stupid dress. So detached from his children, he had not even bothered to come. It did not matter what pleasant memories she remembered. None of them would make up for his absence. She closed her eyes as she dismounted, fighting to keep the bitterness off her face. Exhaling slowly, she turned and watched her future father-in-law step from the keep.

Domhnall, the seventh Mormaer of Mar, was not a small man. Tall and wide, much like his castle, he had a loud voice that filled the room no matter where he was. His even temper and pleasant manner had won Christina over at a young age. Watching him welcome Rob and Neil, his smile warm, her pain lessened a little. Then she saw Gartnait standing beside him.

He had his father's height, but none of his girth, his figure slim and lean. His light brown hair sat neatly against his scalp. Though his lips curled into a smile, Christina could tell it was forcibly given. They had something in common. His desire to be there was just as lacking as hers.

Silently watching the men exchange pleasantries, Christina stood with her sisters a few paces back. It was not that she had to remain behind them; she was more than welcome to step forward. She simply did not want to. She would be courteous, agreeable even, but she would also be true. She refused to give any indication that she was happy to be there. Her stance on this arrangement would be made perfectly clear.

"Are you certain your betrothed is yet a man?"

Distracted by what was happening up ahead, Christina had not noticed Walter Jardine move in beside her. She glanced back at the others. Cailean, Seton and Hay stood with the men of Carrick and Annandale. Their stoic faces stared at her in silence. Uncertain of the question, Christina returned her attention to the man who waited.

From Annandale, Jardine towered above her. With his arms folded across his chest and his stance relaxed, he looked just as wide. He was twice her age and unmarried. If the stories Christina heard about him were true, he wished to remain that way. His fists were seldom idle. Swollen cuts covered his knuckles. Christina watched him scratch the stubble on his face. Keeping his gaze on the men in front of the keep, he said, "He's got no balls. A gust of wind could knock him over."

Christina heard Cailean grunt in amusement behind her. The sound was rare. She could not tell if Jardine was joking, but as he turned his face towards hers, she found not a drop of humour in his eyes. Instead, there was a warning.

Rob calling her forward forced her to leave Jardine and his unspoken words behind. She glanced back at him as she walked. Whatever he was trying to convey, she could not think about that now. Clearing her mind, she followed Rob into the keep. The Countess of Mar greeted her as she entered.

Elen ferch Llywelyn was Domhnall's wife. The natural-born daughter of Welsh king Llywelyn the Great, Elen was older than her husband but just as tall. Her poised demeanor had been passed down to her children. As Christina glanced over at Elen's daughters – Isabella and Margaret – she knew that was not always the case.

Only one year older than Christina, Isabella of Mar was a troublemaker. On the outside, she looked like a queen, locks of blonde hair effortlessly cascading down her back. Her blue-green eyes enraptured even the darkest of souls. Christina had seen how people reacted to her many times. Isabella's presence was a delight. But there was one thing most did not know about the eldest daughter of Mar. Whether it was sneaking to the top of the tower to sleep at night or setting her favourite Highland coo free, Isabella had a wildness in her that ran in contradiction to the body that carried it. Underneath all that beauty was a woman clever and quick.

Isabella stepped forward. "I am so happy you are here." Her smile lit the room.

Christina tried not to like her, but her liveliness was contagious. She smiled back. Ignoring the way her brothers stared, she took her friend's offered hand and let herself be led into the hall.

Over the next two days, nothing happened. Stuck inside the castle, Christina was forced to spin and make pleasant conversation. It felt like torture. She would much rather be out riding with Rob and Neil, visiting the villages and exploring the earldom alongside the men of Mar. Even Mary was getting antsy. She would pick up her distaff only to set it down again. If Christina heard Margaret mention one more time that Maol Choluim, the son of the mormaer of

Lennox, gave her a flower at a tournament in Stirling more than a year ago, she was going to sew Margaret's mouth shut.

A knock on the door interrupted them. Sat in Isabella's chambers, warmed by the fire, Isabella called out for the person to enter. Christina kept her gaze on the window and the view beyond. Spring had arrived. Melting snow fell from the trees. Watching a dotterel fly past, a letter with her name was placed on the ledge.

Christina glanced back at the messenger as he left the room. She caught Isabella's gaze. Christina could tell she wanted to ask who it was from, but Isabella kept quiet and returned to the piece of embroidery in her lap. Margaret was not so composed.

"What does it say?"

Christina ignored her. She had forgotten how annoying Margaret was. Carefully breaking the dried wax that held the letter shut, she began to read.

Lady Christina,

It gives me great pleasure to inform you that the dress you have inquired about has been found. It has been in disuse for a while but will be ready for inspection upon your return in two days' time.

I will hang it in your chambers, in front of the window, where the early morning air will reinvigorate it from the northeast, as is typical of a spring breeze.

Looking forward to your return,

Ena

Deciphering Ena's message, it took Christina every ounce of control to keep the smile from her face. Andrew would meet her northeast of Kildrummy Castle before dawn in two days. Slipping the letter into her pocket, she pretended it meant nothing and picked up the book lying on the dresser. She sat down and began to read. Hope bloomed inside her. She was not married – not yet. And Andrew would help. He would know what to do.

❧

She got dressed in the dark. It was not the first time she had snuck out of Kildrummy Castle to meet Andrew Moray. If everything went according to plan, it also would not be the last.

She did not need a light. The layout of the castle embedded in her mind, she left Mary sleeping in their room and descended the stairs. Her feet were silent against the floor. She was not supposed to know about the tunnel that went underneath the fortress. The small, dark escape route burrowed past the walls and beyond the ravine. She braced her shoulder against the door and pushed. The wood creaked as it opened. Slipping through the gap, she stepped out into the night.

She avoided the road. Keeping within the trees, she stayed well out of the view of the castle. The earth felt soft beneath her feet. A grey fog drifted through the branches. Using the dim light of the moon, Christina spotted the old willow tree up ahead. She turned north.

Moss-covered boulders and fallen logs covered the forest floor. She moved around them with ease, the landscape unchanged. Her heart quickened with each step. It was if she could feel Andrew waiting. Spotting his familiar frame up ahead, she smiled.

Andrew straightened as she approached. Christina came to a stop. They stared at each other, only a few feet apart. He looked the same – black shoulder-length hair, eyes that could devour her whole – but something was wrong. She could tell by his rigid posture and the distance he kept between them.

"We should not be here." His voice was strained.

Christina tried to ignore the alarm those few words caused. She wanted him to smile, to tell her how happy he was to see her after all this time, but that was not what she got.

"We cannot do this anymore." He sounded indifferent. "Nothing good will come of it."

Thinking she knew what he was referring to, she moved closer and reached for his hand. He did not resist. Their fingers intertwined naturally. It felt good to touch him, the warmth of his skin on hers. Suddenly, he removed his hand and stepped back. She watched him in confusion. He was taking the news of her upcoming union harder than she expected.

"We can figure this out."

He turned away, moving farther back as he slowly paced in a small circle.

She did not understand his detachment. She had received a letter from him only a few months ago. Nothing had changed. Watching him move back and forth over the same patch of ground, the muscles in his face twitching, a wave of concern washed over her. She was mistaken. His odd demeanor had nothing to do with Gartnait. It was something else.

"What happened?" She barely recognized her own voice, her words quiet and composed.

Andrew carried on pacing for a while before he stopped. When he turned to face her, Christina fought to still the panic in her chest.

He opened his mouth and then shut it. No sound came. His eyes filling with tears, Christina could not take it any longer. "Tell me."

He shook his head, staring off into the trees.

Her jaw clenched. Fists squeezing tightly in frustration, she repeated herself. "Andrew. Tell me."

"I am married."

As if he had shot an arrow, his words quick and deadly, she unconsciously stepped back. She felt sick. She stared at him to take it back, to tell her he was joking. He remained silent. She saw the truth in his eyes.

"It was not my decision. I knew nothing about it." The information poured out of him. "She is from Ross, the mormaer's daughter. My father arranged it. I was only told a few days before."

Christina never wanted someone to stop talking so badly. Each word felt like a blow. She struggled to absorb the words rushing from his mouth. When it was over, when he was finally silent, an ache filled her chest. She wanted to rip it out.

"Do not hate me, Christina." Andrew's voice cut through her anguish. He took a step towards her. "Please."

"How long?" The question burst from her lips. His soft words failed to placate her. Contempt festered within. Meeting his gaze, she asked again. "How long have you been married?"

His face fell. She had her answer. It was long enough.

A short, sarcastic laugh escaped her throat. She shook her head in disbelief and glared at him. "Of all the things you are, Andrew, I never thought you could be so pathetic." Her words dripped with disgust. "You are such a coward."

His demeanour changed at the insult. Moving closer once more, he held his face just inches from hers. "Is that so?" he asked, his tone mocking. "I am a coward?"

She refused to back down or look away.

"I did what was asked of me." He met her anger. "What my father wanted. And that makes me spineless?"

"You should have told me!" She did not care that she was shouting. She hoped someone overheard and caught him, a Moray, on Mar land. It would give her an excuse to punch him in the face.

"Why?" he yelled back. "So you could tell me to find a way out of it?"

"Yes!" She did not have to think about her reply. It was precisely what she would have told him. Their families would never approve their union, but if they could remain unattached, if they could get out of marriage to another, then maybe – She looked down. Angry tears filled her eyes. It no longer mattered. The hope of any future with him was dead. He had married someone else and broken her heart.

Andrew shook his head in frustration. He ran a hand angrily through his hair. "You just don't get it, do you?"

Christina did not answer. She loved him, and he loved her – at least she thought he did until now. What else was there to understand?

"I am the only son." He spoke each word with conviction, his voice quiet. "My father was not blessed with five sons and four daughters. I am the only one to continue my house, the only one to follow in my father's footsteps." His eyes pleaded with her to understand. "There is no one else. I must do what he asks of me."

The truth did not make accepting it any easier. It did not hurt any less. Christina willed the tears from her eyes. She had nothing to say. Turning away, she left him standing alone in the dark.

∾

The evening meal was a lively affair. They had been in Mar long enough for word to spread, the hall packed with guests. It was not just Rob the people came to see. Christina would be their countess one day. Sitting next to Gartnait near the head of the table, she felt the eyes watching her from around the hall.

The sound of something being knocked over onto the table made Christina glance in Gartnait's direction. Ale ran across the surface. Taken by surprise, she only managed to lift her arms out of the way before the liquid spilled into her lap. The skirt of her dress was soaked, her legs damp and sticky. Those nearby did not seem to notice. Barely containing her anger, she reached over and righted the jug.

The clay vessel hit the table with a thud. The sudden noise silenced the conversations around her. Gartnait was the last to notice. Following the gazes of everyone else, he looked over and saw that she was drenched in malted water. Then he noticed the jug at his elbow.

"How clumsy of me." His slurred words and loose smile told her just how much he already had to drink. "My sincerest apologies."

Christina could feel the stares. She did not have to look at Rob to know he was tense. He expected her to react badly – to yell at Gartnait and call him a fool. Demanding the muscles in her face remain perfectly still, she watched as Gartnait began mopping up the mess he made on the table. It was probably best for everyone, herself included, if she did not lash out at the man she was about to marry. That could wait until after the wedding, when everyone was gone. She would let her new husband know just what she thought of him then.

"Here."

Gartnait offered her a rag. She did not want it. Keeping her arms at her sides, she stared at the table in silence. Gartnait reached down to pat her lap dry.

Her chair screeched against the floor as she abruptly pushed back from the table. The voices in the hall ceased. Everyone stared as she stood. Sat beside Domhnall, Rob's face glowered with apprehension. She saw the look of warning in his eyes. Perhaps her reaction had been a bit too strong, but she had to get out of reach. The thought of Gartnait's touch made her nauseous. A light hand on the back of her elbow interrupted the glaring silence.

"Come," Isabella said softly, an encouraging smile on her face. "We will get you changed into something dry."

Christina wanted nothing more than to leave the room. But eventually, she would have to come back in and she did not know if she could force herself do that. She was tired of being on display and wanted this spectacle to be over. The more she thought about the whole situation, the angrier she became. She was not the one at fault here. Gartnait was the fool, the drunk, the incompetent future mormaer of Mar. People were not stupid; they knew what he was. They had come to see how she would handle him and what kind of countess she would be. They were about to get what they wanted.

Christina snatched the cloth from Gartnait's hand. Running it down the front of her dress, she dried herself off as best she could. She sat back down.

Gartnait mumbled apologies again.

Her posture rigid in the chair, she ignored him, not even bothering to turn her head. If he was going to be an embarrassment, a detriment to his family and the people of Mar, she would treat him the way he deserved. She would marry him, yes, but that did not mean she had to tolerate him or his follies in the slightest. She doubted anyone would object. Catching sight of a few small smirking faces around the room, she reached over and took Mary's untouched cup of wine.

The gathering carried on well into the night. Christina remained where she was, determined to show just what kind of wife she was going to be. Gartnait stood without warning. Wobbling slowly, he leaned her way. Christina flinched. He lost his balance and tumbled towards her.

Cailean stopped his fall. Stepping between them, the Gallovidian grabbed Gartnait roughly and stood him upright. Though Christina could not see Cailean's face, she knew he was unhappy.

"Let me help you find your chambers." It was not a request.

Christina glanced around to see if anyone noticed. Domhnall watched them, his mouth still moving as he spoke to Rob. Even as Cailean held Gartnait up by the back of his tunic, his free hand working to pry the mug from the drunk's grasp, Domhnall did not spare his son another thought. He simply looked away.

Gartnait attempted to say something. His words were garbled and slow.

Cailean did not give him the chance to finish. "It *has* been a long day. Sleep will do you well."

He pulled Gartnait's arm over his shoulder. Jardine helping, the two men half-carried, half-dragged the future mormaer to bed. It made Christina happy, seeing him being taken far away from her. She turned back to the table. Finishing the wine in front of her, she met Rob's waiting stare.

She did not bother masking her anger as she glared back. He was her brother, the leader of their kindred, the one man bound by blood and duty to protect her. Yet there he sat, saying and doing nothing as he witnessed the agony that her life would become.

If it was her father here instead of him, she might understand. Her father owed her nothing. But this was Rob, the brother who had once been so close, the man she used to call her friend. Holding his gaze, she hoped he felt responsible for the pain he was causing. She would not soon forget it.

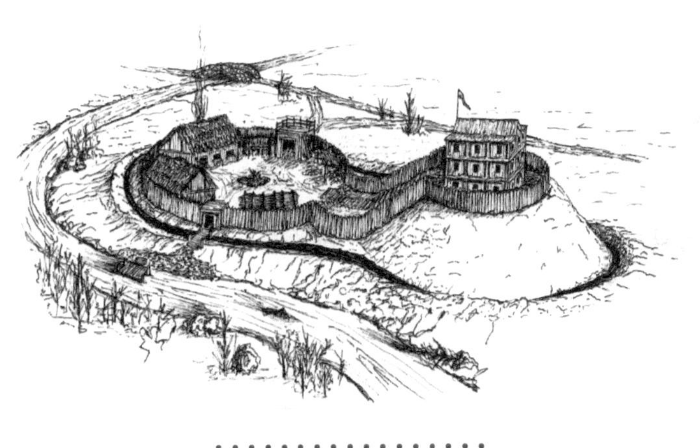

THE BASS OF INVERURIE

CHAPTER FOUR

I T WAS DECIDED. Christina Bruce of Annandale and Carrick would wed Gartnait of Mar in three days.

Rob informed her the morning after the spectacle in the hall. Christina waited for the anger to come, but it did not. All she felt was a numbing sadness. For the rest of her life, she'd be stuck in Kildrummy Castle with *him*. She did not have much time left. Grabbing her cloak, she climbed onto her horse and rode for Garioch.

The sight of Inverurie brought tears to her eyes. She blamed it on the wind, her face stinging as she galloped for the gate, Cailean and Jardine close behind. She wished her grandfather was there. What she would not give for him to be waiting for her in the keep. Entering the bailey and dropping down from her horse, she knew no one could comfort her. Her fate was her own. Only she could come to terms with it.

"Lady Christina."

Her mind occupied as she walked into the hall, she had not noticed Nicholas Biggar at the table. Hesitating near the door, Cailean and Jardine moved past her. Their eyes assessed the older man as they undid their cloaks. Forcing a smile, Christina approached her grandfather's friend.

"Sir Nicholas," she said as she stepped towards him. "I did not know you were here."

Biggar stood. "I am not staying. I only came to give you this."

Placing a letter into her hand, Christina glanced down at the note.

"It is for your grandfather. And only him."

She looked up into his serious face.

"Please make sure he gets it upon your return."

She opened her mouth and then shut it, unsure of what to say as she looked down at the paper once more. Biggar waited for her to acknowledge that she understood. Christina only gave him a strained smile.

"I do not know if you have heard, Sir Nicholas, but I will not be returning to Lochmaben." She fought to keep the tremor from her voice. "I am to marry Gartnait of Mar and will remain in the north, at Kildrummy Castle." It felt suddenly real, saying it out loud. Taking a moment to force the lump from her throat, she handed back the letter. "I am sorry. I cannot deliver it for you. Perhaps there is someone else."

Ignoring the paper in her outstretched hand, Biggar said nothing as he studied her. Keeping his hands clasped behind his back, he smiled. "There is no one else, Lady Christina. It must be you. Your grandfather assured me that you would return."

She could not stop the tears from forming. There was nothing she wanted more than to see her grandfather and Lochmaben again. But that was not possible, no matter how hard she wished it to be. Her vision blurry, she glanced down.

Biggar stepped forward. Taking her other hand, he

placed it over the note. The paper sat firmly in her grasp. "You are the only one he trusts to deliver this letter."

She looked up.

The smile was gone. "Do not let go until he has it."

She should have said something, insisted that he had been misinformed. But as he walked out of the hall, she found no words, her mind disoriented. How could her grandfather make such promises? He knew what she had been brought here for. Standing there, as if frozen in place, his words to resist came flooding back. Still not knowing what they meant, she turned in frustration and walked out of the keep.

Snow fell softly down around her as she stood outside. The men remained in the hall. She pictured them around the table near the fire as she descended the hill. Night was upon them bringing darkness and silence. She cherished them both. Entering the bailey, she grabbed the bow hanging in the rafters of the stable and stepped to face the burlap sack mounted against the wall. The arrow released. She heard Cailean's voice before it even hit the mark.

"Relax your hand."

She did not turn. Taking another dart from the quiver, she nocked it into the bow. Cailean moved to her right. He stopped and leaned against the post.

Her eyes flicked over to the piece of straw he twirled in his hands. Returning her gaze to the target, she drew the arrow. She loosened her grip slightly and slid her fingers back.

She hit the mark cleanly, the narrow stem sticking out of the centre. She drew another. Lifting the bow, the wood sprang forward, feathers silently cutting through the dim light as she exhaled. The fresh air felt nice in her lungs.

Reaching once more into the quiver, she heard the call go up. The men from the tower descended the hill. She turned to watch the gate open.

A single rider came through the wall. She did not recognize Hay until he dismounted. Spotting her by the stables, Hay walked towards her. She faced the target once more.

He stopped a few paces away as she shot. He waited for her to acknowledge his presence. Ignoring him, she nocked another arrow. He spoke as she let it loose.

"There is something I must tell you."

She drew the arrows faster, one after another, refusing to turn. Each hit their mark, the sound rhythmic. She reached for the last one. Hay stepped into her sightline the moment she let go.

The arrow missed his head by less than a finger's width, but Hay did not move. He did not even flinch.

Horrified, Christina lowered the bow.

His ashy-grey eyes stared back.

Looking away from the scar that ran across his forehead, she stiffened her resolve. "I do not care." Her voice was firm. "I am not interested in anything you have to say."

Setting the bow against the post, she picked up the quiver and walked past him to the target. She yanked the arrows out one-by-one. His voice sounded behind her.

"Alan MacBlane."

Still facing the wall, her palm squeezed the wooden stem within her grasp. She had not heard that name in years. Unable to pretend it meant nothing, she pulled the arrow out of the burlap and threw it into the pouch. She turned around. "Are you certain?" she asked. She took a single step towards him. "You only get to use it once."

Hay nodded. Christina took a breath.

Hay's disloyalty to her those years ago was not a simple matter. A pair of oxen had gone missing from Carrick not far from the Gallovidian border. Lost for over a week, they suddenly reappeared, found in the same pasture they had vanished from. When Hay informed her father that Christina had been the one to return them, her father grounded her for the rest of the summer. Trapped inside the castle, her siblings free to roam the land, she had never been more miserable. But the story Hay had told her father was not the whole of it. While Christina had indeed snuck into Galloway and retrieved the Carrick oxen, that was not the reason she had crossed the border. No – that foolish act was because of Alan MacBlane.

She was not supposed to know him – she was from Carrick and he was a Gallovidian. They met by chance, both sailing their small vessels to a beach not far from home. When they realized where the other was from, Hay pointing out the marks on the other's boat, Christina would never forget how the air around her suddenly felt different. For a moment, all was still. Then the tension broke.

Voices rose in anger as they slung insults back and forth. They were not old enough to fight, that was true for all of them. But when a boy called Christina's family a bunch of murderous cowards, she felt the blood freeze in her veins.

It had taken her a while to find out who he was. When she did, she snuck into Galloway in the dead of night and climbed through Alan's open bedroom window. She wished she could have stayed to watch him wake and find the note she had stabbed into the wall above his head. Instead, she returned home, coming across the oxen by chance. While

Hay had betrayed her trust, by not telling her father the entirety of the story he had saved her from the wrath that would have inevitably come. She owed him for that.

Staring at him across from her, she said, "Go on then. Speak."

He hesitated for a moment. "Do you remember when Rob trained in England with the other sons of Scotland?"

Folding her arms across her chest, she nodded.

"I went to visit him at the English court. Gartnait of Mar was there."

Though she wished they did not, his words piqued her interest. She wanted to skip to the end of the story, to get to the point, but she remained silent.

"I did not see much of Gartnait. He was always disappearing after the evening meal." Hay paused. "But when I mentioned it to David Brechin, he told me what Gartnait was up to."

A look of uncertainty fell across Hay's face. It was as if he did not want to continue. Standing there waiting, Christina grew more impatient and more interested by the second. He had her full attention now.

Hay cleared his throat. "Every night, while the others rested, Gartnait would sneak off to play cards and dice games. Brechin followed him once." His brow furrowed, and he pursed his lips. "Gartnait lost more money in a single game of Hazard than a knight earns in a lifetime."

Christina's hopes fell. She was disappointed. Not in Gartnait's behaviour – that was expected. Men like him usually had more than one transgression. For a brief moment though, as Hay spoke, she thought her marriage might be stopped. Hay had wasted what was owed to him.

Her arms dropping to her sides, her frustration returned. "So what?" she asked.

He smiled as though she should know what it meant.

When she remained silent, not bothering to hide her irritation, he took a step towards her.

"Think about it, Christina." He stared into her. "Gartnait has no income, no money to gamble away. Who, outside your family and his, would willingly cover his losses? Who would want the future mormaer of Mar to be in their debt?"

The name came to her instantly. Keeping his gaze, she saw Hay's optimism. There was no way Gartnait was that dumb. If it was true, her family would be furious. She shook her head and said, "It is not possible."

His smile fell. "Maybe not. But if you want out of this marriage, do you not think you should find out?"

She stared at him in silence. What he expected of her was absurd. She could not just reach out to the family hers hated most. Such an act would be unforgivable. Besides, even if she could be convinced to do it, she had no time. "How?"

He ignored her question. "You have ten days."

She almost laughed. "Ten days?" Her tone was bitter. Perhaps Hay had forgotten. "I will be married in three."

He stepped forward, closing the distance between them. The intensity of his gaze was unnerving. When he spoke again, his voice was quiet. "Elen, the Countess of Mar, is dead."

Christina stared at him in shock. She had just been at Kildrummy; she had just seen the countess. She did not understand. Hay offered no explanation.

"The land is in mourning. Your wedding has been

postponed." He paused. "Ten days, Christina. That is all you have. Do not waste it."

Rendered speechless, she watched him walk away. She did not know what to feel. If Elen of Mar was dead, she had a chance to find out who Gartnait was indebted to. It did not make her happy. She would have to go against her family and put herself in harm's way. Hay swung himself back onto his horse. His frame disappearing into the night as he rode from the bailey, Christina was not sure this was what her grandfather meant when he told her to disobey the demands of lesser men. She was not sure he wanted her to be this bold.

"Your heart must ache for Gartnait."

Back in Kildrummy, Christina looked at Anna of Fife beside her. The noble houses had gathered to lay Elen ferch Llywelyn of Mar to rest. They buried her in Saint Bride's Chapel, the parish church two miles from the castle. Anna had come with her grandson Donnchadh, the six-year-old Mormaer of Fife, the fourth of his name. Afraid her answer would sound indifferent, Christina nodded her reply.

It was not that she did not mourn Mar's loss. Elen had always treated her with kindness. Christina knew all too well the pain of losing a mother. But Gartnait and her heart had nothing to do with it – they had nothing to do with each other. She let her gaze drift around the hall. Her mouth went dry when she saw Andrew.

On the other side of the room, he spoke with the person standing next to him. He seemed oblivious to her presence. A young woman came into view. She rested her hand lightly on Andrew's arm. Christina felt her chest constrict.

Dorothea of Ross was the eldest child of William, Mormaer of Ross. She was more beautiful than Christina remembered. Her fair skin and slender frame drew admiring glances. Christina knew very little about Andrew's new wife. Situated deep in the Highlands, Ross was far from any of her family's lands. She stared at the gentle touch shared between husband and wife. She felt as though she would be sick. Setting her cup down on the table, she walked quickly from the hall.

She made it to the stairwell before she doubled over. It felt like a knife was twisting in her stomach. The pain made it hard to breathe. Hearing the footsteps coming towards her, she pushed herself upright against the wall.

Cailean's concerned face rounded the corner.

Relieved it was him, the air rushed from her lungs. Her shoulders relaxed.

Stopping on the stair below her, he reached out and pressed the back of his hand to her cheek. She did not doubt she looked ill. She felt pale. Cold sweat formed on the back of her neck. Ever since the death of her mother, no affliction went unnoticed.

Seeing the way Cailean's brow deepened, Christina removed his hand and said, "I am all right." She looked at him expectantly.

His eyes narrowing with disapproval, he told her what she wanted to know. "He is waiting."

Pushing off the wall, Christina descended the stairs. Walking from the castle, the breeze relieved her warm skin as she moved across the grounds towards the northeast tower. The tension in her body began to melt away. She felt calmer than she expected. If everything went according to plan, she would have her answer before Rob noticed she was missing from the hall. All she had to do was hold her nerve and she would be free. Pulling the door open, the hinges squeaked. Cailean followed her up the stairs.

Reaching the landing, she stared at the room ahead of her. She felt the note hidden up her sleeve. The roll of parchment was precisely where she had placed it earlier that day. Gripping the handle, she opened the door.

John Comyn, son of the Lord of Badenoch, met her gaze as she entered. Stood near the only window, the sun highlighted his red hair as it streamed into the small space. The isolated room had not been used for some time. Cobwebs covered the walls; the scratch marks along the stone were dull and dusty. Her eyes drifted across the floor to the bed of hay in the corner. Feeling Comyn's waiting gaze, she looked up.

He stared at her in silence before he motioned with his head. The man who had come with him into the tower moved past her and out the door.

Glancing back, Christina gave Cailean a similar look. He did not go far. Wedging a rock beneath the door, he returned to the top of the stairs. His eyes never left her frame. Knowing it was the most privacy he would give them, she faced Comyn once more.

A small smirk played at his lips. He straightened, his lean, muscular frame no longer leaning on the wall next to the window.

She knew her request to meet was odd. It went against everything she had been taught. Looking at the man they called the Red Comyn, his eyes dark and thoughtful, she pushed her apprehension aside. He would help her. He just did not know it yet. Unwilling to wait any longer, she asked, "Why would the King of England be making inquiries in the Lowlands?"

Her question seemed to amuse him. His smile widened before he looked down, clasping his hands behind his back.

He would know the answer. The King of Scots was his uncle. But she was not inquiring about what King John knew. She wanted to know what the Lord of Badenoch, the Red Comyn's father and the real power behind the Scottish throne, knew about English activities along the border.

"What do you know about Edward, the English king?"

His directness surprised her. Her father's close relationship with King Edward was no secret. Their ties to England only strengthened when her grandfather refused to swear allegiance to King John. If she was to get what she wanted in return, she could not give the information up quickly. The Red Comyn would have to be convinced of its value. Otherwise, he would not tell her what she needed to know. "Does his inquest into Scotland have to do with the treaty in Paris?" she asked. "The one John signed?"

Comyn stepped closer. He stared at her thoughtfully. "I see your grandfather's friends in the French court have been serving him well. And his affection for you has not changed."

She did not respond. The information had come from a clergyman in Rome. The Norwegians had also confirmed it, but she was not about to tell him that. It was better to let him think he had it all figured out. "Will you answer my question or not?"

He chuckled softly. "Why should I? Anything I say will end up in the English court, whispered into Edward's ear. Why would I tell you anything?"

She had her answer ready. "Because," she replied. "I know what Edward's doing. I know what he seeks."

Stepping away, he smiled. His gaze returned to the window.

Christina waited, well-versed in games of strategy. Her brother had taught her thoroughly. Sometimes, all it took was a little patience. A few birds caught her eyes as they flew by the tower. Their chirps rose upon the wind. The Red Comyn looked at her once more.

"What makes you think we do not know what he seeks?" He paused. "Edward has not tried to hide his activities. His tax collectors and sheriffs govern as if we are in England. What else is there to know?"

It was her turn to smile. If she had learned anything from her grandfather, it was that people's minds worked in similar ways. They liked to think they were smart, that their actions were not predictable. But despite the eloquence in which they spoke and the idea of themselves they wanted to project, she found that most thought in a similar pattern. For example, they did not linger if they already knew everything. She switched strategies. "Is there someone else I should be speaking to? Was I wrong to come to you with this?"

The smile returned, but it did not stay. Looking down at his feet, he crossed his arms in front of him. "Tell me then, Lady Christina." His voice was compliant. "What is King Edward of England doing in the Lowlands?"

She waited a moment before she spoke. She could not falter now. Choosing her words carefully, she said, "Gartnait of Mar. How much does he owe you and your kin?"

He almost laughed before his face turned sour. "I suppose I should not be surprised." His distaste for her was evident. "Would it be too much to ask House Bruce to serve their king?"

She glared in response to the sarcastic question. While his remark did not disparage her family, the suggestion that they were disloyal to the Scottish throne was careless. She risked her family's ire and good reputation by standing here alone with him. But she would bring it all down upon herself if he did not bite his tongue. Her brothers would not take kindly to his opinions. Perhaps it would not be the only death they mourned that day.

Reading the warning in her eyes, he returned to the matter at hand. "Gartnait of Mar." He glanced away. "Tell me about Edward, and I will tell you about Gartnait and what he owes."

Hope burst up. She rejected it. She had prepared for this scenario. It was no surprise that he offered to tell her only after she told him, but she did not trust him that much. She did not trust him at all. Keeping the anger on her face, she said, "I promise you, what I know is worth much more to your father and King John than what you know about Gartnait." She held his intimidating gaze. "You must answer my question first."

The charm he had cloaked himself in earlier was gone. She could tell he was considering her offer, weighing the rewards of bringing his family news about England over keeping deeply desired information from a Bruce. He frowned and adjusted the sleeve of his tunic. "Gartnait of Mar owes House Comyn enough."

"Enough?" She barely heard her voice over the pounding of her heart.

He stared back at her. "Enough to break the ties the bind you."

Relief rushed over her. She smiled ever so slightly. It was over. She could go home. She had found a way out.

"Lady Christina."

The Red Comyn's voice broke her bliss. His face had turned dark and foreboding. Seeing the threatening look, she remembered what she had promised.

"I have to warn you," he began. "If you do not have the information-"

She stepped forward and took his hand. Her unexpected movements cut him off. Pulling the note from her sleeve, she pressed it into his palm.

He looked back at her in confusion.

She explained. "There are Englishmen in the Lowlands surveying castles. They are noting our defenses and the number of men within them." Her voice was quiet. "And as for Wallace-" The sudden look of interest on his face made her pause.

When she had first read the dead Englishman's note by the river in Annan, she barely noticed the name written lightly along the edge. Examining the message later that night, she thought it was nothing of consequence. But as they journeyed through Lanark, English blood running through the streets, she changed her mind. If there was a Scotsman capable of enacting that kind of swift and targeted violence, it would be the twenty-three-year-old outlaw from Renfrewshire. No one hated the English more.

"You might want to warn him," she continued. "He has captured the attention of the English king."

CHAPTER FIVE

THE WIND WHIPPED her hood back, pelting her face with freezing rain. She was tired and cold atop her horse. But none of that mattered. She was going home to Lochmaben and she was free.

Telling Rob about Gartnait's debt had been harder than she expected. Each word had to be carefully chosen. She needed him to believe her. He said nothing at the end, his blank expression staring back as she stood by the door, her hands nervously clasped together. Leaving the room, she worried he did not care about what she had discovered. It was only when he found her in Garioch two days later, his cheeks flushed from riding, did she hear the words she had prayed to the saints for every night.

"Prepare your things. We are going home."

Heading south, they arrived in Paisley on the fifth day. Home to the Stewarts, the town sat in the heart of Renfrewshire, just north of Carrick. It was early afternoon. Clouds gathered on the horizon. Thankful to be off her horse, Christina strolled out into the meadow.

Winter's heartless grip on the Lowlands had finally released. Wildflowers bloomed in bunches, and crops had been sown in the fields. Christina's fingers reached down to lightly caress a cluster of bluebells. A falcon's cry brought her gaze upwards. Following its flight, she watched as it travelled across the open, sun-filled sky, coming to circle above a figure on the hill. A waiting arm stretched out. The winged predator swooped down with precision and latched onto the man's fist.

James Stewart smiled as Christina came to a stop before him. Lord of the land and head of his kindred, he was the fifth High Steward of Scotland, inheriting the role of managing the king's household upon his father's death. Only ten years older than her, he was young for holding so much power. Christina thought it suited him. Like the men of his house before him, James wore responsibility well.

"Spring has found us once more."

Smiling in response, Christina admired the falcon still perched on his hand. Its chest was white, blue-grey speckles spread throughout. The bird's eyes never stopped moving.

"Did you find what you were looking for in Mar?"

Christina's gaze returned to the man in front of her. His knowledge of their journey north was no surprise. Word would have spread of Rob's presence in the Highlands. But as she looked back at James, a small smile on his lips, she could not shake the feeling that his question had nothing to do with Rob or why they went north. He knew something about her meeting with the Red Comyn. She did not like it.

"Yes." Keeping her reply simple, her eyes never left his face.

James nodded. He fed the falcon a morsel from his hand. "Sometimes, the answers we seek come from the most unlikely of places." He smiled again. "It would do Scotland well to remember that." His eyes drifted over the land in front of them. "Maybe then, we will find our way out of the darkness."

He left her there. Christina stood alone in the field contemplating the meaning of his words. It felt like she was being warned. The murder of English soldiers in the Lowlands had only increased in recent weeks. There was a band of men ranging the countryside killing the English at will. While she had her suspicions, she did not doubt James knew who it was. She would be a fool not to heed his advice.

A storm brewed on the horizon. Grey clouds cloaked Paisley in darkness as thunder rumbled. Hurrying back to the village, she was too late. The sky opened. Buckets of water crashed down on top of her. Cold and wet, Christina spotted the abbey up ahead. She ran for shelter. Pulling the door open, she darted inside.

She was drenched. Water dripped off her dress and onto the floor. Shaking the rain from her hands, she looked up into the nave of the priory. The men staring back made her stop.

She did not know who they were, but it did not matter. Her sudden entrance into the abbey had disrupted a private meeting. A man spoke quietly with a monk near the altar. But that was not what troubled her. The threat lay in the three men at the back, close to the door where she stood and in the way their eyes held her. As soon as one of them stepped towards her, she spun and reached for the door.

She was fast, but not fast enough. Arms grabbed her from behind. A calloused hand closed over her mouth, silencing her protests. She wrenched her body as hard as she could, desperate to get free, but it was no use. The man who held her did not budge. Fear thickened in her throat as she was dragged deeper into the church. A voice broke through her panic.

"What are you doing?"

Abruptly sat down on a pew, a pair of hands pressed firmly on her shoulders. Christina watched the monk approach.

He looked at the men standing around her. Anger flashed across his face. He asked the question again. "What are you doing?"

One of the men moved forward. He pushed his dark, shoulder-length hair back from his face. "We caught ourselves a spy." He grinned at her in amusement. "She is stronger than she looks."

Christina glared back, attempting to shrug off the hands that held her down. They remained in place. She was about to demand to be let go when the monk suddenly stepped closer. Grabbing the dark-haired man by the arm, he pulled him aside.

"What have you done?"

Though it was whispered, Christina could hear the monk's concern. He was no longer angry. He was afraid. "Do you not know who she is?"

The other man glanced back at her. A look of uncertainty flickered across his face before it disappeared. Returning his attention to the man of the church, he said, "I do not care who she is. She saw him."

Their voices dropped. Christina could no longer hear them, but it did not matter. They knew who she was. She would not be harmed. Besides, the longer they kept her there, the sooner Cailean would come. She had asked him not to follow – she was only going out into the field – and he had obliged. The storm and her failure to return would bring him looking. He would not hesitate to do whatever it took to find her. No longer afraid, she relaxed in her seat.

Movement at the altar caught her gaze. She had forgotten about the man standing there. The monk had left him to deal with the chaos of her arrival. She watched him descend the small set of stairs. His steps slow and relaxed as he came towards her, the certainty of her impending freedom shattered.

William Wallace, son of Alan, looked down at her. The others went quiet. With a nod of his head, they moved away. The hands lifted off her shoulders.

Christina shivered. Staring at the large man before her, his features distinct and familiar, she straightened her back against the pew. She needed her head despite what her heart was doing. As he lowered his frame down onto the bench in front of her, she recalled the last time she had seen him.

It was three years ago. The tournament in Stirling drew people from across the kingdom. She had become intimately familiar with watching men fight as a young child, the sound of metal clashing a constant in the training grounds at Turnberry Castle. Standing with her sisters around the arena, the largest man she had ever seen entered the enclosure. She swore the longsword in his hands gleamed with menace.

The fight was brief, Wallace emerging as the victor. You could count the number of blows he landed, his opponent's armour dented thoroughly. As Christina looked at him now, his face calm and his body at ease, she saw that the past few months of living in hiding had not diminished his character. He was as unafraid as the day she first laid eyes on him.

"We find ourselves in a precarious position." He hung

his arm casually over the back of the pew. His gaze hovered on the men waiting nearby before he turned to her.

His eyes were kinder than she expected. The stories that circulated made him out to be some kind of monster, a terror that lurked in the night. But that was the English version, the one her younger brothers told to scare Matilda. The tales that originated in the Scottish villages were more heroic. He was a Scotsman, taking a stand and fighting for justice when the king would not. He was doing what they all wished they could.

"You are a Bruce, and I am an outlaw. But seeing as we both have something to lose…" He paused, staring back at her. "I was hoping we could reach an understanding."

She had not expected him to be so honest. She was used to games, of men hiding what they wanted. She saw only transparency in his face. "What do you have in mind?"

Her response made him smile. He looked back over at his men.

They seemed uncomfortable; eyes narrowed, faces grim and untrusting. Christina watched the monk. His finger tapped nervously against the back of his hand. Wallace finally answered.

"I will deny ever seeing you if you do the same."

The solution simple and easy to execute, she nodded. She would say she found refuge from the storm in the abbey, as she had. She would just leave out the part about meeting him.

"We have an agreement?" he asked.

"Yes." Leaning forward, she offered her arm.

He grinned and reached over the back of the pew. His

grip was tight as his hand latched onto her forearm. Squeezing in return, Christina let go and stood.

She had meant to walk out of the church, not knowing or caring if it was still raining. But as she stepped out into the aisle, she hesitated. She turned to face Wallace once more.

"You need to be more discreet," she said.

Already standing, he looked back at her in surprise.

"You are attracting attention. The wrong kind."

"William."

The warning from one of the men was clear, but Wallace ignored it. He took a step towards her. When he spoke, his voice was soft. "And whose attention would that be?"

"Edward's." She was not quite sure why she was telling him this. Wallace would not be enough. One man, let alone one from a minor family, could never bring the King of England to heel. It would take every Scot, united under one aim, under one king, to defeat the beast constantly hammering at their door. Even then, it seemed unlikely. But as she stood there knowing all this, she could not help but admire Wallace and his foolish pursuit of a land free of Englishmen.

"And you know this how?"

The question did not come from Wallace. Christina turned to find herself looking at the man who had held her hostage a short while ago. His reaction to her had changed drastically, the pleased look he had once given her now pure hostility. He looked like he wanted nothing more than to slit her throat. Ignoring him, she faced Wallace again.

"Your whereabouts are being sought in the Lowlands." She spoke quickly. "If you intend to stay, I would advise you to take extra precautions."

He was silent for a moment. "Anything else?"

Normally such a question would drip with sarcasm. But looking back at the giant of a man before her, she saw only genuine intention. "King John…" she paused, trying to find the right words. "If he has given his support, I would not depend on it too heavily." She could not believe she was saying this out loud. It was not treason, but it was close. Something in the way the Red Comyn had reacted to Wallace's name urged her to warn him.

"He has not," Wallace replied.

She looked back in confusion. "Then why do this?"

He smiled at her as if she was a child.

She attempted to explain. "I understand your anger. But what good does killing every Englishman do? What does it do for Scotland?"

An irritated scoff came from the side of the room. Wallace silenced it with a single look. Holding her gaze once more, he asked, "When John was crowned, where were you? Where was your family?"

Her muscles tightened defensively. He knew perfectly well where her family was. They were the only noble house not present as a new King of Scots took the throne. It irritated her to no end that she kept coming up against this, the choices made by the men of her kindred marking her as well. Fighting back the urge to explain her family's actions, she considered her reply. Wallace beat her to it.

"I was there, as were most of these men."

She glanced over at the others.

"With the crowning of King John, we thought that Scotland would be what she once was: independent, strong, and free."

She stared back at him.

"But that is not what we got." Anger danced across his face. "We got English oppression, servitude, and taxes." He took a step back, lifting a hand to rub his cheek. "We have been patient, waiting for those who have the means to do what is right. But Edward has only furthered his invasion, doing so without making a declaration of war, without issuing a call to arms." He looked back at her, his eyes on fire. "We do this simply because others will not. Because our king cannot. Because, Lady Christina, we can wait no longer for those who are supposed to lead to do what must be done."

The door to the abbey squeaked open. Christina froze. Wallace had already turned around, his men disappearing into the shadows as he headed in the other direction. The monk hurried towards the door.

Uncertain of what to do, she remained where she was. She wanted to turn and look but did not trust herself. If it was Cailean or one of her brother's men, she would not be able to keep her nervousness off her face. She was about to take a seat on the bench when the footsteps approached.

"My apologies for keeping her." The monk's voice grew louder as he walked. "We lost track of the day."

Clasping her hands together, she took a breath. The tightness in her face subsided. Feeling calm, she turned.

Seton's stare waited. She expected him to say something. He did not. Refusing to shrink under his gaze, she straightened her posture. Seton may have seen her with Wallace, but that did not mean she would admit to it. Even if he told Rob, there were many ways she could play this out.

The monk glanced between them. "Please tell the Mormaer of Carrick that it was my mistake." There was a slight tremor in his voice.

Seton remained silent, his eyes never leaving hers. Knowing they could not stay like this forever, Christina relented and turned to the clergyman.

"Thank you," she said, smiling at him, "for letting me seek refuge in your abbey. It was a wonderful way to wait out the storm."

Following her lead, he clasped her hands between his and smiled back. "You are always welcome here, Lady Christina. Send my greetings to your grandfather."

Squeezing the monk's hands in response, she walked past Seton and out of the abbey.

The streets were empty as they made their way back to the castle. The rain had stopped, the roads wet and glistening as dusk fell. It was darker than usual. Storm clouds still hovered above, threatening to break open once more. She glanced over at Seton beside her. He kept his gaze straight ahead.

She had become used to his presence in Garioch and Mar. His was an almost constant silence. Even after all this time, she could not figure him out. While the other men did not hide who they preferred to follow – her grandfather or Rob – Seton did not have any tells. He had helped her with the Englishman and said nothing. She had kept her composure in the church, and yet he knew she was guilty of something. Walking into the bailey, noise from the evening meal drifting out of the keep, she could hold back no longer. She needed to know who he was for. She spun to face him.

"What do you want?"

The hostility of her question made him stop. At first, his expression remained unchanged, but as a slight look of amusement emerged, he asked, "What makes you think I want anything?"

She almost laughed. Everyone wanted something, especially when they knew things they should not. Her grandfather had taught her that. It was what she was counting on now. "Just tell me," she said. She folded her arms in front of her. "What will make you forget the Englishman in the river and what you saw in the abbey?"

He no longer found her words funny. His smile vanished as quickly as it had appeared. He looked away. "And what about the Red Comyn?" His eyes found hers again. "Do you want me to forget about your visit with him as well?"

Her face fell as soon as he spoke that name. Any confidence she had disappeared. He knew more than she thought. If she was not careful, her nightmare of being married off to someone she did not want would begin again. And this time, there would be no way out. She was still struggling to come up with a response when he continued.

"You think you know everything." He shook his head in frustration. "But you do not."

For the first time, she did not need to guess what he was thinking. He told her outright.

"I have done nothing but help you, and you still do not trust me. You are more arrogant than Rob."

Surprised anger chased away her apprehension. She opened her mouth to defend herself. He was not finished.

"I know this may be difficult for you to understand since you only think about yourself, but if I wanted to betray you, if I had *any* desire to do it, do you not think I would have done it by now?"

A shout from atop the wall rang out. Christina ignored it, keeping her attention on Seton. His irritated glare radiated back. A rider burst through the gate and into the bailey.

Unable to disregard it any longer, she caught sight of the dark figure rushing towards the tower.

She did not see it at first, the banner obscure in the dark. But as the messenger dismounted and hurried inside, the candlelight from the keep illuminated the fabric draped across the back of the horse. A red x covered a yellow shield. Suddenly, Seton did not matter. She ran after the rider from Annandale.

She failed to catch up. His feet moved faster than hers as he sprinted up the stairs. She tried to dismiss the alarm mounting inside, but it was no use. Nothing good came from a message delivered in the night. Reaching the hall, she spotted the rider as she strode through the door. He leaned down into Rob's ear, lips moving quickly. Finished, he straightened and took a step back. Christina's gaze latched onto her brother.

For a while, Rob did not move. He simply sat there, blankly staring at the table as the conversations around him continued. Her pounding heart drowned out the noise. Rob finally stood.

Bracing his palms against the table, he looked around the room. He stopped when his eyes found her waiting by the door. The moment she saw the desolation within, she knew what it meant. Her heart shattered in an instant.

CHAPTER SIX

ROBERT BRUCE, THE Competitor, the fifth of his name, was dead.

They laid him to rest at Gisborough Priory in North Yorkshire, England. Dedicated to Saint Mary, the monastery had been founded by the first Robert Bruce over a hundred years earlier. Every Bruce who had carried the title of Lord of Annandale was buried here. In the nave with her siblings, Christina nodded numbly at the words of comfort offered by those who came to mourn her grandfather's passing. It did nothing to calm the turmoil within. A storm was brewing on the horizon; she could feel it. There was no one to protect her now.

They returned to Lochmaben. Riding up to the castle, Christina slowed. It felt different. The imposing walls no longer gave her comfort. All she could think of was her father. He would be here soon. Rob had sent a letter to Norway. His reply, arriving ten days later, had been short.

I will return.

Christina never knew three simple words could cause such distress.

"Matilda! You idiot!"

Standing atop the tower, Christina heard the admonishment as she looked out across the loch, Mary's angry voice carrying up from the open window. She had come here to be alone, Lochmaben bustling in preparation for their absent lord's return. Even Rob remained. Catching sight of an osprey as it scanned the water for fish, she wanted nothing more than to ignore the argument happening in the hall below. But she could not. She was responsible for her sisters now. Sighing, she left the broken quiet of the fresh morning air and headed inside.

The commotion only increased as she descended the stairs. Stepping into the room, Christina watched Mary and Matilda lean across the table towards one another, slinging spiteful insults back and forth. Porridge was scattered across the floor, shards of broken porcelain mixed throughout. The moment Matilda called Mary a smelly cow, Christina walked forward and slammed her hand down on the table.

The sound reverberated across the wooden surface. The room went silent. Oblivious to her presence, her sisters stared back at her in surprise. Wrenching the spoon from Matilda's hand, the utensil clenched in her fist like a knife, the youngest Bruce daughter sank despondently in her seat.

Mary was not so easily intimidated. The glare she had been directing Matilda's way was now aimed at Christina. Placing the spoon silently on the table, Christina knelt and began picking the clay fragments up off the floor.

"Matilda," she said, her fingers sifting through the goo, "let Arthur inside."

Matilda did not have to be told twice. Her sour expression disappeared as she ran off to find her favourite dog. Christina gathered the pieces in silence. Finished, she stood and dropped the chunks onto a plate. Wiping her hands clean, she sat down in Matilda's empty chair.

Mary's scowling face met her gaze. She had their mother's eyes, light green and bright, but their father's anger, quick and fatal. They had been at Lochmaben for only a few days and yet Mary's sullen disposition already contaminated the air around them. Everyone was miserable. Christina waited patiently for an explanation. Eventually, Mary gave in.

"I hate it here."

Christina kept quiet.

"This is not my home and it never will be. I wish I were back in Carrick."

Remaining still, Christina let out a long, inward sigh. Mary had been free to do what she wanted at Turnberry. Rob raised his sisters with a kind and tender hand. But that time was over. Their father did not share his son's approach to rearing children. The life Mary was about to experience at Lochmaben would be strict, orderly and seldom pleasant. Shoving her consternation aside, Christina leaned her arms against the table and mustered up the strength to say what Mary needed to hear.

"So, you do not want to be here?"

Mary nodded.

"Do you think any of us get what we want?"

Taken aback by her sharp tone, Mary sagged in her chair.

"You are not a child anymore," Christina continued. "You are old enough to be married, old enough to know what is expected of you. So stop." She sighed again. This time she did not hide it. "Stop fighting everyone around you."

Tears formed in Mary's eyes. Christina pushed herself back from the table.

It was not that she wanted to say these things. She wished she could tell her sister that it would be all right, that they would be happy here. But that would be a lie and Mary needed the truth. She needed the chance to accept her new predicament before their father returned, before he could inflict more pain. Christina walked towards the door. Mary's voice sounded behind her.

"I will *not* forgive him."

Christina turned. Her sister's eyes had hardened once more. "I am not asking you to."

Mary stared back.

"I simply want you to understand that you are not the only one who feels-" She searched for the right word. "-disappointed, in the way things have to be." She looked at the wounded face before her. "You are not alone, Mary. Remember that."

The sound of feet running up the stairs interrupted them. Mary dropped her gaze to the table. Watching the dog sprint into the hall, Matilda right behind, Christina turned from the room. Mary was not the only one who needed to make peace. If Christina was to survive the summer and not end up exactly where she was a month ago – engaged to a man she did not want – she needed to take her own advice. Her father's suffocating hold felt tighter now. Winding down the staircase, she left the keep and walked out the gate.

She followed the edge of the loch. The water was calm. A light current waved throughout as she stepped along the path. Cailean was somewhere behind her. The trees kept him from view. Christina's thoughts drifted once more to her father and the havoc he would bring.

Their relationship had been strained from the start. He wanted her to be like Isabel, obedient and demure, but Christina had other plans. From the moment she could walk, she followed her brothers at every turn, insisting on being taught how to fight, ride, hunt, and track. At first, her parents indulged her – mostly her mother. But the moment Marjorie died, taking her father's joy with, everything stopped. Christina was told to do her duty and learn her place.

A quiet rustle broke the silence. She looked out at the trail ahead. It sounded again, but this time closer and to her left. She barely turned before she saw the blur of a small child running through the trees. Another darted out in front of her. The stirring grew louder, sounding from all directions. She was trying to make out a face between the pines when a small hand lightly touched the back of her arm.

"Run!" a boy yelled.

She knew instantly who it was. Listening to their scattering, she bunched up the skirt of her dress and took after nine-year-old Rory Fletcher.

Excited shrieks burst into the woods around her. They were fleeing, but clumped together, too scared to be caught on their own. The game had started when Rory was young, Christina using it to keep him from following her and his older sister Shona. They had not played much since Shona left to marry a merchant's son, but each time they did, Rory brought more of his friends along. As she chased after them now, she could not help but smirk at their frightened squeals. She caught the first one just as she crested the top of the hill.

Calum Kerr looked terrified for a moment before his face fell in disappointment. Letting go of his shoulder, Christina tossed his hair encouragingly and continued after the others. One-by-one, she captured them. By the time she caught up to Rory, finding him hiding in a hollowed-out trunk of a tree, they were well past the village.

She sank onto the ground beside him. He grinned as she caught her breath. Holding out her hand, he slapped a letter from Shona down into it. She tucked the note into her pocket. A familiar whistle split the air. Unsure of what it meant, she reluctantly pulled herself back onto her feet and headed towards the road.

Cailean was waiting not far from where she had entered the trees. Seeing her emerge from cover, Rory at her side, he took a step towards her, but then stopped and turned in the other direction. The uncertainty of his movements made her hesitate. Placing a cautionary hand on Rory's shoulder, she watched as Cailean's palm wrapped around the hilt of his sword. A rider appeared around the bend.

Spotting the Gallovidian standing there, the man atop the horse slowed. His eyes moved past him to Christina. He urged his horse forward.

"Lady Christina," he called out. "The Lord of Annandale has returned. Your presence is requested at Lochmaben."

He said nothing else, turning back for the castle. She found it difficult to move. Her father was here and he had sent a rider. After three years apart, three years of silence between them, nothing had changed. She was already at fault. Pushing her dread aside, she began the long walk back.

She found her father in the hall. Surrounded by men, he listened to their reports on the land and the villages within.

He looked the same. With broad shoulders and thick, brown hair, his agreeable features were impossible to miss. Perhaps that was why her mother had fallen in love with him so quickly. Watching him from the back of the room, Christina's heartbeat increased the moment his eyes found hers.

"Leave us." His voice was like a thunderclap. It silenced the man speaking and sent those gathered for the door.

Keeping her gaze on her father, Christina felt the men's glances as they walked by. One of them paused beside her. She turned to look.

Jardine stared back. He did not seem pleased. His face held the same look of warning he had given her at Kildrummy. She still did not know what it meant, and he did not explain. The hall growing silent, he walked out. Christina returned her attention to the only man left.

Robert Bruce, the sixth of his name and the Lord of Annandale, assessed her from where he stood. His fingertips rested on the table beside him. For a while, he did not move, merely looking at his second eldest daughter. Then he came towards her.

Reaching out, his large hands gently cupped her face. He ran a thumb down her cheek. A soft smile formed on his lips as he said, "You look like your mother."

Gazing up, she watched tears fill his eyes. His face fell. Letting go of her, he turned away. Staring at his back, Christina was reminded of the love story she knew so well.

At eighteen-years-old, Marjorie, the Countess of Carrick, became a widow. Her husband had died in the Holy Land fighting in the crusades. A knight was sent to inform her. Seated in the hall of Turnberry Castle, Marjorie listened as a young Robert Bruce from Annandale offered his condolences. Before he had even finished talking, Marjorie knew what she wanted.

Barring the doors and locking the gate, she refused to let him leave. She held him captive for days. Every morning and every night, she asked him to marry her. Sixteen times he did not answer. On the seventeenth, he said yes.

Christina watched her father walk away. Time had healed nothing. He was still broken, still afraid to live without the woman he loved. The realization was devastating. It meant he would still demand things from her she was not willing to give.

"Do you know why I have returned to Scotland now?"

Pulling her attention back to him, he sat down in the chair once reserved for her grandfather. He hung his hands casually over the armrests. The ledger was open on the table before him, newly written letters stacked beside. Knowing her answer did not matter, Christina remained silent.

"Your grandfather had many strengths." He stared at the floor. "But he had faults as well." Lifting his gaze, he looked at her for a moment before he said, "What he lacked was the willingness to recognize when to give up."

Christina struggled to keep the contempt from her face. Her grandfather did not know the meaning of defeat. Even when he lost, he never conceded, always working in some way to further his goal. Her father, on the other hand, did nothing but give up. The two men shared the same name and looked almost identical, but that was where the similarities ended. The traits which endeared her grandfather to so many had failed to pass on to his heir. Christina did not know when the disagreements between father and son started. The difference in character and opinion had divided them long before she was born. But it had only worsened in her father's absence. No bond, kinship or loyalty could close the ever-expanding gap that separated them. It had fractured the family in more ways than she could count. Looking at her father now, her heart heavy with disappointment, she wished he had stayed in Norway.

"For too long, your grandfather's actions have placed this family in the crosshairs of not one, but two kings." He sounded angry. "We are neither for John nor for Edward." He paused. "He foolishly risked everything. Not just our lands here, but in England and Ireland as well. All because he would not swear allegiance. All because he would not bend the knee. I have come to rectify his mistakes."

She had been wrong earlier, thinking nothing had changed. This was not the same broken-hearted man who left three years ago. He was colder and uncaring, even to his own kin. He had changed indeed. And this was worse.

His gaze weighed heavily on her. "I suppose you think you are clever, with what you did in Mar."

It was not a compliment. She did not take it as one. If making peace with her had been his intention at the beginning, it certainly was not his aim now. The time for posturing was over. They were drawing battle lines in the heather. He was calling forth his schiltrons. Her archers were falling into place. Straightening her shoulders, Christina lifted her chin and waited for the hammer to drop.

"You manipulated your brother, and you jeopardized this family." His words came out like punches. "What happened with Gartnait will not happen again. The next time I tell you to marry a man, you will do your duty, and you will obey."

He waited for her to nod, to tell him she understood. Instead, she kept still and moved her gaze past him to the wall.

For a while, he stared back at her. She refused to look at him. When he picked up a letter and began to read, she spun on her heel and walked out of the hall.

Descending the stairs, she struggled to keep her emotions in check. She knew what her father would do. As soon as he finished inspecting the land, he would go south and swear allegiance to England. The disrespect he showed his own father enraged her. The man might be gone, but his land and the people who loved him were still here. How could he expect them to bend the knee to a king who was not their own? Striding towards the exit, the afternoon sun blinded her as it streamed through the open door. She collided with someone rounding the corner.

Grabbing onto her arms, Randolph held her upright as she staggered back. He looked down at the scowl etched across her forehead. He gave her a sympathetic smile. "He is a hard man to please."

Christina's anger lessened as she looked up at her nephew. Randolph knew her father's disdain better than all of them. Long before he met her mother, Christina's father had been careless. Boys in his position often were, and a farmer's daughter became pregnant. Refusing to marry her, she was whisked away to a nunnery to live out her sin. She died in childbirth a few months later, leaving a baby girl behind. That should have been the end of it. Her father's lustful transgression should have never been spoken of again. But the saints had a different plan in mind. Fifteen years later, just weeks after Rob had been born, an abbess rode into Turnberry Castle. A newborn baby boy was wrapped tightly to her chest. That night, Thomas Randolph became one of them.

It was not her father's decision. His feelings on the matter were made perfectly clear throughout their childhood, Randolph receiving the brunt of his disdain. Christina had asked her mother once why she had kept him. She simply replied that he was blood. It was all that mattered.

"He will make me go back and marry him. I know he will." Her voice was small. When she saw the confusion on Randolph's face, she elaborated. "To Mar." She sighed. "I will be married to Gartnait before summer comes."

Randolph grinned.

Her temper surged at his reaction. He knew something she did not. She took a menacing step towards him.

"Go find your brother." He placed a hand on her shoulder. "He has something to tell you."

She did not have to ask which one. Moving past Randolph, she stepped out into the bailey.

Entertained shouts drew her to the training enclosure near the back. A crowd had gathered. Leaning against the wooden fence, she searched the faces but did not find Rob among them. Neil walked into the ring. A cheer went up. Knowing what was about to happen, she let herself be distracted and watched her brothers fight.

It was less of a match and more of a spectacle. The soft earth had turned to mud, covering Thomas and Alexander with it. They kept their eyes glued to their opponent as Neil stared them down from across the pit. Her younger brothers crept forward, their bodies low and their arms out. Neil met them in the centre.

They held their footing at first, each leaning against an arm as Neil tried to topple them. Edward shouted for them to use their legs and lean in. Alexander wobbled. He lifted his foot to correct his balance. His eyes widened when he realized his mistake.

The muck now under his boot, he slipped the moment he put weight on it. Neil only needed to shove him lightly to make him fall, the spectators groaning in amused disappointment. It was not long before Thomas joined him in the sludge. They struggled to pull their tired, defeated bodies out. Stepping carefully forward, Neil offered each of them a hand. They latched onto him. Halfway up, he let go. They fell back into the mud one more time.

Christina could not help but laugh.

Grinning, Neil turned, brushing off what little dirt he had on him. He made his way towards her. "Would you like to try it?" He smirked. "I have seen you fight. You cannot be worse than Tom and Alex."

She smiled at the jest before she asked, "Where is Rob?"

For a moment, Neil stared at her, the humour disappearing from his face.

Christina had kept to herself since returning from Mar. She knew her brothers had questions. Even if they asked, she would never tell them how she became aware of the debt Gartnait owed the Comyns. Waiting for Neil to respond, she thought he might question her about it now. But he did not. Instead, he lifted his eyes to the castle wall. Following his gaze, she found what she was looking for. She headed towards the gate.

Climbing the tower, Christina stepped out onto the narrow walkway that lined the barricade. A slight breeze brushed against her skin as she continued down the wall. The banners of their house fluttered overhead. Rob looked out over the loch. Saying nothing, she stopped beside him. He glanced over.

"Do you remember, when we were small, we tried to sail down the River Annan to the sea?"

Christina smiled. Her eyes remaining on the body of water ahead of them, she heard the amusement in Rob's voice.

"You had so many silver plates stuffed in your bag, we could barely float."

"We needed it for supplies," she replied with mock-seriousness. "How else would we make it to Ireland?"

Rob chuckled.

Silence falling between them, Christina looked at her brother. He had been her adversary for so long, she forgot what it felt like to be on the same side, to not be at war. "Randolph says you have something to tell me."

Rob turned to meet her gaze.

"About Gartnait and Mar."

He glanced up at the sky for a moment before he nodded. Looking out across the water, he said, "I love her. Isabella. I've loved her for some time."

Christina was surprised by the revelation.

"But with you betrothed to Gartnait-" Rob shrugged. "Isabella and I would never be together if you married her brother." He took a breath and exhaled. "So when you told me about his debts, I used it." He glanced back at her. "I told Domhnall that Gartnait's folly was unforgivable, that you would never be united with him. But for the sake of both our houses, to keep the ties between us strong, I would marry Isabella instead."

She wanted to laugh but did not find it funny. Her cheeks flushed with anger. All this time, Rob could have been working with her instead of being the one to bring her pain. Of course Domhnall agreed to the arrangement. He had gotten the better end of the deal. In Rob, he gained a powerful son-in-law and still had his eldest son's hand to secure another alliance. Thinking about the poor girl who would be Gartnait's wife, Christina forced her outrage back and told herself to be grateful. She had escaped from her engagement unscathed. Her honour and freedom were still intact. For now.

The thought made her look down into the bailey below. She caught a glimpse of her father as he stepped from the keep. Any relief that remained vanished in an instant. If she was not careful, if she did not pay attention, she would be just another poor girl married to a man others shuddered about.

CHAPTER SEVEN

S HE NEVER KNEW summer could be so miserable. Charged with her siblings' care, Christina was trapped within the castle grounds. Her father's watchful gaze was never far. Even when she managed to slip away, walking across the hills with Cailean in the early morning light, she felt the men following her from the gate.

The sun brought everyone outside. Travellers on the road increased as the air grew warm. The fields no longer empty, oats, barley and kale began to sprout. But that was not all summer brought. Summer also meant hunting, fishing and tournaments.

Rumbling through the congested streets, Edinburgh bustled with energy. The spectacle drew people from all over the kingdom, Rob and Neil among the knights vying for glory. Christina hated travelling by carriage. It restricted her ability to see. Leaning towards the window, Matilda's head knocked into hers for the thousandth time. She moved back against the wooden seat in resignation. She would see it once she was out. Then the fun could begin.

It was not just the competition she was looking forward to. With the noble houses of Scotland gathered in one place

– men young and old, rich and poor – striving to change their fates, no one would be paying attention to her. She looked at her siblings practically bouncing in their seats. For once, they would not be her responsibility. She planned on making the most of it.

Shona laughed as Christina wrapped her arms around her, squeezing her friend tight. It had been over a year since they last saw one another. Christina pulled back to look at her. She was unchanged – her face still slender and her hair still blond.

"Come on," Shona said, looping her arm through hers. "Let us go spy on Rob's competition."

It was as if a new town had been built just outside the burgh. Tents for competitors and their followers dominated the field, large sections of land turned into arenas, spectator stands towering up around them. There was the jousting stage, the archery range and the ring for individual battles such as the Lochaber axe and the longsword. But those were just side events. The heart of the tournament, and Christina's favourite, was the mêlée.

The first time she watched two groups of knights face off against each other, she had been eight-years-old. Sat with her family, she watched in awe as men charged into the chaos, metal slashing and glancing off armour, battling as one. The adrenaline of it all hooked her in. When it was over, she did not have to think about what she wanted. She turned to her grandfather and begged him to train her as a knight.

"There is something you should know."

Shona's voice broke her from the memory. They walked about the temporary market that curved its way through the grounds. As a principal centre for trade and the Scottish administration, the firth Edinburgh sat along opened to the North Sea. Tournaments drew not only spectators but merchants as well. The thousands of people who flocked needed food, mead and a wide selection of wares. It was not just those in Scotland who came. Flemish, German and Norwegian traders also made the journey. Listening to the various accents loudly bartering from their stalls, Christina looked at Shona expectantly.

"King John has lost the throne."

Christina cautiously glanced at the faces nearby. Shona often told her what was happening in the Scottish court through the letters she sent. She never signed them. Only a small mark at the bottom of the paper indicated who they were from. While the busy market gave them privacy, it would only take one person to overhear them.

"The Comyns have taken it." Shona kept her eyes straight ahead. "They call themselves the Council of Twelve."

Christina was silent as they continued to walk arm-in-arm through the market. It did not surprise her that John had been reduced to a figurehead. He had been just that for most of his reign. But if the Comyns had formed a council, removing the decision-making power from John's hands, she had no doubt there would be trouble. They had seized control of the kingdom without lifting a sword. At the very least, her grandfather's allies – even her father – would not react to the news well.

The tournament commenced. Each competitor was introduced, the banners of their House flying high. The crowd broke away as the matches began. Knowing Rob would be participating in the joust and Neil in the poleaxe,

Christina went to watch something she had never seen before – the archers of Selkirk Forest.

They were the best hunters in the kingdom. Unlike the longbows used by the Welsh, their weapons were small and light. Tipped with iron, the arrows only travelled so far, but as Christina watched them lift their bows, she saw that distance did not matter. The archers were quick and deadly. Each arrow hit its mark.

"Christina!"

She turned at the sound of her name being called. Unable to see who it was, she walked away from the spectators. Alexander urgently waved at her from a few yards away. The smile fell from her face.

She could hear the commotion before the tent was even in sight. Several men from Annandale hovered outside, concerned expressions covering each of them. They stepped back when they saw her. Taking a moment to steady herself, she opened the flap.

Neil was on the bed, his elbows propping his torso up. Hay and Jardine stood next to him, hands raised as he yelled at them to get back, the knife in his hand a warning.

Christina did not need to ask what happened. She could see the piece of wood lodged in his thigh from the door. The end of his opponent's weapon had unluckily broken off inside his leg. Hearing Hay tell him it needed to come out, his voice equally as loud, Christina entered the tent. The longer they waited to pull the stick from his flesh, the more painful it would be.

Neil's determination wavered the moment he saw her. The knife in his outstretched hand dipped. She did not stop until she was directly in front of him, the tip of the blade pressing into her stomach. He looked up at her and shook his head. She put her hand over his. Resigning, he let go.

"Do not make me do it," he pleaded. "I am not ready."

His words made her smile as she sat down beside him on the bed. Gently placing a hand on his leg, she looked at the wound. She had gotten her fair share of splinters as a child, and while this was not that, she decided it did not matter. She would use the same tactic Neil had used on her many years ago.

"I saw Maud, the Mormaer of Angus' daughter, at the archery competition today." She kept her voice even and her hand still as she spoke.

The name grabbed his interest. She could tell he was trying to figure out if it was a trick. His eyes searched her face for a clue. She continued.

"I do not know how the archers focused. It was impossible to look away from her in that red dress." She smiled, her face becoming more animated as she spoke. "It must have come from France. I have never seen anything so tight. The way it curved down her body-" She shook her head as if she was still in awe. "But that was not the best part." She leaned towards him. "You should have seen her neckline, Neil. It *plunged*."

Neil leaned back into the bed, his body relaxing at the thought of beautiful Maud in a tight, red dress. Christina grabbed the stick and pulled.

His scream made her ears ring. Bolting upright, he grabbed at the mug of ale Jardine offered, spilling more on than in him.

Christina peered into the gaping hole as he drank. She saw nothing but blood and flesh. Satisfied, she stood and handed the piece of wood to Hay. "Compare it to what is left of the pole, just to be sure," she said. Wiping her hands, she turned to leave. Neil's voice made her stop.

"Christina."

Glancing back, she watched Neil breathe slowly. He glared at her but said nothing else, unable to voice exactly what he felt.

She gave him a knowing smirk. "Cheer up, brother. Maybe now Maud will give you what you want." Listening to Hay fail to stifle his laugh, a choking sound emerging from his throat, she exited the tent.

Without William Wallace to challenge him, Rob easily won the joust and the longsword. Others from Bruce lands also did well in their matches. Walking from their lodgings to the tournament grounds the following morning, Matilda happily skipping along beside her, Christina knew the real test was still to come. The mêlée was that afternoon. The knights of Annandale were ready.

The sight of Andrew stopped her in her tracks. Heading in her general direction, he did not notice her in the crowd. She felt like trapped prey. All she wanted was to run and hide, but her feet would not move. Matilda called out her name, telling her to wait. His eyes found her in an instant.

A few months had passed since they had seen one another in Mar. Though it did not hurt as much, recalling his words still stung. As if he remembered too, Andrew's brows knit together. He aimed towards her.

She did not want to talk to him. Seeing the determined look on his face as he came closer, she knew if he reached her, she would not have a choice. She turned to her sister.

"Do you want to play a game?"

Matilda nodded.

Doing her best to seem excited, she said, "A barking beast hunts us. We must get away." Christina looked back. Andrew was almost within hearing distance. She gave her sister a smile. "Run!"

Grinning, Matilda took off into the sea of tents, Christina close behind. It was cowardly to flee, but she shoved the guilt aside. She owed Andrew nothing – less than that. She glanced back to make sure he was not following. No one was behind her. Satisfied, she turned around but then stopped. She was all alone. Her sister was gone.

"Matilda!"

The silence concerned her. She ran forward, looking down each row for any sign of her sister. Matilda could not have wandered far. A man stepping from his tent pulled her gaze. The colour of his tunic sent a spike of uncertainty through her. Slowing to a stop, she looked up.

Three golden bunches of wheat embroidered on a blue flag waved gently in the breeze. It took a moment for the folly to set in. Her heart pounded as she stared in dread at the Comyn banner. Unease filled her chest. She needed to get out of there. She needed to find her sister.

"Matilda!" This time, her voice was not so loud. Searching with renewed panic, she hurried through the tents. Her stomach twisted into a knot. The pain worsened with each moment she did not find her. She regretted running from Andrew now. If something happened to Matilda, she would never forgive herself.

Her sister's laugh was like a beacon in the night. Christina sprinted towards it. She came to a halt as soon as she rounded the corner.

The Mormaer of Buchan's black eyes stared back at her. Two men stood behind him. His hand rested on Matilda's shoulder. Her sister was oblivious to everything but the large deerhound sitting patiently at her feet.

Christina stepped forward. She glared at the mormaer. "Let her go."

For a moment, he kept his hands where they were, studying Christina all the while. Eventually, he smiled. He held them up in mock surrender.

Christina reached out towards her sister. "Matilda, come." She fought to keep the tremor from her voice. "We must go."

Matilda did not want to. Her face dropped. Giving the dog a few more scratches behind the ears, she walked away begrudgingly, her lower lip pushed out a little too far.

Grabbing her hand, Christina was never so grateful to have her sister within her grasp. Turning to leave, she steered Matilda to walk ahead of her. They did not get far. One of the men blocked their path.

"Move."

He ignored her demand. Instead, he looked over her head to the man behind her.

Christina followed his gaze back to the mormaer. Walking forward, he stopped at her side. "If you do not mind, Lady Christina, I would like a moment of your time."

Despite how it sounded, it was not a request. She was alone with Comyn men. He could ask for almost anything he wanted. She was about to comply when she saw Cailean approaching. The sight of him flooded her with relief. Taking a calming breath, she straightened. "No," she said. "You may not."

Though he smiled, the mormaer's eyes were cold. Vain and cruel, he was the worst of the Comyns. He looked down at the ground for a moment and interlocked his hands behind his back.

"Let me rephrase." He spoke slowly and lifted his gaze. "If you do not stay, if you refuse to do what I ask, I will make a claim against your father. I will tell the king that you invaded Comyn territory and provoked my men."

What little grace he projected before was gone. Christina glared at him.

In her desperation to escape Andrew, she had unknowingly broken a centuries-old agreement between their houses. Bruce and Comyn kept to themselves, whether at tournaments, at court, or any other event where both families were present. It was the only way to keep the peace. Their allies did the same, a clear border forming between the two kindreds wherever they went. She had not entered Comyn living quarters deliberately. No Bruce or Comyn would willingly walk into the other's camp alone. But it did not matter what her intentions were. Seeing the look in the mormaer's eyes, she knew he would follow through with his threat. What was one conversation between enemies when family honour was at stake? She turned to Matilda.

"See Cailean there?" She pointed to where he stood. Less than ten feet away, he silently assessed the situation.

Matilda nodded.

"Go and wait with him. I will not be long."

Matilda looked like she was about to protest. Christina gave her sister a gentle push forward.

Cailean stared back. His expression held a question. She shook her head. Matilda reaching him, he held her firmly by the shoulders. Christina turned around and looked at the mormaer expectantly.

"Your father has been busy since his return from Norway," he began, his voice quiet. The other men remained where they were. "He visits England quite often. I was not aware your father was so committed to his lands in the south."

He hesitated, waiting for her to respond. Staring back, she asked, "Is this why you kept me here? To tell you things you already know?"

He glowered.

She did not balk. "If you have a question, Mormaer Buchan, I suggest you ask it. Otherwise, you are wasting my time."

Not appreciating her tone, he stepped closer, his face only inches from hers. "Listen to me very carefully."

She could feel the anger seeping off him in waves.

"You will tell your father we know what he is doing. We know he is gathering complainants and witnesses against King John for the English court." The words rushed from his lips. "If he does not stop, if he continues to serve Edward and betray his king, he will answer for acts against the crown. You will tell him to heed my warning. He will not get another."

He hovered near her for a moment before he stepped back. She had not a clue what he was talking about. It sounded as if her father was helping King Edward build a legal case against King John. For what aim, she had no idea, but she would not figure it out standing there. She motioned for Cailean to leave. Grabbing Matilda's hand, he headed back towards the road. She went to follow.

"Lady Christina."

She glanced behind her once more.

"Be careful, venturing through Comyn land."

His eyes pierced her skin.

"It is dangerous. You never know what kind of man you might meet."

She did not linger a moment longer. Shouldering past the man still blocking her path, she hurried after Cailean, desperate to get out. More Comyns were wandering around than before. Keeping her head down, she walked faster. The end of the camp was in sight. Cailean and Matilda waited for her along the edge on the road. A relieved shiver ran down her spine. It stopped when she noticed the men closing in.

Gallovidians stared back at her. She opened her mouth to warn them, but there was no need. They knew who she was. She felt their eyes assess her, as if silently discussing what to do with Marjorie of Carrick's daughter. The tournament and the burgh were neutral grounds, but she was still a few feet inside the Comyn camp. She did not think they would be foolish enough to harm her. The looks on their faces told her otherwise.

A low whistle turned their heads. Cailean stood a few feet away, a knife already in his hand. It would not be much of a deterrent. There were four of them and only one of him. He mumbled something in Gaelic Christina could not make out. The Gallovidians no longer looked pleased. Spitting on the ground in anger, they walked away.

Christina watched them until they were out of sight. Her feet finally reached the road. She waited for Cailean to give her an explanation, but he avoided her gaze, tickling the back of Matilda's neck to make her squirm. She decided not to press it. She had had enough for one day. Turning to head to the main square, she collided with a man walking up behind her.

Thomas Dalton, the Bishop of Galloway, smiled as she took a step back. He had been a friend of her grandfather's, serving as his chaplain before he was elected bishop. Christina had encountered him a few times at Lochmaben, and he had been present at her grandfather's funeral in North Yorkshire. But they had never spoken. They had no reason to.

"Apologies, Bishop Dalton," she said. He was a tall man. She had to tilt her head back to meet his gaze. "I did not see you there."

He did not respond, not right away. When he did, it was not what she expected. "Perhaps there is a way you can make it up to me."

She stared at him with uncertainty.

He stepped towards her. "Meet me outside the taverns near the square, after the evening meal." His voice was low. Pausing to search her eyes, he said, "Come alone. There is something I must tell you."

He left. Christina remained where she stood. She had woken up this morning like she always did, and yet, it felt as if she was living someone else's life. She used to think she had a clear grasp of the kingdom and all its moving pieces, but now she was not so sure. The more she learned, the less she knew for certain. She missed her grandfather and his comforting words. Feeling Matilda grab her hand, she looked down into her sister's eager face. The mêlée would be starting soon. Setting her doubts aside, she let Matilda drag her towards the square.

The skirmishes began. In the stands near the centre, Christina watched as knights walked into the arena only to be carried out moments later. The crowd cheered and groaned appropriately.

King John was there. She could see his grey hair curling beneath his crown from where she sat. His kin, the Comyns, surrounded him like thieves. It was no wonder her father placed his faith in England. The Comyns had taken Scotland for themselves.

The Red Comyn met her gaze from across the stands. Feeling a nudge on her arm, she turned to see Rob beside her. He offered her a piece of biscuit bread. She ignored him. Though months had passed, she had not forgiven him for what he had done in Mar. She thought his actions short-sighted and selfish. All he had to do was trust her, but he chose not to. Annandale entering the ring, sans Neil, Christina focused on the match that was about to begin.

They had been paired against Lennox, their allies to the west. The mormaer was not participating, but his son was. As he passed by, leading his men into the enclosure, he touched the end of his axe to Jardine's helmet. There was no need to announce the start. His cocky gesture set everything in motion.

It was more chaotic than usual. Annandale descended on Lennox before the attendants could close the gate. If Christina had not known how pesky their opponent was, she would have bet on a quick battle. But the Lennox men refused to go down. Pushing back from their knees, they regrouped. Christina settled into her seat. It was going to be a long fight.

At the end of it all, Lennox was declared the winner.

Bodies littered the field. Only a few knights on both sides remained upright. Collecting their wounded men and scattered armour, Christina returned with her brothers to their tents. The evening meal was laid out in the centre. She bided her time. It would not take long for everyone to get good and drunk, the last day of the tournament leaving the men tired, happy and full. As soon as the signing started, loud, slurring voice filling the air, she slipped away from the table.

"This is not a good idea."

She stopped at Cailean's voice, her hand still holding onto the flap of the tent. He stepped from the shadows. With everything that had happened, she should have known he would be watching her closely. She ignored his comment. "How did you find me, with the Comyns?"

His eyes searched her face as if he was looking for an answer he could not find. "Your friend from Moray," he replied. "He told me where you had gone."

Thoughts of Andrew filled her head. In the chaos of the day, she had forgotten about seeing him on the road. His presence had taken her by surprise. She did not think she was still in love with him, but that did not mean she was ready to face him. The wound was deep. Even if it healed completely, it would leave a mark.

Cailean gently touched the side of her cheek. "Is there something you want to tell me, a bhobain?"

Her eyes lifted at the endearment. Her mother was the only one who called her that – *my darling*. Finding a sudden lump in her throat, she shook her head. His hand dropped away. She disappeared into the dark.

Thomas Dalton waited for her outside the taverns. It had not been the most pleasant walk. The celebrations grew louder and became more unruly as the night wore on. He did not acknowledge her. Instead, he turned and started walking down the road, heading out of the centre. Christina followed.

With each step, the noise lessened. They moved past the archery targets. The field was empty, and the air was quiet. Dalton finally spoke.

"I grew up alongside your father at Lochmaben." He looked at her, his feet still moving. "Did you know that?"

Christina shook her head. She was learning many new things today.

"Your grandfather raised me as one of his own." Dalton smiled. "When I told him of my intention to join the Kirk, he gave me a chapel." His face sobered. "He is the reason why I have the privilege of being a bishop now."

Christina remained silent. She had heard the rumour surrounding her grandfather and the new Bishop of Galloway. According to the Comyns and King John, her grandfather had rigged the election, bribing the clergymen of Whithorn Cathedral to give the position to Dalton over the man King John supported. It was John's land after all. Even though he was king, he was still the Lord of Galloway. But when he tried to oppose the election of Dalton, he was too late. Dalton had already been consecrated as the new bishop.

Whether or not her grandfather bribed the Kirk of Scotland mattered very little to Christina. His last act of defiance against the newly crowned king was a testament to his character – bold and unapologetic. Though she did not think it was possible, she missed him even more.

Dalton stopped. Standing beside him not far from the treeline, Christina looked up at the moon, the summer night perfected by a light breeze. Lowering her gaze, she found the bishop watching her. She looked back at him warily.

"Your grandfather was unlike any man I knew." He smiled and looked out across the field. "He did not just dream of great things. He acted on them without fear or hesitation." Looking at her, he asked, "Did you know he planned to give you Garioch?"

His question surprised her. She did not. Her silence answered.

"He told your father as much. He intended to give you the land when you wed." He turned and faced her fully. The moonlight set his eyes aglow. "But it was not just his part of Garioch he meant for you to have, Christina. He wanted you to possess the whole of it."

She did not understand. The lordship of Garioch had been divided for some time. A descendant of the Scottish royal family, her grandfather had inherited a third of the land from his mother, Isobel of Huntingdon. Her two older sisters received the remaining shares, their portions also passing down to male heirs. Uniting the lordship under one house was not a simple task. If what Dalton said was true, it meant her grandfather had planned on taking the rest of Garioch from not only the Lord of Hastings but King John himself.

"It is because of your grandfather that I come to you now."

Dalton's voice drew her back to him. She stared up at the man in front of her. His face sobered.

"I will not attempt to guide you, Christina. These are dangerous times. You must choose your own path, no matter how difficult it is for those of us burdened by the truth." He looked up at the sky. The stars were visible in the dark. "I have prayed on it for many weeks now. I trust God has led me to the right decision." He lowered his gaze. "I hope you do the same."

He said nothing else. Turning, he looked at the forest behind him.

Christina suddenly felt uneasy. He offered no reason for coming out so far into the fields, and she had not asked. Anyone or anything could find her here. She could leave, return to the safety of her family, but as she followed his gaze, her eyes searching through the dark, she knew she could not. If she left, if she turned and walked away, she would always wonder what might have happened if she had found the courage to stay.

Two men emerged from the trees. Her breathing increased. Their silhouettes coming closer, she found herself looking into a familiar face.

The man from Lanark stared back at her. His nose was still crooked, his eyes still oddly blue. But he was not the one Dalton had brought her there to meet. A monk stood before her in the moonlight. His smile was warm. She looked to Dalton for an explanation.

"William Lamberton," he said. "Meet Lady Christina Bruce."

She had heard his name before. Assessing the Chancellor of Glasgow Cathedral, she was taken aback by how young he was. Her grandfather had mentioned him more than once. With the way he spoke of him, she had thought Lamberton to be much older.

"I believe you know my friend." Lamberton looked to the man beside him. "Alexander Fraser of Touchfraser and Cowie."

She finally had a name. Fraser's eyes met hers. His face partially hidden by the shadows, she almost swore he was smirking at her.

Lamberton took a step forward. He held out his arm. "Dico tibi verum, libertas optima rerum."

The Latin phrase was oddly familiar, but she could not place it. Lamberton watched her in silence. It was only when she glanced down at his outstretched arm, did she remember.

She was back in Paisley Abbey, drenched from the rain. Sitting in the pew, she noticed the metal clasp on Wallace's cloak and the words stamped into it. *I tell you truly, liberty is the best of things.*

Staring at Lamberton now, she suddenly understood why she was there and what they were telling her. They would not choose John or Edward. Their loyalty lay in only one thing. They were for Scotland. They were for Wallace.

CHAPTER EIGHT

THE COLD TOOK possession of her bones. A frigid spring descended upon them. The dampness seemed to infiltrate every part of Lochmaben. Warming herself in front of the fire, Christina looked at Mary and Matilda bundled tightly together.

They had returned to Annandale after the tournament. Fall came quickly, and her father was called to England. King Edward named him the Governor of Carlisle Castle, the fortress located just south of the Scottish border. It was an important post. Her grandfather had held it once. Knowing her father would reside at Carlisle made Christina happy. But when he took her three youngest brothers with him, their concerned faces looking back at her as they rode out of the gate, her joy disappeared. Their mother would have wanted them to be raised in the land of their birth, trained and mentored by Scotsmen. Staring into the flames now, the heat rising around her, Christina felt like she had failed. A part of their family was missing. She did not doubt her brothers felt the same.

The sound of footsteps broke her from her thoughts. Neil walked across the room towards her.

With Rob returned to his own lands, Isabella of Mar joining him as his new bride just before the winter solstice, Neil had been charged with the care of Annandale in their father's absence. It was not a particularly difficult task. Their grandfather had been an attentive lord, the land was well looked after. Coming to a stop, Neil handed her a letter. Distress marked his brow.

"Scotland has ratified the Auld Alliance with France." He did not wait for her to read it. "King Edward is already assembling his army at Newcastle-upon-Tyne."

Christina took a moment to glance over the message. From their father, it said exactly that. But when she reached the end, she did not understand the instructions at the bottom of the page. She looked up at Neil for an explanation. He complied.

"Two days ago, a summons came from King John." His voice was flat. "It said to gather mounted men and meet him in Selkirk with the rest of the feudal host in five days' time." His brown eyes conveyed his uncertainty. He looked down at the letter. "I just received this letter from Father. We are to ignore the summons. We are to refuse King John."

Air rushed from her mouth in disbelief. Such an act was more than careless – it was absurd. Defying the Scottish crown would leave them unprotected. Annandale would be vulnerable and open to attack. Not just from thieves and warlords, but from the Scottish army itself. She looked down at the paper in her hand for a reason. It gave her none.

"We cannot…" Struggling to form the words, she tried again. "We must not-"

Neil cut her off. "It is done."

She stared at him in confusion. Neil's trepidation matched hers.

"Father has already sent his reply to the king. Even if the English army advances across the border, we are not to oppose them. We are to stand aside."

She felt herself nodding as if this was all very ordinary. Faint sounds of people moving about their daily tasks in the bailey reached her. Annandale was oblivious to what their lord had just done, to what sentence he had proclaimed upon all their heads. They had no choice in the matter, and yet, they would be the ones who paid. Neil's voice pulled her from her spiral.

"I know what this means. I am not a fool." His anguish radiated back at her. "But I need you to say it. I need you to tell me that nothing can be done."

She knew what he was asking. He did not want this. No one besides their father did. His loyalty to England made him blind – blind to what was important, blind to what his family and his people wanted. There would be no convincing him. Not even if Neil rode for Carlisle, fell on his knees and begged him to change his mind.

She folded the letter back up. Stepping towards her brother, she pressed it into his chest. His hand covered hers as he met her gaze.

"We are for England." Her words hung in the air like a proclamation. Unable to take the condemning silence, she turned and walked out of the hall.

Her fears came to fruition four short days later. She was in the church. Sat on the pew, she looked up at the stained glass windows, bright colours shining down around her. She was not there to pray. She had come to feel closer to him.

Her grandfather was often found in the chapel. Dedicated to Mary Magdalene, Christina would listen quietly as he repented. It was not for himself that he asked for forgiveness. He was the most pious man she knew. No, her grandfather's lifelong contrition and acts of penance were for the man who had brought a curse upon them all.

One hundred and fifty years prior, Robert Bruce, the second of his name, ruled as Lord of Annandale. Residing in Annan Castle, an Irish priest appeared at his door one afternoon. Lord Robert was not one to turn away someone in need. Inviting the holy man inside, he gave him a seat at his table.

With a bowl of warm stew before him, the monk listened to the conversation that dominated the hall. A thief had been caught earlier that day. He was guilty, and there were witnesses. In the morning, he would hang.

Going to Lord Robert, the priest asked for mercy. It was not due to luck that he had arrived on the very day a man was sentenced to die. It was a sign; he had been sent there for a purpose. God wanted the man to be spared.

Moved by the monk's conviction, Lord Robert agreed. The thief would be pardoned. Gathering his belongings the next morning, the priest led his horse from the stables and headed towards the gate. A horrible sight met him. The thief's lifeless body hung from the wall.

Enraged, the priest turned, finding Lord Robert on the steps. He cast a curse upon the deceitful lord, one that would follow him and his kin forever.

The winds came as soon as the priest left. The water swelled in the river. Surging over the banks, the River Annan turned into white fury, tearing at the castle, ripping away the mound and half the fortress with it.

Lord Robert fled, never to return to Annan Castle. The curse remained. For generations, it haunted them – sons dying before their fathers, daughters unable to conceive. Christina's grandfather had devoted his life to lifting it. He gave large amounts of land and income to the church. He joined the crusades and fought in the Holy Land next to men half his age.

He had told Christina once that he thought it was over, that he had finally appeased the wrath of Saint Malachy. Even when he was denied the crown, he held onto his belief that the curse was finished. But as she sat there, staring up at the statue of Mary Magdalene, the patron saint of prostitutes and sinful women, Christina was not so sure. Peril and misfortune hounded them like wolves in the night. If the curse of Saint Malachy was indeed over, then something else plagued them. Someone else was responsible for the tribulation constantly knocking at their door.

The church doors burst open. Christina glanced back. Jardine strode towards her like never before, his long strides quickly eliminating the distance between them. She could hear the horses waiting outside. Their sharp whines alerted her to their angst. Stopping beside the bench, Jardine handed her a letter.

His face was blank, as if the reason for his unexpected appearance did not surprise him. Taking the paper, the seal already broken, she unfolded it. She recognized the Mormaer of Mar's handwriting immediately. His note was messy and short.

Bruce lands declared forfeit. Annandale allotted to Comyn, Mormaer of Buchan.

For a moment, she did not move, unable to believe what was happening. She wanted to scream, to pound her fists into someone's flesh. But what she wanted did not matter. Lochmaben and the land her grandfather loved the most was no longer theirs.

"Your brother has gone to Carlisle."

Jardine's voice lifted her gaze.

"You are to return to the castle. You must gather your things."

Bitter resentment overcame her. Her father was the reason they were in this predicament. He could send all the men he wanted back with her brother – it would not change what had been done.

Crumpling the paper in her fist, she rode with Jardine back to the castle. They passed several villagers on the road. She could not help but notice the disgruntled looks as they went by. She did not doubt they knew the Scottish army was assembling at Selkirk. Mounted knights from Galloway had ridden through Lochmaben only yesterday. She wanted to apologize, to offer some explanation for why Annandale was not joining their king. But she had nothing to give them. She did not know the reason why herself. Thinking of what was coming, she urged her horse forward and in through the gates.

The bailey bustled with activity. Tapestries, silverware, and her grandfather's ledgers were being loaded onto carts, horses already strapped to the front. It was not chaos, but it was close, a sense of urgency rife in the air. Cailean met her at the keep. Dismounting from her horse, she walked past him into the tower.

She found her sisters in their room. Matilda ran towards her. Feeling her wiry arms wrap around her, Christina looked over at Mary. For once, her face was not pinched in a scowl.

If Christina did not know better, she would think Mary was scared. Kissing the top of Matilda's head, she pulled back from her embrace.

"Pack only what you need. We are leaving soon." She was not going to wait for Neil to return. With the messenger already come and gone, the Comyns could very well be on their way. Carlisle was not far – only half a day's ride south. She would rather take her chances on the road unescorted than be met by the Mormaer of Buchan. She doubted he would be merciful.

The sound of horses filling the grounds made her go to the window. Her first thought was of Neil, but the notion left her head as soon as it entered. It was not possible for him to be back. Peering through the glass, her stomach dropped. Blue and yellow banners stared back at her. It was too late. The Comyns were already here.

Running to the door, she found Cailean on the stairs. The warning in his face told her everything she needed to know. She motioned for her sisters to come.

"Take them," she said. "Get to the boat."

He did not look happy. She ignored it.

"There is a house across the loch. Mary knows where it is." Glancing at her sister, Mary nodded. "Find a man named Sinclair. He will get you to Carlisle."

The voices in the bailey grew louder. They were out of time.

"Go," Christina said.

She did not stay to watch her sisters leave. Descending the stairs, she walked towards the door, quieting her trembling hands against her dress. It would be better if she came out on her own volition. No matter what happened, regardless of what the Mormaer of Buchan did, she would keep her composure. It was perhaps the only thing she had left.

The sky seemed to darken as she stepped into the bailey. Grey clouds blocked the sun. Mounted men waited for her, the banners of House Comyn draped across their horses. A single rider moved forward. The rest remaining where they stood, she turned her attention to him.

The Red Comyn's dark eyes assessed her from atop his horse.

His presence surprised her. It was unlike the Mormaer of Buchan to give up an opportunity to embarrass her family. Looking back at the man she had spoken with in Mar, the grounds eerily quiet, she knew this would not be like their previous conversation. The stakes were much higher.

He stopped a few feet in front of her. Turning his horse around, he faced the bailey. "By proclamation of King John, the Bruce claim to these lands is now forfeit." His voice rang out in the stillness. "Annandale has been granted in favour to John Comyn, Mormaer of Buchan, now rightful Lord of Annandale."

Christina glanced at the people present. They did not react, their disgruntled faces staring silently at the man who demanded their attention. She knew they were not pleased. The family they had been at war with for generations now ruled over them. When the Red Comyn said nothing else, they turned away. Christina repressed a smirk.

Dropping from his horse, he straightened in his tunic. The other men did the same. The sound of boots hitting the ground eliminated the silence. One walked past her to nail the king's proclamation to the door of the keep. It was only then that she noticed Seton standing behind her.

They had not spoken since Paisley. She had seen him often enough, doing what her father asked of him or training with her brothers in the grounds. She had kept her distance. His bluntness that night had taken her by surprise. She felt vulnerable around him, as if he could see through her carefully-constructed walls. It was not a feeling she was accustomed to, but that mattered little now. Stranded in a sea of Comyns, he might be the only thing that kept her afloat.

"I had hoped to find you here."

The Red Comyn's voice pulled her back to him. She glanced at the man standing in front of her before her eyes drifted over the men in the bailey. The sight of Comyns in Lochmaben was more unsettling than she had imagined. It felt as if her very person was being invaded.

"I will not lie." His smile was tense. "I do not know what to make of you."

His words only caused her more discomfort. He was talking to her as if they were friends, which they most certainly were not. People were beginning to notice. More faces looked their way. She wanted it to stop.

"Perhaps you can enlighten me." He took a step towards her. "How do you know my nephew, Andrew Moray?"

It was as if her guts were a small ship being tossed about by the sea. She struggled to keep the unease off her face. Her mind reeled, trying to figure out how he knew, but she forced herself to stop. It did not matter. She just needed this inquiry to end. "What do you want?"

An amused smile tugged at the corners of his mouth. When he saw that she was serious, expectantly waiting for him to answer, the smile disappeared. He obliged her. "Your father has put you in a difficult position."

She pretended not to notice the people listening.

"He has declared you for England." His eyes held her intently. "But I know that is not what you want."

She did not know what was worse – the accusation that she was against her father or the suggestion that he, the Red Comyn, knew her well. He was clever, she would give him that. She tempered the indignation surging through her. "You know nothing of what I want."

Though quiet, her voice carried enough of a warning to make him shift. He leaned away from her. Tension filled the air.

"You can throw me from the gates of Lochmaben, escort me out of Annandale itself, but you will not speak of what you do not know." She let her anger carry her through. "Do not make that mistake again, Sir John."

She said his name pointedly, expecting him to back down. He did not. He was not done with her yet.

"Then I must warn you. You are on the wrong side. You will regret disobeying your king."

It was all too much, the hypocrisy of such a statement. "My king?" She tried to keep the contempt from her voice. "And what king is that?"

The bailey went still. This time, the silence was not so quiet. More than a few men moved closer to where she stood. Jardine was only a few feet away now. His eyes on the Comyn men, he rested his hand on the hilt of his sword.

The Red Comyn stared back at her. His expression both cautioned and dared her to say more.

"Even you, King John's own family, have pushed him

aside." She let her gaze bore into him. "There would be no treaty with France without your Council of Twelve." She shook her head. "If I refuse to fight against England, it is not my king I am disobeying. It is the Comyn kindred and your father." She lifted her chin, her voice clear. "I have sworn no fealty to you. I owe you nothing."

Not a sound was made. When the Red Comyn finally spoke, his voice was quiet.

"There will come a time when you will have to choose." He stared at her. "No one, not even you, Lady Christina, will be able to hide behind the decisions of your father." He paused, his anger seeming to lessen. He studied her for a moment before he said, "I hope you make the right choice."

She left Lochmaben alone. Riding for Carlisle, Neil met her just north of the border, a body of mounted men behind him. Though she hated to admit it, she was relieved to cross over into England. Her journey had been uncomfortable. The land she knew so well no longer felt welcoming. She had not stopped once.

Approaching the castle, a call went up. The gate rumbled open as they rode across the bridge in the darkening sky. The moment she saw Mary and Matilda, she jumped from her horse.

Her sisters ran across the bailey. Wrapped in their embrace, they led her to the keep. English soldiers moved past them in droves as they walked. Fires were lit on the walls above, guards standing in defensive positions. The gate clanked shut from somewhere behind them. Entering the inner bailey, Christina spotted Rob high on the barricade with their father.

She was disappointed to see him there. Rob's presence meant that Carrick was for England. If anyone might have remained at Scotland's side, it would have been him. He was a mormaer and had the most autonomy. He was also married to Isabella of Mar.

Domhnall, Isabella's father, had answered King John's call to arms. The pull to defend their land was greater than his duty to her family. For the first time in generations, Mar would be against them.

Christina wondered what Isabella thought about opposing her father. She could ask her, Rob's wife would be in the chamber of the keep. Stepping through the door, Mary and Matilda let go of her, their footsteps echoing off the stone steps as they climbed up. Christina went to follow. A figure emerging from the corridor stopped her.

Cailean stared at her. Seeing the anger on his face, she instinctively took a step back.

He did not give her the space she wanted. Coming towards her, he held his nose an inch from hers. "Do not do that again."

She did not have to ask what he meant, his words coming out in a low growl. When she had sent him away with her sisters, she knew he would not like leaving her behind. But the depth of his anger surprised her. She had forgotten how terrifying he could be.

Cailean held her gaze a moment longer before he walked away. She had no doubt he did not want to be there. He despised England and until now, had never set foot in it. Watching him disappear into the shadows, she wondered if he would leave. Her mother was dead. He was beholden to no one. He could go if he wanted. Once the fighting started, there would be no turning back. Those in the castle would remain until it was over, until one of the two kingdoms fell.

Picturing the knights of Annandale on their horses, riding alongside their countrymen, Christina forced her tired legs up the stairs. She might never see Lochmaben again. The thought made her slow, and she reached for the railing. She never thought she would be happy that her grandfather was gone, but she was now. It would have broken his heart to see how far they had fallen.

The call of war woke her six days later. Leaping from the bed, she threw a blanket over her nightdress and hurried down the stairs out of the tower. Rob followed. Running up the exterior steps to the wall, she stopped along the northern edge. Armoured knights filled the field between the village and the castle. Scaling ladders were being prepared. The Scottish army had come to Carlisle.

Her father's voice rang out from somewhere nearby. English soldiers moved into position along the wall. Rob turned back to retrieve his armour as Christina stared at the rows of mounted men.

The banners told her who they were – the lands of Mar and Atholl standing beside Buchan and Badenoch. For the first time in her memory, Comyn and Bruce loyalties had been set aside. Her father was the only one who had not.

Her eyes slowed when she saw Annandale. Of course the Red Comyn would bring her grandfather's men to fight against them. Searching the figures in the distance, she tried to find Seton and Jardine. A blue shield with three white stars stopped her. Her fingers dug into the fabric. Somewhere in the crowd, weighed down by chainmail and metal plating, were Andrew and the knights of Moray.

She did not get a chance to look for him. Pulled back from the wall, Neil escorted her to the keep, archers melding the gap she left behind. Placed inside, the door locked shut. Two guards stood in front of it. She would not be allowed out until it was over. Knowing there was nothing to do but wait, she returned to her chambers to get dressed.

She had never known a longer day. Sat in the hall with her sisters and Isabella, they listened in silence as different sounds filtered in from outside. Her father's commands reverberated around the wall, the men repeating his words like an echo. A shout rose up. Then everything went quiet.

The silence rattled Christina the most. She hated not knowing what was happening. She paced more than she sat. Matilda bit her lip absentmindedly as she hugged her knees in the chair. Mary pretended to read a book. Only Isabella seemed to be at peace. Leaned back into her seat, her hand resting gently on her small, round stomach, she looked perfectly content.

The door opened well past midday. The battle was over – the Scots had failed to break through the wall. Her father and the English had won.

Outside once more, Christina watched Rob and Neil give chase to the fleeing Scottish army. It was only one battle, the war was not over yet. Little did she know as she stood there, feeling both relieved and disappointed, just how much Scotland's insurrection against England would cost.

CHAPTER NINE

ONE MONTH. THAT was all it took for the rebellion against England to begin and end. One month and King Edward had Scotland in a stranglehold. Looking around the ransacked hall, Christina sighed and picked up a chair.

King Edward responded to the Scots' attack on Carlisle four short days later. With his army behind him, he rode into Berwick-upon-Tweed and slaughtered the town. Man, woman, or child – he did not care. Tens of thousands perished in a single act of vengeance.

The Scots retaliated in kind. Invading England once more, they covered Northumberland in blood, trying to draw the English king south. But he did not move.

The two armies finally faced off against each other on the eighth day of April in a field near Dunbar. Calling it an English victory would be an understatement. The Scottish were defeated in a single charge, their casualties great. But that was not all King Edward won. Besides the dead men that littered the field, he took over a hundred lords and knights prisoner. The mormaers of Buchan, Atholl,

Ross, and Menteith were sent south in chains. The rebellion against England was over. Everything had been lost.

"Think the Comyns did this?"

Christina looked up at Neil standing next to the table. Cailean hovered near the door. She shook her head.

Their Scottish lands had been restored to them following the defeat at Dunbar. Her father ruled once more as Lord of Annandale, and Rob had returned to Carrick. Riding back to Lochmaben had been bittersweet. She was happy to be home, but the price that had been paid was too high. Standing in the hall, looking at the broken candleholders and torn tapestries strewn about the room, everything of value gone, Christina felt an overwhelming sense of loss. Nothing would be as it had been.

It took the rest of the day to clean the hall. No one else was there. When they arrived in Lochmaben, they had found the gates open and the castle empty. Going outside, Christina shook the dust from a tattered tablecloth. She hesitated when she saw a figure standing at the entrance of the bailey.

Rory's gaunt face stared back at her. Seeing his eyes red and swollen, she moved quickly towards him. She was about to ask if he was all right when he stepped forward and took her hand. Turning, he led her towards the village.

Christina watched him as they walked. He said nothing. Uncertain of what was wrong, she kept quiet. Her unease grew when she saw the people lingering outside his house.

The stares felt hot on her back as Rory pulled her through the crowd. She followed him inside. He closed the door behind her.

Christina had been here many times before. Shona and Rory's mother made the best oatcakes in the village, and

Christina's childhood was filled with burnt fingers snatching hot biscuits from the pan. Taking a few steps into the house, the only light a single candle on the table, she stopped when she saw the woman sitting near the cold hearth.

Ada Fletcher's gaze was lifted, but her eyes were empty. Her husband stood looking out the window on the other side of the room. Approaching his mother, Rory gently touched her arm. The feeling made the older woman turn. Her stare found Christina near the door. Her face hardened as if Christina's presence made her ill.

"She's dead." Ada's sharp tone cut across the room. "Shona…" Her voice broke. She lifted a hand to her mouth.

Christina stared at Ada in disbelief. Her chest constricting and her throat tight, she struggled to remain standing. Tears filled her eyes in anguish.

Ada attempted to collect herself. She began again. "She was in Berwick when the English came. They cut her down."

Her last four words reverberated through Christina's head. She stepped back, her fingers reaching for the wall. Thousands of people had died in the massacre – she knew that. For some reason, she never thought Shona could be one of them. The possibility had never entered her mind. Picturing her friend's throat being slit, her body tossed into a mass grave with hundreds of others, she felt sick. She wanted to vomit.

"Your family was there."

The tears in her eyes made it difficult to see. Ada was just a blur. For the second time, Christina did not understand.

"Your father's men rode with Edward. They were there when my daughter died. They killed her. *You* killed her."

Christina's mouth fell open. She wanted to say it was not true, but the words would not form. Ada was not wrong

– her father *had* sent men with Edward to Berwick. But they were English. They had been under his command at Carlisle. It was not the same.

"I will never forgive you." Ada's arms shook as she pushed herself from the chair.

The hatred emanating off her tore into Christina.

"Get out!"

Tears spilled unhindered down her face. She wanted to beg Ada to take it back – to try and convince her that her family had nothing to do with it. But Ada turned away.

Christina left. Shutting the door behind her, a guttural sob burst from her lips. She leaned against the house and hugged her stomach, trying to quell the heartache within. It was no use. Shona was dead and her family had a part in it. The pain was overwhelming.

By the time she stood up straight, it was almost dark. She brushed the moisture from her cheeks and took a steadying breath. No one else was around. The blue sky was still visible in the fading light. Shouting in the distance caught her attention.

The village centre was just a bit farther down the road. Hesitantly walking towards the noise, a crowd came into view. The villagers had gathered, and they were angry. Her stomach hardened once more when she saw who was in the middle.

The English soldier could not have been much older than Mary. His face was bloodied and he looked terrified, his eyes desperately searching for a friendly face. Hands bound in front of him, he wobbled where he stood. The crowd pulled him up onto the large stone dais in the middle of the square. Hearing a rider approaching, Christina looked back.

She stepped to the side as her brother passed. Neil did not wait for his horse to slow before he dismounted. He pushed his way through the crowd. He was still a few feet from the platform when a rope was looped around the Englishman's neck. The boy began to sob.

"Wait!" Neil yelled over the din. "Wait!" He jumped up onto the stone.

The voices quieted at the sight of him.

Gathering himself, Neil looked over the faces before him. He exhaled. "I know you are angry."

It was the wrong thing to say. They let him have it, shouting back at his failed attempt to appease them.

"You know nothing!"

"Coward!"

"Traitor!"

Christina's legs felt heavy as she stared up at her brother. She wrapped her arms around herself to stop her hands from shaking.

"I know you are angry," Neil repeated, yelling above the noise. "But this is not right." He pointed back to the soldier. "This is not justice!"

"He is a murderer!" someone yelled out, the others voicing their agreement. "A defiler!"

Neil took a moment to look at the boy. The English soldier's face was marred with blood, dirt, and spit. When Neil returned to the crowd, Christina knew what he was going to say. Her hand lifted nervously to her throat.

"Look at him!" he challenged the horde. "He is a child!"

They did not agree, shouting all at once, fists raised in anger.

Neil struggled to keep his voice heard. "He is not the enemy you seek!"

Finding Christina amongst the faces, his eyes pleaded for her to do something, to not leave him standing up there all alone. She did not move. She knew he was right – that the boy was not responsible – but it did not matter. Thousands of unanswered deaths kept her still. Deep down, she was just like them. She wanted someone – anyone – to pay.

The crowd surged forward, pushing past Neil as they released their rage upon the only person within their grasp. Jostled by the people rushing by, her brother did not seem to care. He never looked so defeated.

They strung up the soldier. His eyes bulged in terror as he clutched at the rope cutting into his throat, his mouth gaping.

It took a while for him to die. His limbs twitched long after he had taken his last breath. Christina stayed as the mob dispersed. The elation of what they had just done was gone. Even when Neil paused in front of her, his horse taking him back to Lochmaben, her gaze never left the boy. She could not break away from the judgment his lifeless eyes cast down upon them all.

On the eighth day of July in the Year of Grace, one thousand, two hundred and ninety-six, John Balliol, King of Scots, abdicated the throne and surrendered to England.

King Edward treated him cruelly, ripping the arms of Scotland from his surcoat as John stood in humiliation before him. That final act marked John forever. From that day forward, he was known as Toom Tabard, the king with the empty coat, King Nobody.

Imprisoning John in England, Edward took a victory tour through the newly vanquished land. He did not do it to make a good impression on the kingdom he had coveted for so long. He ransacked it like an honourless thief, stealing archives, royal regalia and even the Black Rood of Saint Margaret. He destroyed the Great Seal and took the Stone of Scone, the very seat every King of Scots had been crowned upon since Cináed mac Ailpin. Appointing English sheriffs and justiciars throughout, the Lowlands brimmed with English soldiers. Even the northern castles were occupied. King Edward was not endearing the Scots to his rule. He was trying to hammer them into submission.

Annandale teetered on the edge of dissent. With each passing day, more soldiers arrived. It only stoked people's hatred for the English king.

Neil was gone more often than not. Riding for the villages, he tried to maintain the thin veneer of peace that held the violence at bay.

Christina felt the tension each time she left the castle. She had witnessed, on more than one occasion, villagers pelting soldiers with whatever they could get their hands on as they rode through. Standing in the armoury, the blacksmith not yet returned to Lochmaben, she took stock of what remained. It would only be a matter of time before her brother's appeals for calm were utterly ignored. They would need every blade they had.

Hearing someone holler, she looked up. She could not see what was happening, the armoury tucked near the back of the bailey. Setting the steel down, she walked towards the gate. She arrived in time to watch a throng of people rush through.

Everyone was yelling. Neil stepping from the keep, panicked eyes looked at him and then to the woman in the middle.

Christina recognized Morna Kerr instantly. Her husband had died not long after the birth of their youngest, leaving her with three children to raise on her own. Many expected her to return to her family or remarry, but she did neither. Instead, she stayed in the home she had built with her husband. Christina often saw her out working the fields. She stayed longer than anyone else.

The group parted to let Neil through. It was only then Christina saw the boy in Morna's arms. His neck was covered in blood and he was not moving. It was Calum, Morna's son.

"What happened?" Though spoken softly, Neil's voice rang out.

Movement drew Christina's attention. A young girl was pushed forward. She glanced at the faces around her. Then she began.

"We were by the river when we heard them on the road." She paused. "Calum got there first." She hesitated again, as if she was afraid to say more. A nudge from someone behind her made her continue. "We tried knocking things from their horses with sticks. We called them tailed dogs. They cut him."

Neil moved closer to Morna. He looked down at her son in her arms. "I cannot imagine the pain this brings you." His words were slow. "It was a senseless death. I am truly sorry for your loss."

"We did not come for an apology."

Neil lifted his eyes to the man stepping forward.

"A boy is dead." His ire was palpable. "Something must be done."

Waiting for Neil's answer, the grounds fell quiet. He stared back at the man for a moment. Eventually, he nodded. "I will write to my father."

The people began to murmur. It was not what they wanted to hear.

Neil spoke louder. "He will know what can be done."

Their dissatisfaction only grew, voices rising in anger.

"Your father will do nothing!" someone called out.

"He does not care what happens to us!" another said.

Neil remained in their midst, trying to reassure them that their lord would seek justice. It was not working.

"Your grandfather would have never stood for this!"

"What do you want from me?" Neil's frustrated question rendered them silent. He looked around at the faces. "I cannot go to the English king and demand recompense. I cannot hunt an English soldier through the Lowlands. I do not even know his name!"

A saddlebag hit the ground at his feet.

He looked up in confusion.

The man who had spoken earlier smirked at him with satisfaction. "The girl knocked it from the bastard's horse before he rode off. His name is written inside. We know who he is."

Christina could feel Neil's apprehension from where she stood. Finding the soldier would still be a monumental task, but with a name, it was possible. She waited to hear what her brother's answer would be.

Neil reached down and picked up the bag. "I will hand

this to my father myself. He can use it to make a claim in court."

The grounds erupted. Irate, the crowd spit insults at Neil as he retreated towards the keep. Several of the men stood close by, Jardine and Seton among them. It did not look like they wanted to be there. Grim looks covered their faces. Her family's allegiance to England was tearing the land in two, pitting men sworn to their lord against their own people. By the time Cailean found her, pulling her away from the uprising, Christina knew her father would never care about Annandale the way her grandfather had. The Lord of Annandale would not get recompense for the family. He would not seek justice. Safe inside the keep, Christina decided. She knew what she wanted to do.

She waited until dark. The evening meal finished, she followed Seton out of the hall. It was one of the quietest gatherings Christina had ever attended. The men were silent, and Neil glowered in his cups. Watching Seton enter the stables, the outline of his silhouette visible in the night, Christina stiffened her resolve. He would help her, of that she was sure. Because it was something they both wanted.

Seton carried her brother's saddle out from the back as she entered. Neil had decided to go to Carlisle at first light to speak to their father. Preparations had to be made. Ignoring her, he placed the seat on the ground and turned back to gather more things. Christina leaned against the wall and waited.

The tension between them had only worsened since she returned from Carlisle. Seton had been with the other men of Annandale at Dunbar when they lost against England. More than a few knights had been taken hostage. Having to ransom their freedom from King Edward, their return home was slow.

It was not an easy transition for her family back into ruling power. Though they acted as if nothing had happened, the devastation and loss in the Lowlands were too great to ignore. Everything and everyone had changed – even Seton.

"I need you to do something."

He glanced at her only momentarily, the saddlebags in his hands. When he went to walk away once more, she tried again.

"I need you to find Wallace."

He stopped. Lifting his head, he stood still for a moment before he turned. "That name, I would not-"

"I have a message for him." Knowing he was going to tell her to be careful, she cut him off. Others already did that and did it often. She did not want to hear it from him.

He looked back at her in silence.

She held his gaze. He could assess her all he wanted; it did not change anything. She had a message for Wallace and she needed someone to deliver it.

"Why?" he asked eventually. "What could you have to say to him?"

She considered lying or obscuring the truth in some way, but as she looked at him, his words came flooding back to her. He had kept every secret she had, even helped her hide a body. If she could not trust him now, she never would.

"I have the saddlebag with the Englishman's name on it."

His face lifted in surprise.

"I want you to give it to him – to Wallace – along with my note. He will know what to do."

Seton said nothing for quite some time. He just stared back at her. When he spoke again, his face became unreadable once more. "You think Wallace will find him?"

She did not know. It was a lot to ask from a man she barely knew. She shrugged.

He nodded. "I will do it."

Christina smiled. Part of her had expected him to push back, to tell her that she was foolish – that was what most men would have done. But as he held her gaze, the determination in his eyes telling her he was serious, her grandfather's words came back to her. From now on, she would make her path. She was done following in the footsteps of foolish men.

CHAPTER TEN

STOOD INSIDE THE door of the keep, she watched
the autumn rain drench the earth. Seton had been
gone for almost a month. His absence made her more
nervous by the day. Finding Wallace would not be easy – she
knew that. He could be dead, rotting away somewhere near
the fields of Dunbar, unbeknownst to anyone.

She did not actually believe that was true. She would
have heard of his demise if it was. Wallace's name had only
grown in recent weeks, men flocking to the outlaw. He was
the only hope Scotland had left. She prayed Seton had found
him by now.

A flash of light split the sky, thunder rumbling its
response as the rain grew heavier. Pools of water collected
throughout the grounds. Christina felt restless, her muscles tense.

Scotland's relationship with their English overlords had
only worsened. More soldiers had come, trying to quell the
small uprisings that emerged throughout the Lowlands. She
had never seen so many Englishmen in armour, and it did
not take long for the small fires of resistance to die out.
To King Edward, it must have seemed like a success. But

what he and his men did not realize was that a rebellion was indeed growing. She could hear it in the way people whispered. She could see it in how they stopped fighting all at once, all together.

Stretching out her hand to catch the rain, her mind drifted once more to Seton and where he might be. The possibilities were endless. Watching the droplets split against her palm and fall to the ground, she turned and went inside.

The castle was still. The weather made everyone sleepy as they hid from the rain. Neil had gone to visit Rob at Turnberry. Isabella was due to give birth any day now. Christina was writing a letter in front of the fire when a light knock sounded on the door. She lifted her head.

Fergus Reid stood in the doorway. Close in age to her father, he had been appointed steward of Lochmaben upon their return. His quiet eyes studied her for a moment. "You have a visitor." He paused. "They are waiting in the bailey."

Though she thought it odd, she pushed herself up out of her chair and descended the staircase. Her quick footsteps were the only sound. Spotting the man waiting for her just outside the keep, she slowed. She no longer wondered why he had not come inside.

Sir William Douglas, the Lord of Douglas, lifted his chin as she moved through the door. Three of his men stood behind him. Her stomach knotted at the sight.

Glancing anxiously around her, she saw Cailean and Jardine standing nearby. Their rigid postures and somber faces told her they were just as uncomfortable as she was. Cailean took a step towards her. Christina walked out into the rain.

"Lord Douglas," she said, trying not to shrink beneath his gaze. "We were not expecting you. My brother is-"

He cut her off. "I did not come for your brother. I came for you."

A fearful chill ran down her spine. Suddenly, she was cold, and it was not from the rain. Despite herself, she could not help but think of the last story she had heard about William Douglas.

He had ridden to Tranent and surrounded a castle. According to the tale, he was going to destroy it and burn the land. But besides the baron and his wife trapped inside, a wealthy widow was visiting from England. She had come north to collect the rents from her Scottish lands. When Douglas heard she was in the castle, he did not ravage the fortress. Instead, he abducted the widowed Eleanor and carried her off.

King Edward was furious. Eleanor's late husband had been a distant relation of his. The king demanded that the Guardians of Scotland arrest Douglas and deliver Eleanor to him directly. But nothing was done. As Christina looked at the crusader before her, she tried to remember if any news had come of Eleanor's death. She hoped she was not about to meet a similar fate.

Douglas said nothing, merely holding her gaze as he stood there, his black hair plastered against his face.

Christina had two choices. She could dismiss the man known as the Hardy, a man who was kin to the Morays and no friend of House Bruce. Or she could invite him inside and hear what he had to say. Glancing at Cailean once more, she said, "Come," and walked back into the keep.

It was no longer quiet or still. The sound of men filling the hall reverberated through the castle. With Cailean and Jardine beside her, Christina sat at the head of the table. It felt odd to be in this position, staring down a man three times her age. She straightened in her chair and waited for him to tell her why he had come.

Douglas paid her no attention. He stared at the two men who had followed her in. When he had assessed them to his satisfaction, he turned to her. "I did not come to have ears listening in."

Christina fought to keep the smile from her lips. If he thought she would willingly be alone in a room with him, he had greatly misjudged her. She was not a fool. "Do you trust your men, Lord Douglas?"

Finding her question ridiculous, he scoffed.

She smiled. "Then we will remain as we are."

A small smirk spread across his face. He placed his calloused hands onto the table. "I was at Berwick when Edward massacred the town."

She stared passively back. He would make his point eventually. She just had to wait.

"I swore fealty and placed my seal on the Ragman Roll." His black eyes focused in on her. "Our king is gone. Every nobleman has bent the knee. And still, Edward keeps our men as hostages."

If there was one thing King Edward was good at, it was war. He played the game well and usually won. His recent conquest of Wales was swift and unforgiving. He demanded hostages as often as he could, knowing it was the surest way to keep control. No house would rebel against him if the head of their kindred was wasting their days away in an English prison. After John abdicated, over fifteen hundred mormaers, lords, bishops, and knights swore fealty to Edward on the Ragman Roll and recognized him as King of

Scotland. Only two names were missing in all the land – the brothers, Malcolm and William Wallace.

Knowing all this, she asked, "What do you want from me?"

His answer was blunt. "I want you to go to Carlisle and convince your father to ask for Andrew Moray's release."

Christina was certain she had misheard. At first, she thought her mind was playing tricks on her, her father and Andrew Moray's names coming out of nowhere. But as she stared back at the man who followed no one, loyal only to himself, she saw that he was entirely serious.

"Your father refuses to see me, despite my repeated requests."

She had not asked for an explanation, but he was giving her one nonetheless.

"I am beginning to think he does not like me."

Unsure if that was an attempt at humour, she stayed silent, refusing the urge to shift in her seat.

Douglas grew serious. "Your grandfather and I often disagreed, but he always faced me like a man. He never hid behind his walls like a coward."

Christina glanced at Jardine warily. The insult to her father was nothing insignificant. Jardine had every right to defend his lord's honour. She did not doubt statements like that got Douglas in more than enough trouble. When Jardine's face did not change, his eyes remaining on the men who had accompanied Douglas into the hall, she returned her attention to the difficult man in front of her.

Douglas stared at her. "I am told you are not like your father. I am told you disagree."

The reprieve she felt vanished. It unsettled her to know

that someone was speaking her name. Such a thing was fine for her brothers, their names and deeds constantly talked about. But it was different for her. She was a woman – a loose tongue could inflict irreversible damage. She needed to watch what she said. She needed to be careful.

"I apologize, Lord Douglas, but I do not believe you fully understand my father." She hesitated, choosing her words meticulously. "He is currently out of favour with the English king. Even if I were his most trusted man, I would not be able to convince him to ask Edward to release a Scottish prisoner." She paused. "Especially for someone from Moray, a Comyn."

"I heard he asked Edward for the crown."

Once again, his words made her bristle. She had heard the same, though not from her father. With John's abdication, the throne was empty, and her father had taken it upon himself to remind the English king of the Bruce claim. It had not gone over well. Edward rebuked him for it. If what she heard was true, Edward had responded by asking her father if that was all he thought the English were good for – winning kingdoms for the Bruce family. Irritation flowed through her. Her father was damaging their reputation faster than they could fix it.

"Your grandfather would not have been so weak."

Douglas' voice brought her out of her misery.

"The moment John surrendered, he would have ridden for Scone with an army of men, sat himself down on the Stone of Destiny and declared himself king."

The image made her smile. For the first time since entering the hall, her concern lessened. Her grandfather would have done precisely that. Above everything – the competition for the crown, the rivalry with the Comyns – he would never have accepted that the Scottish crown was Edward's to keep for himself or give away to another. The throne belonged to the Scots and the Scots alone. England be damned.

"We need that boldness now more than ever."

She stared at him.

Holding her gaze, Douglas leaned towards her. "I do not care, Lady Christina, about Bruce or Comyn. As long as a Scotsman sits on the throne, it makes no difference to me." He paused. "But if we do not act now, we will never be free of England." His hands pressed down on the table. "Trust me when I tell you, we cannot win our freedom back as long as Andrew Moray sits trapped in a cell."

Christina glanced down. She had heard whispers of what was happening in the Highlands. While both Andrew and his father had been taken prisoner at Dunbar, men still flocked to the Moray banner at Avoch Castle. The north was their stronghold and had been for centuries. Their influence grew even now. She was not surprised people looked to them to lead.

"I have come to you because there is no one else left."

Her gaze lifted.

His stare consumed her. "If you care at all for this land, if you are anything like your grandfather, I ask that you do all you can. Help me, so we can live freely as God intended."

She could not get his words out of her head. Even when she closed her eyes at night, all she heard was William Douglas' voice urging her to do something.

But that was not all that kept her awake. Her grandfather appeared almost nightly in her dreams. He would be standing in the field, calling out to her for help, but she could never reach him. The ground would always fall out from under her right before her fingertips brushed his.

For days it continued. She slept less and less. She was standing outside, snowflakes falling around her when Neil's face appeared in front of her. The concern seeped off him. He spoke quickly. As soon as he finished, she forgot about the warlord and rode for Turnberry.

The birth was troublesome from the start. Too much blood stained the sheets as Isabella pushed. She fought long and hard, her determined screams filling the room. The baby's first cries tumbled out. Christina felt Isabella's hand slip from her grasp. Looking down, her heart sank. The Countess of Carrick was gone.

Rob was inconsolable. He did not eat and barely slept. He spent his days sitting in the hall staring into the fire. Christina tried to talk to him, tried to get him to hold his daughter. He refused.

The baby was a week old when Christina wrote to her father. It hurt her pride to ask him for anything. Their time together in Carlisle had only pushed them farther apart. But Rob was weakening by the day, and the baby still did not have a name. She needed help. She needed the only person Rob would never turn away from.

Matilda's arrival could not come soon enough. Walking into the hall with Mary, she rushed forward and threw her arms around Rob's neck. His grief broke open. He sobbed into his youngest sister's embrace. The sight filled Christina with relief. She had made the right decision. The healing could finally begin.

Seton appeared at Turnberry two weeks later. Christina

stopped in surprise when she saw him at the table. It took every ounce of control to not rush towards him.

He said nothing as she sat down across from him. Holding his gaze, she reached for the jug of ale. He looked different with the beard, his face partially hidden by the dirty-blond hair. She slowly glanced around the room. Finding no one else there, she said, "Well?"

It looked like he was smirking, but she was not sure. He leaned back in his chair. "I found him outside Paisley. The monk helped."

Taking a drink, she indicated for him to keep going.

"The soldier was in Irvine." He paused. "It is done."

It seemed a bit ridiculous, all that stress and anxiety for three words. When he did not elaborate, she pressed him for more. "Is that it? Are you not going to tell me the rest?"

He did not answer.

"What if she asks?"

His eyebrows rose slightly. "You are going to tell Morna then?"

She had not entirely decided, not knowing how to say it. But she had sent Wallace after the man for a reason. Morna deserved to know what had befallen her son's killer. Looking back at Seton, she realized why she had not figured it out. "You should tell her."

His eyes moved past her. When his gaze returned, he said, "No."

She smiled. It was not just the beard that was different. He seemed more like himself, more like the man she knew before the English had arrived. She did not doubt time with Wallace had something to do with that. "You were there. You found him. She would want to hear it from you."

He said nothing for a while as he looked back at her. His eyes were no longer dark and heavy. Finally, he nodded. Standing, he was halfway to the door when her voice stopped him. "Are you going back to Lochmaben?"

He turned. "Yes."

"Neil was worried when you did not return."

A slow smile formed on his face. Glancing down, he asked, "Was Neil the only one concerned I was gone?"

The heat rose in her cheeks. Caught off guard, she fumbled for an answer.

He smiled as she squirmed. Turning, he walked out of the hall.

Days passed. Fall brought winter and with it calm. Many of the soldiers returned to England, the men who remained holing up in the castles they garrisoned. Christina took advantage of the mild weather in Carrick whenever she could, often walking about the land with her sisters, baby Marjorie bundled up tightly against her.

Rob had finally given his daughter a name. Marjorie seemed to love being outside. Her eyes were always open as they traversed the hills, but it was when they got close to the sea that she came alive. Her soft coos always made Christina smile as she stared in wonder at the vast body of water. She had been aptly named; Christina's mother had also been infatuated with the sea. Looking down at the small head in front of her, she hoped Marjorie learned to love the land of her grandmother just as much as she did.

A sharp whistle made her turn. Seeing Randolph beckoning, they made their way back. Christina's eyes latched onto the horse as soon as they walked into the bailey. She recognized that banner. Holding Marjorie a little bit tighter, she entered the keep.

Randolph led her to the hall. Unwrapping Marjorie from her body, she handed her to the waiting muime. She recognized the rider as soon as she stepped through the door. He had been with Douglas when he came to see her at Lochmaben. Named Robertson, he was one of Douglas' most trusted men. Seeing her there, he walked towards her.

He handed her a letter. Saying nothing else, he left the hall.

Christina opened the envelope as soon as he disappeared from view. It was not what she expected. Unfolding the piece of paper, she quickly understood what William Douglas was trying to tell her.

Issued by Hugh Cressingham, the announcement detailed the new system of rule the Scots were now under. Cressingham had been made Treasurer of Scotland by King Edward in the summer. Charged with the collection of taxes, his proclamation arrogantly explained how any rents owed were now due. He did not care that the people had just been at war and that English soldiers still roamed the land, taking what they wanted at will. The more Christina read, the more irritated she became. By the time she reached the end, she had changed her mind. She knew exactly what she wanted to do about Andrew Moray.

DOUGLAS CASTLE

CHAPTER ELEVEN

SHE SENT A rider north once more. This time, it had nothing to do with Wallace.

Christina had not heard from William Lamberton, the Chancellor of Glasgow Cathedral, since the night they met in Edinburgh. He had not told her much – simply asking that she pass on any information that may be of interest to the Kirk. But she could not help him. She had nothing to tell. Aware of the risk she was taking, she hoped Lamberton was not insulted by what she asked of him now.

She left Turnberry as soon as the messenger returned. The cloth bundle in his saddlebag told her Lamberton's answer. The monk had not let her down. Telling Rob she was returning to Lochmaben had been easy. Convincing her sisters to stay was harder, but as soon as she casually mentioned that she was thinking of visiting their father at Carlisle, they no longer wanted to come with. Cailean beside her, they headed south.

They did not speak, not even when they rode past Lochmaben in the dark. She had altered her appearance as well as she could. She kept her hood up and her clothes simple, all Bruce symbols hidden. Approaching the village of Annan, she slowed when she spotted two riders in the middle of the road. Seton and Jardine's faces came into view.

"Did you find it?" she asked.

Jardine reached into his cloak. Pulling out a pouch, he tossed it to her.

The coins clinked as she caught it. She weighed the bag in her hand. Her grandfather was never one to be unprepared. He had more than a few hidden nooks inside the castle. She had found a couple as a child, coming across the secret compartments as she tried to delay being put to bed. Feeling the fabric against her fingers, she doubted this was what her grandfather had in mind when he had stashed the silver. She lobbed the bag back to Jardine.

They rode all night, needing to get across the border before the next day began. Christina could picture her father sound asleep in his bed as they quietly rode through the streets of Carlisle. She pushed the image away. She could not think of him or anyone else – not now. Otherwise, she might lose her nerve. Giving her horse an encouraging nudge, she hurried after Jardine.

It took four more days to get to Chester. They slept inside whenever they could, staying at the inns bordering the villages they passed through. It was not difficult to avoid being noticed. Few others travelled in the dead of winter, even on the king's road. Christina had kept her mind quiet the entire journey. But as the English town came into view, Chester Castle illuminated by the setting sun, doubt and uncertainty overwhelmed her. She did not know if she could do this. Fear clogged her throat. Jardine glanced at her behind him. Seeing him waiting, she swallowed her apprehension and continued down the road.

The tavern was loud and disorderly. They were in the poor part of town, away from the main street and the accommodations reserved for noble families and burgesses. Besides the anonymity the area allowed her, the brothel was only two houses down. Seton and Jardine had left for it some time ago. Seated in a darkened corner, Christina looked down at the slop in front of her. She was not hungry, and the bowl of gruel did not help. Cailean gave her a look from across the table. Knowing he would force her to eat, she lifted the spoon and took a bite.

She never thought pottage could be ruined. It was a simple dish made of boiled vegetables. Even she knew how to cook it. But this was unlike anything she had ever tasted. It was burnt and had an odd texture she was not quite accustomed to. A chunk of something stuck to the back of her throat. Fighting the urge to vomit, she drained the cup of mead in front of her. She pushed the bowl away.

"I do not like this."

She watched Cailean slowly eat his meal. His eyes never left her face as he continuously lifted the sludge to his mouth. He had grumbled the entire journey to Chester. At first, he refused to wear the clothes that made him look less like a Gallovidian warrior and more like an English villager. When she told him that she was going with or without him, a stream of Gaelic curses was cast in her direction. She had never seen him so sour.

She did not respond to his statement, aware of how he felt. He did not like her idea from the start. He had called her foolish. Fool or not, she would see it through, and for once in his life, he would do as he was told.

Jardine sitting down across from her interrupted their

silent conversation. Seton followed. A tavern worker approached the table, bowls of soup in her hands. Christina tilted her face away. The woman set the food down and left. Christina looked expectantly to the two men.

"It has been arranged," Jardine said. His voice was low. "We are to meet just before dawn. She will bring what we need."

Satisfied, Christina nodded. That part of the plan was relatively simple. Seton and Jardine would go back to the brothel in the morning to retrieve the clothes of two English soldiers enjoying themselves there now. It was not usual for men to stay the night, but when the guards woke in the morning, heads pounding and stomachs lurching, they would not remember a thing. All they would know was that they were still in the brothel and their clothes were gone.

"And then you will go to the castle," she said.

Jardine glanced over at Seton and nodded. "Then we will go to the castle."

Christina exhaled. Her anticipation began to build. She wanted it to be over, but she also was not ready for it to start. Having nothing else to do but wait, she pushed herself up from the table and went to get some sleep.

It did not come. The more she tried, the harder it was to rest. When she heard the soft knock on the door, indicating that she should get up, she was still awake. She sighed in frustration. Throwing back the covers, she rose to get dressed.

Annoyed did not begin to describe it. She had managed to get on most of the habit, the grey tunic cloaking her body entirely, but the scapular was a struggle, the long woollen cloth tight against her head. Her hair needed to be hidden beneath it. The more she tried to tuck it back under the opening around her face, the worse it got, the strands refusing to comply. Groaning in frustration, she opened the door to find Cailean.

Seton's stare met her. He was barely visible in the dark, the rest of the tavern asleep as he waited for Jardine in the corridor.

"I cannot do this." She looked down at the fabric in her hand.

He did not answer. Pushing himself off the wall, he stepped through the door.

She tried once more to fix her hair, but her fingers would not cooperate. Her hands shook whenever she attempted to lift the scapular. She dropped her arms in frustration. "I cannot… It will not stay back."

He lifted the scapular from her head.

Christina watched as he untwisted it. He glanced up at her once. Motioning for her to lean back, she smoothed her hair down. He gently pulled the scapular on.

Standing, she glanced at her reflection in the mirror. Every strand of hair was tucked out of sight. She looked like a nun. Relieved, she turned to thank him. The concern on his face made her stop.

"I will not try to change your mind," he said. "You have already decided what you want." He hesitated. "All I ask is that you make your peace before you enter those grounds." His stare was unnerving. "Once you are inside, you cannot run out. You will be on your own with no one to help you." He paused. "Be certain. Be ready."

He walked from the room. Watching him go, she could not deny the truth in his words. If she was not prepared, if she was not calm, she should not do it. Not even her father could save her from the retribution that would come. Feeling the extra clothes hidden beneath her tunic, she took one more look at herself in the mirror and left.

The town was quiet as she made her way towards the castle. A few others were about, but they gave her no more than a passing glance, having their own reasons for being up before the sun. Cailean had said not a word when she had exited the tavern. His hands flexing at his sides told her just how uncomfortable he was. Despite being told not to, he would follow her there, she knew he would. Thinking of Jardine and Seton dressing in the soldiers' clothes, she picked up her pace.

Seated along the River Dee, Chester Castle was built to protect England from the Welsh. Though it no longer served that purpose, King Edward conquering Wales ten years earlier, it was still an imposing stronghold. Christina walked across the bridge. The gate to the castle rose with the sun. Her hands quivering, she tucked them behind the folds of her skirt.

Attempting to appear casual, she waited for the people ahead of her to enter the grounds. The worst thing she could be was noticeable. One of the guards nodded to her as she walked through. She told herself to remain calm. She was a nun, and nuns were the epitome of restraint. Straightening her posture, she headed towards the inner bailey.

She kept her eyes forward as she walked. Guards moved all around her, their figures visible atop the wall. She gave no indication she noticed them. Lifting the hem of her dress as she crossed the second bridge, she entered the small courtyard at the heart of the castle.

Built of stone, Agricola Tower stood to her left, its rectangular shape rising up into the sky. A small chapel occupied the main floor, but Christina was not here to see the vaulted ceiling. Closing the door behind her, she quickly searched for the entrance to the crypt.

It did not take her long to find it and she did not hesitate. Pushing the door open, she hurried down the steep staircase.

She could barely make out the pathway. The open door above her let in some light, but it soon faded, the corridor becoming blacker the farther she walked. Turning a corner, a torch glowed on the wall ahead. She made her way towards it.

The gaoler looked up as she came to a stop in front of him. Taking a moment to look her over, he seemed confused. "It is a little early for morning prayers, is it not Sister?"

She gave him her sincerest smile. "I hate to admit it, but I think I might be lost." She glanced down the dark hallway ahead of him. "Did you see an abbess here earlier?"

He looked at her as if she was of unsound mind. Not wanting to offend a woman of the church, he attempted a smile and shook his head. "No one down here but me. I am certain you will find her somewhere in the grounds. Just go back the way you came."

It was a clear dismissal. Christina panicked. She could not leave, not yet, and so she remained where she was, struggling to come up with a reason to stay. The gaoler watched her strangely.

Shouting from the bailey was like a sign from God himself. The gaoler stood, slowly approaching the bottom of the stairs to listen. Something was happening in the grounds up above. The noise drifted down towards them in the dark. As he turned, his mouth open to speak, Christina smashed the chair he had been sitting on against the side of his head.

He crumpled, the weight of his body toppling him onto the floor. He went down faster than she expected. Tossing her weapon aside, she dropped to her knees. She struggled to roll him over. Using her shoulder to leverage his arm, she eventually got him onto his back. Ripping the keys from his belt, she grabbed the torch off the wall and ran into the dark.

"Andrew!"

She tried to keep her voice quiet, but it was impossible. It echoed off the walls in the crypt. Peering through the bars of each cell, she searched for him. Some of the rooms were empty, but most were not. She could not tell who they were. The prisoners sat facing the wall, their backs the only visible part of them. Holding the flame up against the bars, she whispered his name louder. They did not move. Knowing she could not linger, she moved on.

She wanted nothing more than to get out of there. The farther she went, the more panicked she felt, the crypt seeming to darken with each step. Stopping at the next cell, she saw a man lying on the floor wrapped in a blanket. His unruly beard partially hid the dirt on his face. Relieved excitement filled her. Her fingers fumbling, she dropped the keys.

"Shit." Crouching down, she scooped them up. Her palms were clammy. Bringing the torch close to the bars once more, she watched Andrew squint at the light. Recognition came over his face.

She did not wait a moment longer. One by one, she inserted each key into the slot. The pressure built with every one that did not turn. She heard him walking towards her. The light shuffle of stiff legs told her exactly how close he was, but she did not slow. The key in her grasp suddenly turned. The bolt slid open with a solid 'thunk.' She pushed her way into the room.

Andrew said nothing as he stared at her. He was only a few feet away, his face a mixture of suspicion and confusion. He did not appear to believe she was real. Lifting his arm out towards her, Christina stepped into his reach.

He jerked his hand back the moment he touched her shoulder. She did not doubt he was struggling to understand, but they could not wait for him to comprehend what was happening. Reaching up under the skirt of her habit, she untied the string that held the hidden clothes to her torso. She handed them to Andrew.

"Here," she said. "Put these on."

He stared back at her. The moment she saw the tears filling his eyes, she walked forward.

She squeezed his hand firmly in hers. "Please," she said. "Do as I say."

He nodded. Turning, she kept watch at the door.

He dressed quickly, the monk's outfit dwarfing him. He still looked like a prisoner, his face too thin and skin too pale. Wiping the dirt off his face, she lifted the hood up over his head. It would have to do. The torch in her grasp once more, she led them out of the crypt.

The gaoler was where she left him. Returning the flame to its holder on the wall, she tied the keys back onto the man's belt. If they were lucky, the pile of hay Jardine had set fire to near the stables would still be alight. With Andrew behind her, she climbed the stairs.

She watched the doorway at the top as they ascended. They were not going as quickly as she would like, Andrew's movements slow. He had been imprisoned for almost a year now. If the changes in his face were any indication of what had happened to the rest of him, he would need a lot of rest and food before he was himself again. She did not hear any footsteps near the entryway. Slowly opening the door, she walked out into the chapel.

All was quiet. Voices no longer called out for help from outside. Hurrying through the pews, Christina stood on her tiptoes and looked out the window. Besides the grounds being a bit busier than before, everything seemed normal. Nothing was out of place. Satisfied, she turned to Andrew.

"You will go out first." She spoke quickly and firmly, making sure he heard what she said.

The climb up the stairs had reddened his cheeks.

"Two soldiers will be waiting with four horses near the gate." When she saw his eyes lift in uncertainty, she said, "They are not English. They are my men. Walk straight towards them. Do not look back. I will be right behind you."

She waited for him to nod. When he finally did, she placed her hands on the sides of his shoulders and gave him an encouraging smile. If they did get caught, if an ambush waited for them in the grounds, she had made it this far at least. It would not help her in the English court in front of King Edward, but it would comfort her nonetheless. Andrew opened the door. She followed him out.

They walked through the inner bailey towards the bridge, Christina making sure to stay a couple of steps behind him. The sun had risen, but it was still cold, a thin veil of clouds preventing warmth from reaching the ground. People nodded to them as they passed. Some even greeted Andrew, calling him father and smiling as they went. Reaching the plank, he walked across the moat. Christina stepped up onto it. A voice behind her made her stop.

"Sister!"

The rebuking tone drove fear into her once more. She glanced back.

A determined frown met her. The nun came hastily towards her.

Unsure of what was happening, Christina glanced at Andrew. He had stopped to wait for her on the other side of the bridge. Her heart thumping in her chest, she swallowed the panic down. "Go."

His eyes were wide. He shook his head.

She forced a smile, her gaze insistent. Her voice dropped as she repeated herself. "Go."

He turned just as the nun came to a stop. Forcing herself to look away, Christina faced the woman who had come for her.

The nun looked down at Christina with annoyance. "The hours are upon us, Sister. It is time for prayer."

It took Christina a moment to understand what she was saying. The realization suddenly dawned on her. Wiping the anxious look from her face, she nodded. Unwillingly, she followed the nun back to the chapel.

Several others had already gathered inside the church. Their faces were contrite as they prayed. It was not difficult for Christina to mimic what they were doing. As soon as her eyes were closed, the words rushed forward, her appeals to God numerous. She prayed the gaoler was still unconscious. She prayed Andrew had made it to the gate. Most of all, she prayed she would get out of here alive. The nuns rose. Mass had ended. The older woman gave her a hint of smile as she stepped out of the pew. Christina took that as permission to leave. Not waiting any longer, she hurried out the door.

For a second time that morning, she walked through the bailey. This time, she was not so calm. Telling herself to slow down, she repeated those two words over and over until she stepped from the gate. Jardine and Seton were not there. Neither was Andrew. Sending another prayer upwards, she ran for the tavern.

She did not make it to the inn. Turning off the main road, she stopped when she saw the men waiting up ahead.

The look of relief on Seton's face was palpable. Andrew stopped pacing. Still dressed in his monk's outfit, Christina bit her lip to keep from smiling. He looked ridiculous. How had she not seen that before? Approaching Cailean, she took the reins he offered in his outstretched hand. Jardine smirked at her. Swinging herself up onto her horse, they headed north.

They rode as fast as they dared through the streets of Chester. None of them knew how long it would take for the English to notice a prisoner was missing. They were not willing to find out. Jardine moving past her as they reached the outskirts of town, Christina urged her horse into a sprint.

This time, they slept beneath the trees. Stopping for the first night, Christina did not bother dismounting before she ripped the scapular from her head. Cold, fresh air soothed her itchy scalp. Dropping down onto the wet ground, she pulled on every piece of clothing she had brought with and threw her blanket over her shoulders. There would be no fire tonight. Huddling close to Cailean, her head on his shoulder, she fell asleep.

Cailean's voice woke her. The forest was still dark. Ignoring the desire for more rest, she sat up. He handed her a piece of dried fish. She chewed on it absentmindedly as she stretched out the kink in her neck. Jardine and Seton untied the horses. The thought of riding all day disheartened her. Every part of her ached, even her toes were sore. Untangling herself from the blanket, she stood. Then Andrew stepped from the trees.

He hesitated. No longer in the monk's clothes, he looked more like himself. His face was washed and his eyes were bright.

Christina stared back at him. She tried to think of something to say. Noticing the way the tunic hung off his frame, her face pained in sympathy. He was skinner than she thought. The confinement of the crypt had worn him down to the bone. While it did not appear that he had been mistreated, he had not been well taken care of either. She took a step towards him. His gaze dropped, but not before she saw the anguish on his face. Moving away from her, he wrapped himself in his cloak and climbed onto the horse.

They crossed into Scotland on the third night. Stopping to rest the horses, Christina looked up at the dark sky, the stars visible behind the thin curtain of cloud. They still had a long way to go. Douglas Castle was over fifty miles northwest from where they stood. Movement made her turn. Jardine stopped beside her.

"Think Neil will be suspicious?" she asked.

He shook his head. "He thinks I was in Kelso helping my brother. He told me to take as long as I needed."

She nodded. They could not arrive in Lochmaben together. That would arouse suspicion. Jardine would return while Seton helped her get Andrew to William Douglas. Holding out her arm, Jardine gripped it tight. Swinging onto his horse, he headed west. Christina dug her heels into her mare for one last push north.

It took the entire day, the road treacherous and cold, the weather miserable and wet. As relieved as she was to get out of Chester, she could not wait until Andrew was no longer her responsibility. They could not be caught now. The pressure mounted. The closer she got to the end, the more anxious she felt.

Night fell once more as they entered Douglas. The fortress was not far now. The darkness brought a storm, thick droplets of rain falling down upon them as they galloped for the gate. Cailean yelled at the guard to open it. The man on the wall did not move. Pulling back her hood, Christina watched his face fill with recognition. The metal barrier clanking as it lifted, she rode into the bailey.

Douglas Castle was as menacing as the lord who governed it. While not as large as Lochmaben, it was an impressive fortress. The keep and its surrounding walls sat atop a hill at the head of a valley, a river running just west of it. It was not very old. Christina had been born before the wood and stone that formed it were set into place. But as her eyes latched onto the large frame stepping from the keep, she forgot about all of that. She dropped from her horse.

William Douglas said nothing as she approached. His eyes flickered over to assess the three men dismounting behind her. Turning, she motioned for Andrew to come forward. Douglas' face transformed when he saw who it was.

Hurried into the castle, they were placed in front of the fire. She did not think they could get any closer. Heat radiated outwards as blankets were wrapped around them. Christina could barely move from all the weight, but she did not have to. A woman appeared at her side the moment she twitched a finger. Warm stew was pushed towards them. Grateful for a hot meal, Christina dug in. Her stomach full and warm, she leaned back in her chair and fell asleep.

She woke with a start. The hall was dim and silent. Seton, Cailean, and Andrew slept in their chairs. Watching their chests rise and fall rhythmically, she struggled out of the layers and stood.

The muscles in her legs groaned in agony. She stepped away from the smoldering fire, her movements stiff. She got as far as the table before she noticed Douglas standing in the doorway.

He leaned his shoulder into the frame and watched her approach. "Come," he said, his voice soft. "Fresh air will do you good." Taking the cloak from his outstretched hand, she followed him outside.

Light filtered slowly into the sky as they walked through the gate. Her breath turned white as it left her lungs. Following Douglas down the road through the trees, Christina relaxed and tucked her hands into her cloak.

It did not take long for them to reach the small loch just south of the castle. The village rested in the valley below, wispy strands of smoke rising up as day began. It looked peaceful and serene, as if she had not ridden with a fugitive through those very houses the night before. Distracted by a sudden motion, she caught sight of a red squirrel scurrying up a tree in the distance.

"I thought I knew who you were, back at Lochmaben."

She turned at Douglas' voice.

He stood with his hands behind his back, the same dark eyes that had assessed her only months before holding her again. "I know you did not go to your father." He paused. "And yet, Andrew Moray is with us once more." He stared down at her. "Tell me what to make of this."

She returned her gaze to the village. Looking over the land of Douglas, she did not know what to say. It was complicated and very simple at the same time. While going to her father seemed like the safer and easier choice, it was not. Not for her. The moment she asked for Andrew's release, she would have to give a part of herself in return, regardless of the outcome. As much as she still cared for Andrew, she could not do it. It was not worth the risk. She loved herself more.

"You asked me to do what I could." She glanced at Douglas again. "This I could do." When he did not answer, she knew it was enough.

They returned to the castle. Cailean was already mounted. Her cloak with the Bruce crest was draped over her saddle. Removing the one around her shoulders, she noticed Seton standing to the side. His arms were crossed in front of him. His horse had not been prepared. As he walked towards her, her stomach clenched. She already knew what he was going to say.

"You are not coming."

Stopping in front of her horse, he smiled, but it quickly fell. He placed a hand on the mare's neck. "You do not need me."

It was not what she wanted to hear. Perhaps she had

asked too much of him with what they had done in England. He had seemed like himself when he returned from Wallace, but now he was changed again. She felt it in the way he looked at her, and in the way he did not.

"I will ride with Douglas to Bothwell," he said. "Ensure Moray reaches his uncle."

Christina quietly contemplated the plan. Andrew's uncle was the Lord of Bothwell and one of the most powerful barons in Scotland. With no children of his own, Andrew was set to inherit it all. But there was more to it than that. While Andrew had sat in the crypt, men continued to go to Avoch, seeking refuge and guidance under the Moray banner. His father, the Lord of Moray, was not in the Highlands. He had been captured alongside his son and sent to the Tower in London. His time there would not be kind. He might not make it out at all. Looking at Seton before her, Christina knew seeing Andrew to Bothwell meant more than just returning a Scotsman to his home. The Highlands finally had a man to lead them. She hoped Andrew was ready.

"And then?" she asked.

A soft smile crossed his face.

She nodded in understanding. Wallace.

While the Morays drew men in the north, the outlaw's following swelled in the south. English taxes and sheriffs dispossessed people throughout the Lowlands. It was not just the loss of Scotsmen to prisons that impoverished them. The area around Selkirk Forest had been ravaged in the fighting, the fertile land and crops suffering heavily. With no goods to sell or trade at the markets, they did not have enough to feed their families. But King Edward did not care. His inhumanity was building a rebellion.

Staring back at Seton, she wanted to say something meaningful. No words formed. She did not want him to go. Despite his absences, she had come to depend on him. She always looked for him in the grounds. But this time was different. She did not know if or when he would come back at all. Looking up into his face, his smile soft, she felt like he was leaving her behind.

She moved her horse towards the gate. Her hands on the saddle, she swung herself up. A voice called out her name.

"Christina."

She did not need to turn to know who it was. The mood in the bailey changed, the men watching her with renewed interest. He should not have said her name – not like that. Glancing over her shoulder, she looked at Andrew standing in the door.

He had just woken up, his clothes wrinkled and his face disheveled. He stared back at her.

She had hoped to avoid this. Whatever he was struggling to say, she did not want to hear it. She had not gone to Chester just because Scotland needed him. So many things between them had been left unsaid in Mar. She went for herself – she needed an ending. Andrew dying in England would not have given her that. The guilt of not doing something would have ripped her apart.

He remained silent, unable to find the words he required.

Christina suddenly wanted to be home. Unwilling to look at his pained expression any longer, she galloped out of the gate.

It was dark when the towers of Lochmaben came into view. Riding towards the bailey, she could not wait to climb into bed and sleep. The sight of English soldiers swarming the grounds made her stop.

She failed to keep the alarm from her face. Spotting Jardine near the armoury, he shook his head to caution her. A soldier approached. He latched onto her reins.

Indicating for her to dismount, Christina reluctantly slid off her horse. Cailean stood beside her. She could feel the animosity surging through his veins. The soldier waved them forward. Exhaling slowly, Christina lifted the hem of her skirt and walked towards what waited for her in the keep.

CHAPTER TWELVE

CHRISTINA HELD HER head high as she entered the tower. The English had already made themselves at home. Supplies loomed up in every available corner. Men walked about the castle as if it was theirs. Moving through the door of the hall, she stopped when she saw the man sitting in her grandfather's chair.

The man did not acknowledge her. He continued to read the ledger in front of him. The hair on top of his head was thin, making his fat cheeks look even more pronounced. Books were stacked in an orderly fashion on the table. A soldier waited at the door. Knowing she was not allowed to leave, Christina straightened her posture.

"Christina Bruce, I presume."

Shifting her gaze over to him, the man smiled. She wished he would not. The expression was unnatural. If he was attempting to disarm her, it had the opposite effect. "Where is my brother?" she asked.

He studied her for a moment before he answered. "I do not believe we have met." He placed a hand on his chest. "I am Hugh Cressingham, the Treasurer of Scotland. King Edward has appointed me to collect taxes owed to the crown." He paused. "I will hold court here at Lochmaben. All debts must be repaid in full. Your brother, Neil, has gone to notify the people of Annandale."

She wanted to rip that tongue from his mouth. Afraid of what she would say, she remained silent.

"Your father informed me that my presence here would not be an inconvenience. He is very-" He searched for the right word. "-appeasing."

Watching him smirk, Christina's jaw clenched. He was not like the English noblemen she was accustomed to. Though he said all the right things, he did not bother hiding what he actually thought. His lousy opinion of her father was clear. Unwilling to be near him a moment longer, she turned to leave. She reached the door when his voice stopped her.

"You will be there."

She expected him to continue and say, "I hope," but he did not. Glancing back, his waiting stare met her.

"It is important for the ruling lord to be present. The people must see your undying loyalty to King Edward. And since your father is not here and your brother has more important tasks, you will stand in their place."

She imagined her knife against his throat, his rosy cheeks paling in fear. It would not take long for him to die. The skin on his neck was soft and supple. She could easily slice into his flesh. The thought of him not being able to speak another word made her smile. Holding his gaze a moment longer, she let him feel the malice in her expression. Turning, she walked out of the hall.

Cressingham did not waste any time. The gates of Lochmaben opened the following morning to those who had come to pay what they owed. Neil still gone, Christina had no choice but to attend. She watched with resentment as people who had nothing gave an English king money that was not his.

She wore black on the first day and the next. Cressingham noticed but said nothing. It was only on the third day, the line growing longer as word spread of the tax collector's presence, that he let her know he was not happy with her attire.

His scowl met her as she stepped from the keep. Smoothing down the front of her dress, she smiled back. She was in mourning. The kingdom was dying. Black was appropriate.

"Please, sir, I-"

The man's voice broke Christina from her daze on the fifth day. The line of downtrodden people having no end in sight, the bleak proceedings wore on. She had started to block it out, unwilling to witness what was happening before her. Cressingham sat behind a table in front of the keep. His book spread out before him, his finger hovered beneath a name and an amount.

"You are grievously behind on your rents." His voice carried out across the bailey.

Silent faces watched with a mixture of fear and anger.

"I understand that your lord has been lenient." He glanced back at Christina before he continued. "But that is no longer acceptable. You will pay what you owe."

Cressingham was not wrong. Christina was responsible for the extension of payment granted towards this man. He and his family had lived in Annandale all their lives and were good tenants, never once behind in rent. But then his son died. A fever took him in the night. The man was too old and frail to take his son's place.

He had offered his only ox as payment, but Christina refused. His land was unworkable without the animal. She told him to find a man to marry the wife his son had left behind. His payments to her family would resume only then. Knowing he had not found a suitor yet, Christina could no longer ignore what was happening. She anxiously waited for the older man's reply.

"I cannot," he said. "I do not have enough."

Cressingham stared silently at the man. His finger tapping against a piece of paper, the steady rhythm filled Christina's ears. It suddenly stopped.

"Rents owed to your lord are rents owed to Edward." He leaned towards the man. "And your king does not tolerate such insolence. Twenty lashes for the crime of withholding payment."

Everything seemed to move in slow motion. The disbelief on the man's face reflected in the others present. Soldiers stepped forward. They dragged him towards the post.

Unaware that one had been built, Christina watched in horror as they bound the man's hands together. His arms were raised above his head. Her breath short and fast, she prayed for Neil to ride through the gates. A soldier pulled out a whip. The man's legs buckled. The moment she heard the crack of leather, the man's skin splitting with ease, Christina broke from her stupor.

She reached him as the fourth strike came down. Placing herself between the man and the soldier, her forearm took the brunt of the blow. The pain shocked her. It was not like being cut with a knife. The agony was profound and spread through her limb like wildfire. She looked down at the wound. Blood flowed from her arm. Feeling unsteady, she dropped to her knees. The bailey erupted.

She saw nothing, but the sound of people shouting was unmistakable. There was a skirmish not too far from where she was, the boots of the soldier moving towards it. She felt nauseous. Despite her best efforts to stand, she could not. Cailean's face appeared in front of her.

He stared into her stunned gaze. Wrapping her arm with cloth, a silent cry rushed from her mouth in anguish as the bandage pushed the ripped skin together. Helping her to her feet, Cailean directed her away from the altercations in the grounds. Two soldiers latched onto her arms. Cailean was pulled back.

The English swarmed him, swords out and at the ready. Cailean assessed his odds.

Shaking her head, Christina wanted him to do nothing. A blade stabbed into him. She choked back a scream.

He wobbled and fell to his knees, the knife still sticking out of his thigh. She tried to go to him, but could not. The hands that held her dug into her shoulders. The last thing she saw before Cressingham blocked her view was the butt of a sword smashing into his head.

She tried to see around him. Cressingham grabbed her face. His fingers gouged her cheeks.

"You have no right," she said.

He smiled. "I have *every* right."

"My father-"

"Your father is an obedient mutt and he will do what he usually does." His face hovered close to hers. "Nothing." He released her from his grasp. "Lock her in the tower," he said to the men holding her. "She needs time to think about what she has done."

Christina fought as they dragged her inside and up the stairs. She squirmed, kicked and thrashed, but they did not slow, determined to get her into the cell. Reaching the top floor, they pushed her into the small room. The dust kicked up around her. Rushing towards the door as it shut, she heard the deadbolt slide, locking her in. Her fists pounded against the wood. Sinking down onto the floor, a despondent scream burst from her throat.

She was told nothing. The soldiers refused to answer her questions when they came to bring her food. They simply shoved the plate across the floor.

Neil finally returned two days later. His distraught face looked at her through the bars of the small window. Hearing the door open, she picked herself up off the thin mattress and rushed towards him. He hugged her tight. Letting go, she moved for the door. The soldier standing in the frame stopped her.

"He will not let you out," Neil said. His voice was strained. "He says you interfered with his orders, which is an act against King Edward. You must repent and swear to him that you will obey or he will take you to the English court to be tried."

Her relief at seeing her brother was gone. Cressingham was a bastard. He could not get away with this.

Neil cupped her face in his hands. "Just say the words," he whispered. "You do not have to mean it, Christina. Just tell him what he wants to hear."

She sighed and pulled away. As easy as it seemed, she knew she could not do it. The moment she stood before him, looking at his greasy scalp and arrogant smirk, the words would not come. All she would want to do is spit in his face.

"I am sending a message to Rob."

Her head jerked up. "No." Whatever happened, Rob could not know. If he found out Cressingham had imprisoned her in her own castle, refusing to let her go, there would be no telling what he would do. She would not have him go to war against the entire English army. Not for her, not for this. "Promise you will not."

Neil looked at her with frustration. She could tell that he did not want to. Eventually, he nodded.

"Where is Cailean?" She had asked that question every time someone came to the door. She received no reply. Looking at her brother, her eyes begged him for an answer.

"He is somewhere in the village," Neil said. "Jardine will not tell me where." Seeing her concern, he continued. "He will be all right, Christina. It will take more than a few English soldiers to kill that man."

Christina attempted a weak smile. Not knowing if Cailean was alive or dead had kept her up at night, the blow from the sword replaying in her mind. If he could bide his time, then so could she. Neil left the room. Wrapping herself in the thin blanket, she sat down on the mattress, ready to wait out her sentence.

Sleep came easier as the days wore on. In the beginning, she would stand on her tiptoes, gripping the window ledge with her fingers to watch the people lined up in the grounds below. With each passing day, the number dwindled. So did her strength. The wound on her arm festered. It was angry, the cut red and swollen. Ripping a strip from the bottom of her dress, she replaced the bandage, wrapping it as tight as she could. The pain made her sweat. Exhausted from the effort, she pulled the blanket back over her.

The days melted into one another. She rarely moved. Relieving herself was a struggle. She had to squat over the bucket while bracing herself against the wall. Her thighs shook the entire time. None of the food interested her enough to eat. The best part of her day was watching the mice scurry over her plate, whiskers twitching in excitement.

"Christina."

She heard her name being softly called. It felt like a dream, and so she kept her eyes shut, hoping to stay asleep a little longer. A hand touched her shoulder. She reluctantly left her peaceful state and looked up in the dark.

Jardine stared down at her.

Unsure if he was real, she reached out and touched the beard that covered his face.

He smiled. "Come. It is time for you to go."

Sliding his arm under her shoulders, he lifted her off the mattress. She did not protest. Wobbling a little, she was set on her feet. Moving for the first time in days, her body cried out in agony. The bandage on her arm was soaked again. Jardine at her side, she leaned into him and descended the stairs.

There was no light, no sound of movement in the entire castle. It looked like all the English had gone. Reaching the landing, Christina walked slowly on her own. She stopped when she saw the soldier slumped against the wall.

"We put a little something in the ale," Jardine whispered. He grinned. "They will feel worse than a dog's arse in the morning."

She smiled for the first time in how many days, she did not know. Moving past the hall, they stepped down the last set of stairs to the entrance of the keep. The light May breeze floated in through the open door. She turned to Jardine.

"Is he here?"

Knowing who she was referring to, Jardine shook his head. "No. Cressingham left this morning."

She hesitated. "Wait for me. I will not be long." Not staying to hear him tell her no, she hurried down the dark corridor.

The door to the cellar creaked as it opened. Carefully peering through the crack, she scanned the room. Cressingham spent a lot of his time here. At the end of every day, when the taxes had been collected, he would return to the basement to write down accounts and review the ledgers. She had seen him do it three times before she was locked up. Hoping the books were still in the chest, she stepped into the room.

Her eyes adjusted to the dark, she easily picked out the shapes of things. She headed towards the corner. The ledgers were exactly where he had left them. She was tempted to take them. She could burn them or throw them into the sea. Fumbling around for a match, lighting the small candle against the wall, she resisted the urge. There was only one thing she wanted. Cressingham could not know she had it. Not until it was too late.

"What are you doing?"

Her muscles tensed, sending jolts of pain down her body. She looked up. Neil stood just inside the door. Her fear vanished. She dropped her gaze back to the pages. Her fingers quickly traversed over the marks.

"We need to go."

She ignored him. If she left without the information, she would regret it. It was the only thing that would make all the pain and agony of the last few days worthwhile. Flipping the page, she hesitated when she saw the note. She read the sentence five times over to commit it to memory. Closing the book, she snuffed out the candle and followed Neil out of the keep.

They walked inside the shadows along the wall. There was no one there, but they did not risk it, Christina leaning against the stone to keep her upright. The gate had been left partially open. The bottom rungs were just high enough off the ground for someone to crawl through. She fit easily, Jardine pulling her out from the other side. Neil followed. Crossing the road and into the trees, she smiled when she saw the man standing beside the horses.

Cailean only grunted as she hugged him. Letting go, she stared at his face closely. There was a cut on the left side of his head near his hairline. He looked well despite the bandaged wound on his leg. Giving her the slightest smile, he reached out and touched her cheek.

Christina turned to her brother. "You should not stay."

Neil smiled. "I am not." He walked over to where his horse was standing. "I am coming with you." Looking back at her, his face fell. He sighed in irritation. "You are not going to Turnberry, are you?"

She glanced at Jardine and Cailean. Their waiting stares told her they were ready for whatever she wanted to do. She turned back to Neil. "Not yet," she said. "There is something I need to do."

She rode as fast as she dared. The muscles in her legs shook as they fought to keep her upright in the saddle. She was freezing despite the double layer of clothes she had on. Ignoring the pounding in her head, she tightened the thick cloak around her and hurried to keep up.

Neil had gone to Turnberry without her. He promised not to say anything to Rob about what had happened at Lochmaben until she arrived. Rob would be furious. Christina needed to tell him in person. Cressingham would not have to guess where she went. Turnberry Castle was the obvious choice. But Christina was confident he would not go after her, in Carrick or anywhere else. Despite his posturing, he did not have enough evidence to charge her. Her actions were easily explainable even to King Edward. People might not think much of her father, but he was still an essential ally to England. It would take much more than interrupting a whipping to see her tried in any court. Besides, she had been a thorn in his side. Cressingham was likely just as happy to be rid of her as she was of him.

The roads were bare as they travelled through Selkirk Forest, the snow long gone. Wallace had moved into the thick wood a few months earlier. His presence was no secret. The vast woodland and dense foliage made him difficult to uncover. Following Jardine off the main road onto a lightly used hunting path, Christina hoped they found him and quickly. What she knew was worth the trouble.

A pained sigh left her mouth as she dismounted. They had ridden through the night and all morning, finally stopping to rest by a small stream in the heart of the woods.

The journey had taken more out of her than she expected. Feeling the heat radiating from her head, she removed her cloak and splashed water over her face.

"Wait here," Cailean said. "We are going to look around."

She did not reply, too relieved as the water cooled her neck. The back of her dress was soaked. The shivering started once more. Finding a sunny spot nearby, she lowered her aching body down on the grass and let the sun warm her bones.

She had never known a more peaceful rest. It was as if she was in a cocoon of warmth, the cloak cushioning her back as she leaned against the tree. She could hear leaves rusting from somewhere across the stream, but she did not move. When a shadow crossed over her, interrupting her direct line to the sun, she reluctantly opened her eyes.

Cailean's concerned expression stared down at her. Crouching, he reached out and touched her cheek with the back his hand. "You are too warm."

She knew what that meant but did not care. She had to keep going. Only when she found Wallace and told him what she knew, then she would rest. She forced herself back onto her feet.

They continued on, riding deeper into the forest. Nervous whines from the horses made them slow.

Four soldiers lay across the path. They had not been dead for long; there was no foul odor in the air. She looked down at the plundered bodies as her horse carefully stepped around. They were getting close.

The sun's strength waned as afternoon came and went. The trees thickened along the path. She did not know how far they would have to go to find him. Her arm aching, she wanted to rest. Jardine pulled to a stop. Looking past him, she saw the men waiting on the trail ahead.

There were only three of them, but that was not what concerned her. Jardine already had his hand on his sword, his eyes scanning the trees. Christina did the same. Bandits and gangs of thieves were commonplace in the Lowlands. They liked to hide in the forests, taking travellers by surprise and relieving them of their goods. People often died. Their appearance on the road usually meant that more of them lurked in the trees. Christina slid her hand down to the knife tucked in her boot. She wrapped her fingers around the handle.

One of the men stepped forward. "Have you not heard, Lady Christina," he began. "It is dangerous in the forest. There are thieves and murderers about." He paused. "And that is just the English."

Laughter filled the air. Christina relaxed her grip. She moved her horse forward, Jardine and Cailean following close behind. A man with a crooked nose came into view.

Alexander Fraser smirked up at her. Closing the distance between them, he ran his hand slowly down the neck of her horse as he had done in Lanark.

"Are you lost?" he asked.

She smiled as if he had told a joke. She stared at him for a moment. "Where is he?"

The smirk only grew. When he did not answer, one of the other men did.

"You and your family are for England. Why would we tell you anything?"

The implication in his tone was clear. Nothing changed the fact that she was still a Bruce. Ignoring the man, she kept her eyes on Fraser. He would be the one to decide.

The smile faded from his mouth. "Get off your horse," he said. "Let's take a walk."

Stepping off the path, Christina followed Fraser into the trees, everyone else right behind. No one spoke as they went. The sound of horses plodding along filled her ears. They encountered another of Wallace's men not long after they left the trail. The man nodded to Fraser and stared at her as she passed. The farther they walked, the more men they encountered. By the time she stepped into the camp, the sunless sky darkening the woods around them, she could not count the number of men fast enough. Wallace had an army.

Seeing Fraser ahead of her, she handed Cailean her reins and caught up to the Scotsman. She walked alongside him as they went deeper into the camp.

"There is something you must know." The humour was gone from Fraser's face. "We returned from Lanark not long ago. Wallace is not himself."

His words worried her. Keeping her voice quiet, she asked, "What happened in Lanark?"

He looked conflicted, as though he was not sure how to explain. Eventually, he said, "He went there to see his wife. He stayed too long." Fraser's face was grim. "The sheriff, Heselrig, almost caught him. He killed Wallace's wife instead."

It was far worse than she imagined. Her heart sank. She had not known Wallace was married. She did not doubt he wanted it that way, trying to keep his wife safe from harm. It still was not enough to save her.

Fraser cleared his throat. "Heselrig is dead, as is his son and every other Englishman there." He stopped in front of a tent and turned to her. "But Wallace is not the same."

She nodded, understanding what he was trying to tell

her. Whatever she said to Wallace would not garner the same reaction as before. She might not get what she wanted.

Pulling back the fabric opening, Fraser stepped through. The conversation stopped as Christina entered. A mixture of familiar and unfamiliar faces stared back at her. Wallace stood at the front, a head taller than most. Her eyes drifted around the room, noting Robertson, William Douglas' right-hand-man. She was distracted by the Mormaer of Lennox coming to greet her.

"Finally," he said. "A Bruce is present." He clasped her firmly on the shoulders. "Scotland has been waiting."

Pain from his touch snaked through her arm. She did her best to smile at the burly man she knew so well.

Lennox was allied to House Bruce and had supported her grandfather when he made his claim to the throne. It did not surprise her that he was here. The mormaer cared not for any kind of indentured servitude, to England or anyone else. Indicating that she should sit, Christina complied. The conversation resumed around her.

"You are ridding the Lowlands of Englishmen, and that is good. But it is not enough."

Christina listened as the clergyman spoke.

"We have no desire to answer to the Archbishop of York. Edward must not be allowed to give Scottish benefices to English clergymen. Killing soldiers will not prevent this. You must do more."

Wallace did not reply. His arms were folded in front of him as he kept his gaze on the ground. He looked tired. When he remained silent, the man next to him spoke.

"And what about Andrew Moray? Have you told him the same thing?"

Though she had never met him, it was obvious he was Wallace's brother. A little bit older, but not as tall, Malcolm had the same light brown eyes and the beard to match. His relaxed temperament felt familiar and put her at ease.

The clergyman shook his head. "His father's standard has just been raised. His rebellion has only begun. We do not yet know what Moray will do."

Christina felt Robertson's eyes on her. She did not look over.

Wallace lifted his head. "What exactly are you asking?"

The clergyman could not help but squirm. Wallace's gaze was not particularly friendly. His eyes seemed clouded over, as if the light within had burnt out. There was not a trace of warmth to him.

"We need an army," the monk finally answered. "More men join you every day to fight against the English. Train them."

Malcolm scoffed. "With what?" he asked. "We do not have the means or the time." He smiled sarcastically. "Or has the Kirk suddenly decided to open up its coffers and give us what we need?"

The clergyman frowned. "No."

He shrugged. "Then you have your answer."

Christina softly cleared her throat. The men looked back at her expectantly, but there was only one man's attention she wanted. When Wallace finally met her gaze, she said, "Perhaps I can help you with that."

⁓

"You do not look like yourself."

The others had left, Fraser the only one remaining in

the tent. Wallace moved to the seat across from her. She could feel how pale she was despite the way her arm burned. Slightly amused by his words, she said, "Neither do you."

He grunted but did not smile. His eyes focused on the space behind her. He said nothing.

"What was her name?"

He looked down at the table. Folding his hands on the surface, he raised his head. "Marion."

Her attempt at a smile fell flat. She nodded instead. Feeling suddenly tired, she sighed. "Hugh Cressingham, the so-called Treasurer of Scotland, resides at Lochmaben."

His eyes flickered. He remained silent.

"He has been-" she struggled to find the right word, "-quite proficient at collecting taxes for the English king. His methods are very effective."

She watched the muscles in his jaw clench. Before arriving in Scotland, Cressingham was already well known throughout the kingdoms. He had made a name for himself during the English invasion of Wales. It was there he developed a liking for flaying those who refused to cooperate under the new administration. So horrid were his tactics that even the English hated him. He was precisely the man King Edward needed to subdue the Scots now.

"But that is not why I am here." She adjusted in her seat, her muscles stiff from sitting too long. "Ornesby, Edward's appointed Justiciar of Scotland, is responsible for the treasury. It sits with him at Scone."

She expected Wallace to react. But when nothing changed, his face remaining the same, she leaned forward.

"William." Her voice was soft. "Cressingham has taken every single shilling, every item of value from across the

Lowlands." She spoke slowly, desperate for him to under-stand. "March, Lothian, Annandale, Renfrewshire, Galloway and Carrick have all been emptied." She watched the realization manifest on his face. "He has sent everything to Scone. Go and get it."

Wallace leaned back in his chair. Fraser took a seat at the table.

She could tell he was considering it, his fingers rubbing against the wood as he stared off into the distance. If he could do this, if Wallace could steal back the treasury, every moment in Cressingham's presence would be worth it. As soon as she saw him smirk, she knew she had him.

She was back on her horse the next morning. She had not slept much, the meeting carrying well into the night. It had been difficult to stay awake. But as soon as Robertson stood at Wallace's request for mounted men, she smirked with satisfaction. She did not doubt the Lord of Douglas would be more than happy to help them rob the English crown.

She gripped the reins tighter. It felt like she was spin-ning. Her skin was on fire. Desperate for water, she reached for the flask at her side. She swayed in her saddle. By the time she realized she was tipping, it was too late.

She hit the ground hard. Gasping for air, she regretted it instantly, the movement racking her torso. She clutched at her side. Blurry faces appeared above her. She could not make out what they were saying. The pain spiked again.

Fading in and out, the agony continued. The discomfort spread throughout her limbs. Occasionally she heard a voice. Most times, nothing. When the abrupt movement finally stopped, the sensation of being carried soothed her aching bones. She leaned into the frame that held her and let go.

CHAPTER THIRTEEN

THE SMELL OF wine woke her. She squinted at the sunlight streaming through the window, the room bright. She looked around her. Nothing about this place was familiar. Glancing at the thin nightdress she was in, her skin stained red, she swung her feet down onto the floor.

Her legs trembled as she stood. She held onto the wall for balance. A plate and a knife sat on the small table beside the bed. Seeing the dried blood on the blade, she brought the arm that was not bandaged close to her face. Small cuts dotted her skin. They were not from the fall off her horse. Wrapping the blanket around her, she headed towards the door.

She could barely pull it open, her arm shaking from the effort. It was even brighter in the corridor. Temporarily blinded by the sudden light, she scrunched her eyes up again as she stepped through the hallway. The smooth stone cooled her bare feet. She ran her hand along the wall as she headed towards the door of the keep. She could not wait to taste fresh air. The door already open, she walked outside.

Gallovidians stared back at her. Their eyes narrowed as they scowled.

Every muscle in her body tensed. Anxiously looking over the faces around her, she took a step back. She did not understand. She should not be here. Her panic was interrupted by Cailean striding towards her.

"You should not be outside," he said. He glanced around them.

She had so many questions, but could not form a single one. It was hard enough just remembering to breathe.

"Christina of Carrick."

Her name boomed across the grounds. If people had not realized she was there, they did now. She turned hesitantly.

The cross face of an older man stared at her from inside the door. "Come."

It was the last thing she wanted to do, but when he did not move, waiting for her to indicate that she would obey, she knew she did not have a choice. Pulling the blanket tighter around her shoulders, she followed him back into the keep.

He led her to the hall and took a seat in the middle of the table. Wanting to keep her distance, Christina pulled a chair out near the end. He shook his head. A bony finger pointed to the seat across from him. Stepping forward, she lowered herself down into it.

He did not speak. His hands folded neatly across his lap, he stared at her in silence. A woman entered. Christina stiffened as she approached. Reluctantly, she let her take the blanket off her shoulders.

The woman said nothing. Clucking and humming to herself, she looked Christina over, running her thumb across every cut on her arms, feet, and hands. When she removed the bandage on her forearm, Christina could not stop herself from looking down.

The smell was gone. The wound was no longer red or swollen. It still hurt when the woman touched it, but the pain was nothing like it had been before. Her arm no longer felt like it was on fire.

The woman gave her a small smile. Tucking Christina's arms back against her body, she wrapped the blanket around her once more. The fabric tight against her shoulders gave her comfort. Watching the woman leave, her footsteps echoing throughout the hall, Christina turned back to the man sitting across from her.

"Do you know who I am?"

They had never met, but she could easily guess. He was Alan McDowall, great-great-grandson of Uhtred, son of Fergus, the King of Galloway.

She could trace her own lineage to the Gallovidian king. Her mother was the great-great-granddaughter of Fergus' other son, Gille Brigte. But with the way Alan was looking at her, like he wanted nothing more than to gut her right on that table, no one would ever think they were kin.

Under Fergus, the earldom of Carrick and the lordship of Galloway had been one. The land was known only as the Kingdom of Galloway. But when he died, the conflict between his sons was too great to overcome. They turned against each other and Uhtred was gruesomely cut down by Gille Brigte's son. Peace was made ten years later, and the land was divided. Uhtred's son took Galloway and Gille Brigte's son took Carrick.

While Christina's family still ruled, Alan McDowall was

not the Lord of Galloway as his grandfather had been. His father, Thomas, was born out of wedlock and therefore not allowed to ascend to the lordship. The Gallovidians did not see it the same way, even going to war with the King of Scots over it. They wanted to remain as they were – independent from the rest of Scotland. But when Thomas' rebellion failed, the lordship was split between his three legitimate half-sisters and Galloway was absorbed into the kingdom. As Christina stared back at the older man, seeing the loathing in his eyes, she knew their defeat and the loss of the lordship irked the Gallovidians to this day.

She finally answered. "Yes."

Alan leaned forward. "Your grandfather was a contemptible man. That is why he had no sons."

She did not reply to the insult against her mother's father. Nothing good would come of it.

"The only reason why your head is still attached to your body is because my children are soft." He said each word pointedly, as if he was spitting out a curse. "They cherish honour over vengeance. That is why you are sitting here, at my table, still breathing."

She stared back at him. If he was still in charge of his kindred, she had no doubt that her head would be detached. But he was not. His son had replaced him when the older man could no longer climb atop his horse.

Leaning forward once more, he said, "You tell that brother of yours to not get too comfortable at Turnberry. He will not be sitting there much longer."

Slights against her family she could put up with. Threats, she could not. She opened her mouth to warn him when a figure moved into the frame of the door.

Donnchadh McDowall stood watching. His gaze moved from his father to Christina and then back again. He did not need to speak. The older man rose from his chair. He gave Christina one last smirk before he left the hall. Her eyes followed him out. Walking towards the table, the younger McDowall took his father's seat.

Donnchadh's grey eyes assessed her in silence as his father had done. He scratched his beard slowly for a while before his hand dropped down to the armrest. He took a breath. "Why is your brother riding for Douglas?"

She tried to keep the surprise from her face. Not knowing what he meant, she answered truthfully. "I do not know."

He smiled like he did not believe her. Leaning forward, he said, "When Cailean arrived with you in his arms eight nights ago, you were barely alive. You had no strength left in your legs and your skin was too hot to touch." He seemed to stare into her. "My father wanted nothing more than to let you die. But I decided against it." He jabbed a large finger down into the table. "You will tell me what I want to know. Otherwise, you will not leave Galloway in one piece."

She glared at him as he sat back. She did not know which McDowall she disliked more, the father or the son. But his threating words were not what bothered her most. He said Cailean's name as if they were very familiar. It unsettled her enough to ask, "How do you know Cailean?"

McDowall smiled again. It was clear he found her question amusing. "I have known him since I was a boy." He relaxed into his chair. "His father died shortly after he was born. My father raised him here as one of his own." He observed her carefully. "But that should not surprise you. He is the son of Gille Ruadh, after all."

She pretended to be unsurprised by the name, as if it meant nothing. But it was significant. Gille Ruadh had led the Gallovidian rebellion against the King of Scots, fighting for Thomas to be lord and keep the land together. If Cailean was his son, then that meant – she did not know what it meant. McDowall's voice interrupted her thoughts.

"I will not ask again. Why do men of Carrick march against Douglas?"

She tried her best to find an answer. It did not make sense. Rob had nothing to do with the acts of disobedience against the English crown. There was only one possibility. "What happened at Scone?"

His face grew rigid at her response. Seeing the caution in his eyes, she quickly elaborated.

"You said I arrived eight nights ago. If you tell me what happened, I might be able to explain why Rob is heading for Douglas."

His knuckles tapped against the wooden surface, the sound filling the room. Finally, he replied. "William Wallace attacked the English justiciar at Scone. Ornesby escaped, but he left the treasury behind. Wallace rode off with the whole of it."

She could not stop the smile from tugging at her lips. Wallace had actually done it. Understanding now what had happened, she returned to McDowall. "William Douglas rode with Wallace to Scone. He would have been there for the attack." She held his gaze. "Carrick has no quarrel with Douglas. Rob would only lead his men against a Scottish lord if he had been ordered to do so."

"By King Edward?"

Though the command most likely came from her father, it meant the same thing. She nodded.

McDowall tossed a letter onto the table. It slid to a stop in front of her. "Tell me then." His hand clenched and unclenched repeatedly. "What do you make of that?"

For a moment, she did not move. She was not sure she wanted to tell him anything more. Curiosity overcame her. She picked it up. The paper unfolded easily. Recognizing the mark of Douglas, she began to read.

It was a short note. William Douglas' writing mirrored his speech, quick and to the point. He was inviting the Gallovidians to join him at Irvine, along with James Stewart and the Bishop of Glasgow. They would face off against the English army in a week. Finished, she placed it back down onto the table. McDowall did not wait for her to answer.

"Why would Douglas remain at Irvine when his own lands are under attack?" His gaze pressed heavily upon her. "Even if Galloway answered his call, it would not be enough to defeat the English. Why is he so eager to fight them now?"

It did not take her long to find the answer. She remembered what Malcolm Wallace had said in the tent in Selkirk. "He needs time."

His brow furrowed.

"Wallace," she explained, "has the treasury. He can now train an army. But he does not have the time to do it. Douglas is in Irvine to distract the English. The more men he has, the longer he can hold their attention. That is why he wants you there."

His fingers made circles on the arm of his chair. He was not looking at her anymore, his mind occupied. When his eyes found her across the table again, she could not help but ask, "Will you go?"

He hesitated. "No."

She had no right to feel irritated by his response. She was nevertheless. "Why not?"

"Wallace does not fight for us. He fights for Scotland. Why should I bring my men there to die when Galloway will still not be free?"

She almost laughed in disbelief. Galloway had been a part of Scotland for over sixty years. They just could not let it go. "The former King of Scots, John Balliol, is your lord and kin. How does Wallace not fight for you?"

He smiled at her as if she did not understand. "John Balliol may be called Lord of Galloway, but he is not and never will be a Gallovidian." His smile disappeared as he stared back at her. "A yoke is still a yoke – Scottish or English, it does not matter." He leaned forward. "We are the descendants of kings, you and I. They may not be Norman or Anglo-Saxon, but they are kings nonetheless. Carrick may have chosen to forget, but we have not. We have every right to rule over our land and our people. Galloway is for Galloway, and no one else."

Christina stewed in frustration as he exited the hall. She could not believe he was being so short-sighted. But when she thought about Rob marching on Douglas, her anger lessened.

If her brother had taken the same stance as McDowall, choosing to remain loyal only to Carrick, he would not be attacking the land of another Scottish lord at the behest of an English king. It would never be that simple for them – she knew that – their family and allegiances spread across multiple kingdoms. Riding for Turnberry later that day, Cailean and Jardine beside her once more, she could not help but think it would be easier if it were. If they were loyal to one thing, one land, the path ahead would be clear. Cresting the hill as Carrick came into view, she stopped when she saw the fires.

❧

There were too many men to count. Directing her horse down the ridge, she walked through the camp. Men nodded to her as she passed. She recognized most of them, knights of Annandale and Carrick filling the field. Their presence here concerned her. They were exceedingly close to the Gallovidian border. Spotting Hay up ahead, she rode towards him.

At first, he looked surprised and then concerned. His face turned hard. "Come on," he said.

Dropping down from her horse, she followed Hay into the heart of the encampment. She spotted Neil first. Randolph stood beside him outside the tent. She smiled as soon as she saw Rob.

He did not wait for her to reach him. His long strides eliminated the distance between them. Feeling his arms wrap around her, she leaned her tired body into his. When he continued to hold onto her, she looked over his shoulder at Neil and glared at her other brother. He gave her an unapologetic shrug. Rob knew about Lochmaben. He knew what Cressingham did to her.

Stepping out of his embrace, she said, "You are supposed to be in Douglas."

He rested a hand on her shoulder and smiled. "And you are supposed to be in Carlisle."

She raised her eyebrows in confusion.

"Father sent a messenger," he explained. "Seems he has found someone for you to marry."

His words startled her. She adjusted her stance nervously.

"I am supposed to deliver you to Carlisle." His expression was serious. "I am to drag you there if I must."

Filled with fear, her relief at seeing Rob dissipated. She tried to distance herself from him. His grip kept her where she stood.

He stepped closer. Taking her face in his hands, his eyes filled with tears. "You should have sent for me." His voice was barely a whisper. "I would have come."

Surprised at the change in conversation, she stared back at him. He would have done just that and more if she had called him to her aid at Lochmaben. Her worry lessened. "I know," she said.

Nodding, his hands dropped away from her. His gaze never left her face. "Sit with me."

She hesitated. No longer restrained, she could attempt to escape. Running from her brother would not be easy, but anything was better than being married off to whomever her father had chosen. Assessing her brother, she decided against it. He seemed uninterested in following their father's orders. Christina lowered herself onto the log next to the fire.

"Mary's at Turnberry."

He surprised her again. She took the cup of ale he offered.

Her sisters had not lived in Scotland since the rebellion. After Rob's wife had been buried in Carrick, Mary and Matilda returned to Carlisle. It was not by choice – their father insisted they remain in England with him. Christina doubted he had willingly let Mary go now.

Rob gave her a small smile. "She showed up not long

after you left Lochmaben." His face grew grim. "She went there by herself. She was looking for you."

The thought of Mary arriving at Lochmaben alone terrified her. Her heart beat faster. "Was he there?" she asked.

The smile returned. Rob shook his head. "No. I asked her when she arrived. She said Cressingham had been gone for a while."

Christina exhaled in relief. Mary had been lucky. Traveling alone was foolish, especially for a young woman like her. She had no doubt their father was furious. Thinking he should have sent men after Mary, Christina stretched out her aching legs. She was still sore and her strength had yet to return. The woman in Galloway had given her a liquid to help her sleep, but she doubted she would need it. She was exhausted. She could sleep for days. Rob silent, she let her eyes drift around the camp. Her thoughts returned to the men. She looked at her brother once more. "What are you doing here, Rob?"

He stared into the fire. "I was in England while you were with Wallace." His voice was quiet. No one interrupted them. "Edward is not taking the theft of the treasury lightly. He told me to raze Douglas to the ground." He looked over at her. "I marched my men all the way there. But I could not do it. How could I go against the land of my birth? The only home I have ever known?"

Though her smile was sad, happiness filled her. For the first time, Rob had decided for himself. He was not blindly following their father's path. She was proud of him, but more so, she was relieved. There was hope for their family yet.

"I asked the knights to join me against England." He looked out at the campfires around them. The sound of light conversation wafted through the air. "These are the ones who said yes. We ride for Irvine in the morning. William Douglas and James Stewart await us there."

Thinking about the warlord, she wished she could be there to see his reaction when her brother rode in. He would not believe it until he saw it. She could see the smirk on his face now.

"I need you at Turnberry."

She turned at the statement. Rob's face was grave.

"As soon as I raise my standard at Irvine, Carrick will be open to attack." He stared into her. "I need someone I can trust to make the right decisions while I am gone, for my daughter and my land." He paused. "Please, Christina. I need you there."

She looked back at the fire. The seriousness of his words made it feel suddenly real. The throne was empty. Noble or peasant from north to south, the kingdom was united against a common enemy. Bruce or Comyn no longer mattered. If Scotland ever had a chance to break free from England, it was now. The Red Comyn's words came flooding back.

Looking at Rob, she nodded. She made her choice. She was for Scotland and no one else.

TURNBERRY CASTLE

CHRISTINA RETURNED TO Turnberry, but the usual calm of being in her mother's home did not come. She tried to pretend that two armies were not facing off against one another just north of where she sat, but it was impossible. She hated waiting. Especially when so much was at stake.

Watching Marjorie play in the grass with Mary outside the walls of the castle, she heard a whistle. She stood. A rider galloped for the fortress. Spotting her, he changed course. Her stomach clenched when she saw Hay's face. He did not need to say anything. The urgency in his eyes told her everything she needed to know.

Picking up Marjorie, she hurried to the castle to gather their things. The Scots had lost; they were surrendering to Edward. Though she had prepared for this, it did not make what she had to do any less difficult. Her mind drifted to Rob and Neil. She hoped they were not caught by the English when they snuck out of Irvine. Placing her concern for them aside, she handed the baby to Mary and ran into the keep.

They left Turnberry on foot. Marjorie made not a sound

as she looked out across the land from the safety of Christina's arms. Hay led the way, Cailean bringing up the rear, the two men carrying all they would need. Christina turned to glance at the castle by the sea one last time. Mary stopped beside her. The stone walls towered magnificently into the sky. The flag of their house swayed in the light breeze off the water. Her heart squeezed. She prayed to the saints she would see it again. Tightening her hold on her niece, she withdrew into the wilds of Carrick.

Night fell as they reached Glengennet. A personal demesne of her mother's and the mormaers of Carrick before her, the estate sat southeast of Turnberry along the River Stinchar. Christina had been here only once as a child. Looking across the meadow, the wooden structure unfamiliar in the dark, she hesitated. A man stepped from the shadows. His red hair shone in the moonlight. She smiled.

Áed Ó Néill's mischievous grin met her in the field. He seemed to have more freckles than the last time she saw him if that were possible. Not waiting for her to come to a stop, he cupped her face roughly between his hands and planted a loud, wet kiss on her lips.

"I have missed you, mo ghràdh," he said.

She first met Áed when she was six-years-old. A member of the Ó Néill clann, he had come over from Ireland to visit her family. They were kin, Christina's great-grandmother the daughter of the Tir Eoghain king, Néill Ruadh mac Aodha Ó Néill. As she had watched Áed step from the boat, his brilliant red hair and light green eyes striding towards her, Christina could not look away. By the time he taught her to sail a few short days later, she was infatuated. She did not care that he was thirteen years older. She *would* marry him.

She had told him exactly that as she stood next to him on the shore, waiting for the ship that would take him away from her come in to land. He had smiled and reached out, placing his hand on top of her head. Turning to leave, he uttered the words he would say to her again and again, each time they met. "Mo chridhe, mo ghràdh." *My love, my heart.*

She had outgrown her childhood obsession. But as she looked at Áed standing before her now, his hands still cradling her cheeks, she was happy he was here.

He stepped back. Looking down at Marjorie sleeping against her chest, he feigned concern. "Is there something you need to tell me? Have you been unfaithful to the man you love across the water?"

Smiling in amusement, she ran her hand over the top of Marjorie's head. Rob had sent for Áed before he had left for Irvine. If the Scots lost, Rob had two choices – he could surrender and sit in an English cell himself, or he could give up his daughter as a hostage. Rob had no intention of doing either. He would simply disappear into the land that had raised him, surrounded by men he trusted. Edward could try to hunt him down all he wanted. Once they were in the heart of Carrick, the English king would never find the mormaer. Not even if the people gave him up.

"Come," Áed said. "There is stew waiting."

Christina slept well. The long walk carrying her niece had tired her out. They would wait here for Rob before journeying deeper into the hills. It would take him a few days to arrive. He first had to get to Carrick from Irvine. Then he would leave Turnberry on foot just as she had done. Sitting at the small table in the kitchen, rubbing the sleep from her eyes, she heard the sound of horses approaching. Alarmed, she ran to the door.

She could see the riders coming across the field towards the house. Cailean, Áed, and Hay were already outside, their swords in their hands. She thought about disappearing with Marjorie out the back when Áed stepped forward. He sheathed his blade.

Rob pulled to a stop, Neil and Randolph right behind him. He glanced at her with uncertainty as he dismounted. She only understood why when her gaze found the two riders following them through the field.

Reaching them, Jardine swung down to the ground. He had joined Rob after Douglas, going with other knights of Annandale to fight at Irvine. Christina was pleased to see him. But as she looked up at the only rider still atop his horse, Christina waited for Robertson to explain why he was there.

He handed her a letter.

She stepped forward to take it. Breaking the seal, she read the three words written on the paper.

Protect my son.

Not understanding, she looked to Robertson for an explanation. He complied.

"Lord Douglas has been arrested. He is imprisoned in Berwick Castle. The English will release him only when they have his son."

The news worried her. King Edward acted fast. He was not taking any chances with the rebellious Scottish lords.

"We must hurry. You need to come with me now."

His task was urgent, of that there was no doubt, but she still did not understand why Douglas was asking her for help. He should have gone to the Comyns. They were his kin – they were obligated to come to his aid. She dismissed the thought. Douglas was a smart man. If he had a better option, he would not be coming to her. Turmoil surged within her. Conflicted, she folded the paper slowly. "I cannot. My family needs me here."

Robertson glanced at the others around them, his mouth set in a hard line. No one spoke. Moving his horse directly beside her, he leaned down. His beard almost touched her face.

"Douglas has been invaded. English soldiers look for the boy now." The anguish in his eyes was clear. "They will not suspect you. You are the daughter of the Governor of Carlisle Castle, a friend to the crown." He implored her to reconsider. "You must help me. Help me get James to France."

"Christina."

Rob's voice made her turn.

Though his face was grim, there was an understanding in his eyes that had not been there before. "Go," he said. He glanced at Robertson. "Take the horses. Return when you can."

He held her gaze a moment longer before he walked towards the house. She watched him leave. Scotland may have failed to defeat the English, but the fight against England was far from over. Not even Rob was willing to go back to the way things were. He disappeared through the door. Her eyes shifted. She met Áed's gaze.

He looked at her with interest, a slight smile on his face.

Much had changed since he had seen her last. She was no longer the young girl he always left behind.

❧

By the time they arrived in Douglas, Christina knew what to do. She sent Jardine east to Berwick and Robertson north to St Andrews. If everything went smoothly, James Douglas would be halfway to France before the English realized he was gone. She galloped past the village towards the castle. Cailean behind her, she rode through the open gate.

Eleanor de Lovaine stepped from the keep as Christina dismounted. A young boy clung to her fingers. With long legs and prominent cheekbones, the Lady of Douglas was stunningly beautiful. Christina understood now why Douglas had not been able to let her go. But that was not what grabbed her attention. Eleanor's stomach curved outwards. The Lady Douglas was heavily pregnant.

"Lady Christina." Eleanor smiled. "My husband said you would come."

Stopping before her, Christina was surprised by Eleanor's calm demeanour. Her husband was in prison. The English were coming for his son. It looked like she could give birth at any moment. But Eleanor was serene.

"Please," she said. "Come with me."

Walking into the keep, Christina expected to be taken to the hall. But as soon as they were inside, Eleanor handed her son to the woman who waited and entered a small, dark corridor. Glancing at Cailean behind her, Christina followed the Lady of Douglas down the steps.

The air smelled musty and dank as her foot hit the landing. She could not see much. Only Eleanor's outline was visible as they continued farther down the passageway. It seemed to go on forever. Their footsteps echoed off the walls. Christina did not think they were in the castle any longer when a sliver of light broke through the dark. It grew wider as the door opened. The bright light making her squint, Christina stepped out of the tunnel.

Trees surrounded her. She turned to see how far they were from the castle, but she could not see anything. The forest blocked her view. Cailean exiting, Eleanor sealed the entranceway shut. Christina followed her once more.

The soft ground muted the sound of their feet as they walked. Christina did not notice the small lodge until they were almost upon it. Made of wood, it practically melted into the trees. Two men stood outside. They straightened as Eleanor approached. She entered the cabin alone.

Christina glanced around her. Seeing the horses saddled and waiting, she knew they would not be returning to the castle. Movement near the door drew her gaze. She watched Eleanor step out.

A dark-haired boy followed. Placing a hand on his shoulder, Eleanor guided him forward. He looked about ten-years-old and absolutely miserable. Christina studied his face. The scowl was all too familiar. She had no doubt he was Douglas' son.

"James, this is Lady Christina," Eleanor said.

He did not reply. His angry eyes staring back at her, Christina was reminded of her youngest brothers.

Thomas and Alexander were not much older than him. There were many times she had to talk them into doing something they did not want to. Contemplating James' glare, she knew what had worked with her brothers would not work on him. He was too much like his father already. He could not be convinced.

She returned her attention to Eleanor. "What about you? Will you remain here, in Douglas?"

Eleanor smiled and looked down at James still in her grasp. She lovingly smoothed the hair on his head. "Despite the things they say, I love my husband. I love my home." She met Christina's gaze. "I would keep James with me if I could. But he does not have my blood. I cannot save him from Edward." She kissed the top of his head. When she spoke again, her voice was not much louder than a whisper. "This is what we must do until your father returns."

James turned then. He looked up at the woman who raised him. Eleanor held his cheeks in her hands and gave him an encouraging smile. For a brief moment, his anger was gone. But as she nodded, pressing her lips to his forehead, James turned to face Christina. The frown reappeared.

Christina took a step towards him. "So, James," she said. "How fast can you ride a horse?"

When she saw the ire dissipate, his scowl turning into smug confidence as he crossed his arms in front of him, she smiled. They would get along just fine.

It took two days to reach St Andrews. The summer roads were dry and the weather was fair. They were rarely alone, a constant stream of travellers going both north and south. English soldiers seemed to be everywhere. Their numbers increased near Edinburgh. Each time a group of them passed, Christina could not help but tense. She hoped they did not notice the boy seething in his saddle beside her. Crossing over Stirling Bridge, she relaxed slightly. They were through the Lowlands and the worst of it. Turning off the main road, she headed east towards the largest diocese in Scotland.

Robertson met them just outside the town. Christina almost missed seeing him in the sea of people. Hundreds of years before, Saint Regulus had fled to Scotland, bringing with him the bones of Andrew the Apostle. Óengus, the King of the Picts, built a monastery to house the relics. While the church had been rebuilt many times over the years, the shrine and the people's devotion to Saint Andrew only grew. Pilgrims came from all over Europe to be cured of disease or blessed by the saint. Directing her horse to where Robertson waited, she followed him into the burgh.

St Andrews Cathedral sat along the North Sea. The town was directly west. With the wealth and power the diocese afforded, the bishop of St Andrews held the most important seat in the Kirk of Scotland.

His influence reached far beyond the kingdom. It was why the elderly man was still in France. He had gone there two years earlier to press the French king for an alliance against England. It had worked; the Auld Alliance had been ratified. But England still ruled over them, and so he remained. The bishop's loyalty to the Scottish cause and his connections with the French court had made Christina come here. James would be protected in St Andrews. The Kirk was his best chance at making it out of Scotland.

Leaving their horses outside with Cailean, Christina walked into the cathedral. She kept James close as they followed Robertson. He stopped to speak with a clergyman near the side of the chapel. He beckoned them over. She pointed James in his direction.

The monk said nothing as he looked down at the boy.

Indicating that they should follow, he turned, moving towards the back of the chapel. He led them to the residence, passing other men of the Kirk as they went. A long corridor waited for them at the top of the stairs. When the clergyman stopped at the end, taking a key from his pocket to open the door, Christina turned to James.

"You will stay here with Robertson until the ship arrives."

His uncertain face stared back at her.

"I will return when its time. Until then, you must do everything he says. Do you understand?"

James nodded.

She gave him a quick smile. "Good." The door to the room opened. "Go on. Get some rest."

He walked in, glancing about the room. It was small and plain, two cots pressed against the wall. Robertson nodded to her as he passed. He shut the door behind him.

"How long?" the monk asked.

She followed him back down the stairs. "I do not know. I am still waiting to hear."

He nodded. "We will keep him out of sight and make sure he gets enough to eat." He stopped at the door that led back into the chapel and handed her a small piece of paper. "I suggest you do the same."

She watched him walk away before entering the main room. The church was full of people. It would not do her any good to be recognized here. Tucking the note into her pocket, she kept her eyes down as she moved towards the entrance. She found Cailean exactly where she had left him. Taking the horses, they disappeared into the burgh.

They stayed at an inn the monk had recommended. On the northern side of town, the tavern was quiet and unassuming. Christina found it difficult to rest. She was both anxious and bored. The days seemed to drag on as she waited impatiently. She was standing outside near the sea, the wind tossing hair across her face when Cailean approached. The sight of Jardine behind him lifted the weight off her shoulders. Stopping in front of her, he gave her the letter.

Gripping the paper tightly, she took care not to rip it as she broke the seal. It contained only a date and two names, but it was enough. She had everything she needed. Looking out across the horizon, William Douglas' face came to mind. His son would be safely tucked away in France and out of Edward's grasp before the month was over. She hoped it would be enough.

The ship landed at St Andrews a week after Jardine's arrival, just as the letter said it would. Finding the merchant along the docks had been easy. He was expecting her. Fetching James and Robertson from the cathedral, she walked with them towards the boat. She was waiting for them to cross the plank onto the deck when James turned around.

"I do not want to go."

Robertson's reply was blunt. "You are going. It does not matter if you want to or not."

Seeing the troubled look on the boy's face, Christina knelt in front of him. A lesson her grandfather taught her came to mind.

"Sometimes, when you are fighting for what you love, you are not always going to win. Sometimes, James, you need to run."

His despondent face stared back at her.

"When you are losing, the best thing you can do is give yourself time. Time to recover, time to gather more men, time to find a different way to win." She straightened the cloak around his shoulders. "So when you are in France, James, use the time your father has given you wisely. Become the kind of man you want to be. Decide who deserves your loyalty. Think about what you will do when you return to the land of your birth, to the land that is yours." She smiled up at him. "Then come back. Scotland will be waiting. I will be waiting for you."

Walking along the shoreline, the sand soft beneath her feet, she watched the ship leave. Her eyes never strayed from the sails as they grew smaller in the distance. She felt suddenly lost, as if she no longer knew the path forward. She would return to Carrick, but what then? Would she remain in hiding forever?

The vessel disappeared from view. Leaving the seaside, she made her way back to the inn. Perhaps going to Carrick was for the best. She could help Rob decide his strategy. She stopped when she saw Alexander Fraser step from the stables.

He said nothing. Staring at her for a moment, he turned back inside.

She knew he wanted her to follow. Glancing at Cailean and Jardine, she moved away from the tavern door and entered the barn.

He was leaning against a post as she walked in. No lighthearted comment greeted her this time. When he spoke, his voice was low. "You are a long way from home."

Unaccustomed to the seriousness of his blue eyes, she remained silent. She did not have to explain herself. She did not answer to him. And yet, she replied. "I was asked to do something for a friend."

He held her gaze for a while. "I know what you have

been doing," he said. "The clergyman told me. How else would I find you here?"

She had misjudged how intertwined Wallace was with the Kirk. From Whithorn to St Andrews, they seemed to support him fully. Everything that happened in the Lowlands found its way back to him. Fraser stepped towards her. She set her irritation for the monk aside.

He stood quite close, much closer than he should. His eyes level with hers, he said, "Gather your things, Lady Christina. I am taking you to Dundee."

Watching him walk out of the stables, she did not bother asking why. While Douglas, Stewart, and Rob had been surrendering to the English at Irvine, Andrew Moray took control of the Highlands, one castle at a time. According to the rumours circulating the streets of St Andrews, Dundee Castle was the only English stronghold left north of Stirling, the gateway to the Highlands. She had not known how much of the hearsay was true. The tales varied depending on who told them. But with Douglas imprisoned and Rob hiding in Carrick, there was only one man who would summon her. She returned to the inn and prepared for the journey north.

Fraser did not wait for morning to depart from St Andrews. It was a hard ride. They spent most of the night in their saddles, moving down the empty road towards the large trading port along the eastern coast. They reached Perth before light the next day. Stopping only to water the horses, they crossed the River Tay and continued on. It was well past noon when she spotted the Dundee Law. The large mound of earth towered in the distance just west of the town. Following Fraser as he rode off the path and into the woods, she pulled to a stop a few feet inside the trees.

Tents covered the forest floor. Smoldering fires sent bits of smoke into the air. They had entered Wallace's camp. Men moved about, but they were not in a hurry, the odd one glancing at her as they walked by. Fraser dismounted. She did the same. He approached the group of men standing up ahead.

Looking outwards from the edge of the trees, their eyes were on the town. The murmur of their voices drifted back to her. Remaining by the horses, Christina did not recognize any of them beneath all their armour. Fraser walked up. Their heads turned. William Wallace looked back.

He came towards her. Stopping halfway, he removed the plates of steel tied around his body until only the gambeson and the sword on his back remained. He looked at her with sincerity. "Tell me, Lady Christina." He adjusted the collar around his neck. "Could you outrun the English in that dress?"

She hesitated, uncertain of what exactly he was asking. "Yes."

He smiled. "Good. There is something I want you to see."

She followed him through the camp. There were more men present than she expected – sharpening blades, cooking food, repairing injuries they had accumulated. One of them had an arrow sticking out of his shoulder. He screamed as they pulled it out, hands holding him down.

"Are you coming?"

Distracted by everything around her, she had fallen behind. Wallace was already a few lengths ahead. Turning, he disappeared deeper into the forest. She hurried to catch up.

The ground sloped gently at first. Moving upwards and out of the trees, the sun setting in the distance, she stopped to look at the Dundee Law before her. She understood now why Wallace had asked if she could run. Out in the open and a ways from the camp, they would be easily spotted by any patrol. She began to climb. Reaching the top, her legs burning, she stared in awe at what lay before her.

Men besieged the castle next to the water, Wallace's army of Scots attacking from the burgh that surrounded it. She could see them attempting to hoist scaling ladders onto the walls. Archers shot from nearby buildings. There were men everywhere, down every street and inside every building. None of the inhabitants seemed to mind; some of them even participated in the fighting. The only resistance came from the castle and the English garrison trapped within it.

Christina glanced at Wallace beside her. "Will it hold?"

He smiled and nodded. "Yes."

She returned her gaze to the castle. Her admiration turned to worry. "Then the English will come." When he did not answer, she looked at him once more.

He was not watching the attack. His eyes were on her. "I need you to go north."

"Why?" The question was out of her mouth before she could stop it. He had never asked her to do anything before.

He smiled again, but it disappeared when he answered. "Andrew Moray."

She stared at him for a moment before she shifted her gaze. Biting back her irritation, she looked out across the sky. There was only one person who would have told Wallace about her connection to Andrew.

Thoughts of Christopher Seton filled her head. She had no doubt he was fighting somewhere in the town below. He was so close to her and yet so far. Resisting the urge to ask about him, she turned back to Wallace.

"You are right," he said. "The English are coming. An army marches towards us as we speak." He paused, holding her gaze. "We cannot defeat them on our own. We need more men. We need the Highlands."

His answer did not change her reluctance. No matter what happened, no matter what she did, she could not get away from Andrew. She sighed in frustration. "Can you not send someone else?"

Reaching out, he placed a hand on her shoulder. His grip was heavy and firm. "No," he said, "I cannot. I do not know where he is. Every man who claims to know gives me a different answer." He smiled. "But you know him. And he trusts you. You will find him for me."

Staring back into his brown eyes, light within them once more, her disinclination waivered. She knew Wallace would not take no for an answer.

CHAPTER FIFTEEN

THE PLEASANT WEATHER had passed. A soft drizzle fell down around her as they journeyed north. It took two days to get to Garioch and another to reach Cullen in Moray. Riding along the path positioned between the sea and the castle, she slowed her horse. Her eyes studied the tower atop the mound. The outer rampart surrounding the motte was still in place. In fact, it looked completely undamaged. Confused, she glanced around. Spotting the man on the road ahead, she walked her horse towards him.

Paying no mind to the three riders that followed, he watched her approach. He held the day's catch in his hands.

She slowed as she met him. "Is the English garrison still in Cullen?"

He seemed unbothered by her question. His expression and pace remained unchanged. "They are not."

Turning to look at the fortress once more, the stone walls whole, she said, "I thought the castle had been destroyed."

This time he stopped. His thoughtful eyes assessed her. He then looked at the men.

She could tell he was unsure of what to make of them.

Besides Cailean and Jardine, Fraser was with her as well. Wallace had sent him. A noblewoman, a Gallovidian, a knight, and an unkempt Lowlander made for an odd group. She waited for his answer.

"They came in the night." His eyes returned to her. "The English sat at their evening meal." He turned and pointed to the barricade that surrounded the castle. "They scaled the wall and entered through the open windows." He looked at her once more. "Not much is left inside. The fire took most of it."

Nodding, she stared up at the castle. She could imagine the dark shadows of silent men climbing the walls, the soldiers unaware they were under attack. Andrew was smart to avoid open battle, but his tactics were bolder than she expected. No wonder he had taken the Highlands so quickly.

"Are you of House Bruce?"

The man's question made her turn. She had forgotten he was there. Uncertain of the response it would get, she said, "Yes."

He nodded but did not indicate what he thought. "Has your father returned to Scotland then?"

She stiffened unconsciously. "No."

He did not react. Keeping his eyes on her, he said, "Edward will come. Best to have everything sorted before he does."

He left, continuing down the road without another word. Pressing her legs into her horse, Christina could not help but wonder if his advice was for her or for himself.

They reached Elgin the next morning, the burgh only twenty miles west. She spotted the cathedral before anything else. The two towers jutting up into the air, the cruciform shape of the sanctuary dominated the landscape. The royal castle was less than a mile down the road. She slowed as soon as she saw the wreckage.

The wooden walls had been destroyed. What little remained was black from the heat. The tower was still standing, but only partially. Watching a few villagers walk amongst the rubble, picking up whatever was left to find, she heard Jardine's voice behind her.

"We are getting close. It has not been like that long."

She agreed. Turning her horse, she galloped for Duffus Castle.

Five miles north of Elgin, the fortress sat on top of a man-made hill along the coast. Inland from the shore and surrounded by bog, the castle had a vantage point around it for miles. It had been built by the Moray family over one hundred and fifty years earlier. Primarily made of timber, it was one of the most guarded fortifications in all of Scotland. As Christina rode out from under the trees, the keep suddenly in view, she spotted the smoke. She urged her horse to go faster.

The heat from the fire forced her to stop before she even reached the gate. A pungent smell stung her nose. The secondary buildings were already ablaze, and the wood crackled as it burned. Hearing the horses slowing behind her, she tore her eyes away from the destruction and scanned the boggy ground of the coastal plain.

Nothing moved. Even the birds stayed away. Christina glimpsed their feathered bodies in the distance over the water. She did not know if Andrew had done this, but as close as he might be, she would not find him here. Turning once more, she returned to Elgin.

They stopped at the river. Kneeling along the edge, she cupped her hands in the water and washed her face. The heat in her eyes dissipated. Her skin felt cool once more. Considering what to do next, she looked out across the water. Fraser spoke.

"He is probably back at Avoch."

She glanced over at him sitting in the grass.

He elaborated. "All the English are gone. Any castles left standing are under his control. Why would he remain here?"

She looked down at her hands in the stream. Fraser could be right. With every castle in the Highlands taken, Andrew might have simply returned home. But there was also a good chance he was not there, or in any of the castles he had conquered. For some reason, she felt he would be here. Wishing she could ask his uncle in Bothwell, it suddenly dawned on her what she had missed. Her head lifted in realization. Leaping onto her horse, she rode for the cathedral.

The chapel was quiet as she entered. It had been recently enlarged, a fire tearing through the old structure twenty years prior. But she was not here to see the renovations. She was here because she remembered just exactly who lived within these walls.

Waiting near the back of the church, she admired the high ceilings. A clergyman found her there. A pleasant smile covered his face. She recognized him instantly. From the way he carried himself to the hair on his head, he looked like a Moray. He looked like Andrew.

"Forgive me," David Moray began. "I do not believe we have met."

Smiling, she shook her head. "No. But I know your nephew. The one burning down all the castles."

The corners of his mouth twitched. There were other canons in the chapel, but his gaze never left her. He seemed unconcerned that they might be overheard. Clasping his hands behind his back, he said, "Tell me. What does a Bruce want with the future lord of Moray?"

"I have a message for him, from William Wallace."

Looking down, he nodded. When he met her gaze once more, the smile had reappeared. "Meet me here at nightfall." He turned and walked away.

Returning to the cathedral at dusk, they headed south into the forest. No one spoke. David kept a good pace, the thick underbrush not slowing him down. The sky grew darker with each step. Christina could barely see in front of her. Wondering how much farther they had to go, she saw the orange glow of a fire ahead. A low whistle announced their arrival. She bit the inside of her cheek nervously.

The whites of a man's eyes peering at her from a few feet ahead almost made her jump. The closer they got to the camp, the more men emerged from the trees. They stared at her as she passed. Following David into the small clearing, she did her best not to wilt under the scrutiny. She spotted Andrew near the fire. Everyone else faded away.

As though he were being held down, Andrew slowly rose from his seat. He stared as she walked towards him. The men around him stood as well. Seeing their hands on their swords, she stopped. David approached alone. Andrew's eyes finally let her go.

Their conversation was quiet. Feeling like she was eavesdropping, she averted her gaze. She looked around at the camp. The men stared silently back. One took a menacing step towards her, but when his eyes shifted to something in front of her, he stopped.

She turned to find Andrew there. He looked well, much better than the last time she had seen him. He was no longer scrawny, the muscles in his frame returned to their normal girth, his face lightly browned by the sun. Freedom had breathed life back into him. He glanced over at Fraser and Jardine. It gave her the time she needed to collect herself. She opened her mouth to begin.

"Wallace is besieging the castle at Dundee."

His gaze dropped to her.

"Edward's army marches north to relieve it." She paused, forcing herself to take a breath. Her hands were clenched, nails digging painfully into her palms. Andrew waited for her to continue. Her fists unfurled. "I have been sent to invite you to Perth. Wallace is wondering if you would like to join him in taking on the English."

The mood in the camp suddenly changed. It no longer felt tense, excitement beginning to build around them. The Highlands had been cleared of the English. They had no one left to fight. The small smile on Andrew's face told her what his answer would be.

He stepped back. "What do you say?" he asked the men. "Would you like to go south to spill some English blood?"

A shout of support answered him. The united sound sent a chill up her spine.

Andrew returned his attention to her. He stared at her for a while before he said, "Come with me, to gather the men. I want you to see what we have done."

She smiled at the invitation. Not too long ago, it would have been all that she wanted. But their time had passed.

She had come to the realization in Galloway. Lying on the bed close to death, Andrew had not entered her mind once. She did not belong beside him anymore. "I have been riding around the Highlands looking for you." Her voice was quiet as she spoke. "I have already seen what you have done."

Though he smiled, it fell.

She could tell he wanted to say something, the struggle written across his face. But when he remained silent, the noise building as the men prepared to leave, she turned away. She was tired. And she wanted to go home. Immediately thinking of Lochmaben, she took one last look at the men who would fight the English for it. She wished them well. She had done all she could. Turning, she walked out of the camp.

She returned to the Lowlands with only Cailean. Jardine and Fraser stayed to ride south with Andrew to meet Wallace in Perth. It would be the largest gathering of Scots in recent memory. Even when John was king, his rebellion against England did not have this many men. Little did Christina know just how much it would change.

A narrow bridge made of wood was all that separated English from Scot. The English were undefeated, heavily outmatching their northern opponent not only in strength and mounted men, but in experience. Edward's obsession with expanding his kingdom ensured their constant state of war, both outside and within England itself. The army Wallace and Andrew brought was made of commoners. They fought not because of servitude or loyalty, but because they wanted to be free. As Christina would learn later, it was not brilliant strategy or undeniable bravery that won the day. It would be Wallace and Andrew's ability to recognize and take advantage of an opportunity handed to them by Hugh Cressingham himself.

The Earl of Surrey had settled the English army just south of the bridge. He attempted to negotiate with the Scots waiting on Abbey Craig, the hill that dominated the land north of the river. But the Scots had not come to surrender like the others at Irvine. They were there to fight. Cressingham became impatient. Not willing to delay any longer, he advised the earl to send the army over the river at dawn.

It would be a fatal mistake. The bridge was only wide enough for two men to cross at a time. Limited by the slow movement, the Scots descended upon the English as they came, encircling those who made it over, isolating them from the rest of the army. The earl and the men that remained could only watch as Scottish spearmen slaughtered their fellow men-in-arms. They were cut down or sent over the bridge, the weight of their armour drowning them in the water below. It was too disheartening a sight. The English had no desire to continue.

Ordering the bridge destroyed, the earl fled south for the border, abandoning his men on the battlefield and the garrison trapped in the castle. His retreat would not go unpunished. James Stewart and the Mormaer of Lennox were on the English side. They had been forced by Edward to join the earl and Cressingham against the Scots as punishment for their rebellion at Irvine. But as soon as they saw the earl fleeing, they turned. Attacking the supply train, they killed the English soldiers as they fled. In one fell swoop, the Kingdom of Scotland was free.

Christina was in Douglas retrieving her brother's horses when she heard what happened at Stirling. She had planned to return to Carrick, but as she listened in disbelief to the messenger, his voice radiating across the bailey, she knew there was only one place she wanted to go. She rode for Lochmaben.

A trail of destruction led her there. At first, it was hardly noticeable – a few trampled fields and a smattering of debris littering the road. But the closer she got, the worse it was, the hasty retreat of English soldiers becoming more desperate and careless as they neared the border. Maneuvering carefully past an abandoned cart and out of the trees, the fields of Lochmaben appeared before her. Her heart surged when she saw the castle.

The gate was open, but it was oddly quiet, no men atop the wall. She had not seen an Englishman since St Andrews. Hoping she would not find any here, she warily walked her horse into the grounds.

Reid did not notice her enter. His attention was solely on the sow in front of him. With the help of the swineherd, he struggled to get the pig back into the enclosure. The sow did not want to go. She grunted in irritation as he moved closer. The swineherd gave her backside a light tap. She darted into the pen.

He turned to find Christina near the keep. Still on her horse, she dismounted. He smiled as he walked towards her. He did not waste any time. "We are behind on the harvest. Our stores are low. There is not enough meat to last the winter."

She nodded and glanced around. While the grounds were not in shambles, they were disorganized and unkempt.

A few men worked to fix the damage that had been done. Noticing the partially collapsed roof over the stable, she returned her attention to Reid. "And the English?"

"Gone," he replied. "Most rode out with Cressingham. Those that stayed fled south only yesterday." He paused. "They will not be back anytime soon."

She did not doubt the truth in his words. With the summer ending and their defeat fresh, the English army was unlikely to ride north until the spring. Annandale may see more soldiers, but they would not stay, not with what Christina had seen in the villages on her journey here. Armour, weapons and horses were being prepared. The Scots would take English subjugation no longer. Nodding once more, she asked, "What do you need me to do?"

Sweat trickled down her back as she walked through the field. The scythes worked in unison, the sound of blades cutting filling the air. Her feet kept time with the rhythm. Dropping the sheaves of barley onto the cart, she returned to gather more. She had just bent over to pick up a bundle Cailean had tied when she heard a whistle.

She straightened. Shielding her eyes from the sun, she looked towards the castle. Reid stood several feet from the gate with a rider beside him. His outstretched arm pointed towards her. Picking up a few more bundles, she headed towards the road.

The rider approached as she placed the sheaves on the cart. He stopped but did not bother to dismount. Leaning down, he handed her a letter.

She knew who it was the moment she saw her name written on the front. Watching the messenger turn and leave, she slowly opened the note from her father.

Come to Writtle.

She lifted her gaze and looked out over the landscape. For the past few days, she had done nothing but toil in the fields. Every able body in the village worked to help salvage what remained of the crops. From dawn until dusk, she was out here with the others, praying that the rain stayed away for one more day. She was exhausted. There were parts of her that ached she did not know could. Thinking of her father sitting in comfort at his estate in Essex, her younger siblings around him, she tucked the note into her pocket. He could send all the letters he wanted from England. She would not willingly leave the land of Scots again.

The evening sky cast a dark blue light down upon her as she walked towards the castle. They had eaten their evening meal outside in the field, the day's work finally done. She longed for the soft, warm bed waiting for her inside the keep. Her fingers loosened her braided hair. She stopped when she saw the horses in the bailey.

Glancing up at the hall window, the light from the candle flickered. If she stayed perfectly still and closed her eyes, she could hear the voices faintly, the sound drifting from inside the keep. She wanted nothing more than to ignore whoever was in the hall. Cailean moved past her. His frame disappearing through the door, she pushed aside her reluctance and followed.

The voices grew louder as she ascended the stairs. Each step reminded her of how much her feet hurt. She still did not know who had come. The sound of men laughing greeted her as she reached the door. They clearly were not waiting for her. Straightening her shoulders, she entered the room.

William Wallace stared at her from the head of the table. Sat in her grandfather's chair, he looked more than comfortable. A slight smirk moved onto his lips. The rest of the men noticed her there. Their conversations stopped.

"You need better watchmen," Wallace said. "Thieving Englishmen are about."

"How odd." She feigned confusion. "I did not realize you were English."

His smile grew wider. He pushed himself up. Stepping away from the chair, he grabbed a small pouch off the table. "I brought you a gift."

Walking forward, she watched as he unknotted the strings, his large hands doing nimble work. He waited until she reached him. Holding the bag out, he dumped the contents onto the table.

A shriveled tongue hit the surface. Uncertain she saw correctly, she bent down for a closer look. Though it was no longer pink, there was no denying what it was. The thick chunk of flesh could be nothing else.

"It used to occupy the mouth of Hugh Cressingham."

She turned her head in surprise.

He smiled again. "I thought you might want it. I know how much you enjoyed his company."

Christina smirked at the sarcasm. More news of what had happened at Stirling reached Lochmaben every day, but it was hard to know what was true and what was not. Glancing once more at the severed appendage, she asked, "And where might the rest of him be?"

A hand slapped the table. She looked up as Alexander Fraser stood.

"You will not be able to put him back together, if that

is what you are wondering." He raised the mug in his hand. "We have been tossing pieces of him all over the Lowlands!"

Cheers and pounding fists met his remarks. Amused, Christina looked at the faces around her. Jardine was present, as were several others from Annandale. But someone was missing. She turned back to Wallace. "Where is Seton?"

Pouring her a cup of ale, he indicated that she should sit. He took the chair next to her. "He is at Avoch Castle." He slouched in his seat. "With Andrew Moray."

Christina stared back at the outlaw in silence. She did not understand why Seton would choose not to return to Lochmaben. And go with Andrew no less. The revelation both hurt and surprised her. She found it difficult not to take it personally. At the very least, Seton could have sent a letter, offered her some sort of explanation. Attempting to hide the pain on her face, she took a long drink from her cup. Wallace watched her intently.

"I am going north to join Andrew there," he said. "Fraser and the army will remain in Selkirk Forest. They will need help over the winter. I am hoping you can give them that."

She understood now the reason for his visit. While there was enough game in the forest to feed the men, they would need tents, blankets, and feed for the horses. Thinking about where she would find the provisions, she asked, "And what about the rest of the Lowlands? What about Carrick and Galloway?"

A smirk formed on his face. "Your brother has the southwest well under control. I do not think there is a single Englishman left in it. Even Gallovidians ride with him. A family trait, I see."

Her eyes drifted over the room, trying to find Cailean.

Rob had come out of hiding the moment he heard about Stirling. Leading the men of Carrick, he attacked English strongholds before retreating back into the wilds, using his knowledge of the land to thwart their pursuits. While he had not yet returned to sit at Turnberry Castle, he was still very much the mormaer of the land. The people thought of him as nothing else. Wallace's voice distracted her.

"Edward's army has gone, but they will return." He paused. "We need to be ready."

She took his words to heart over the next month. Finished harvesting the crops, they stored at much as they could. Hunting parties went out almost daily for meat to smoke and dry. When the weather finally turned, grey clouds replacing sunny skies, she travelled to every castle her family owned in Annandale. She took all the blankets and armour they could spare. She was returning from the forest with Jardine, having delivered the goods to Fraser, when she saw Reid waiting for her outside the keep. The moment he told her who was inside, her stomach knotted. She walked nervously to the hall.

Seton's back was to her. He stared out the window as he waited.

Entering the room silently, Christina studied him. He looked different, his stance wider, his shoulders thicker. But the changes of the past year did nothing to prepare her for the moment he turned around.

Green eyes held her where she stood. His smile was brief.

She wanted to move closer. The troubled expression on his face kept her in place. She did not understand the tension between them. If anyone had the right to be angry, it was her. Almost a year had come and gone since she had last seen him in Douglas. In moments of silence, she often found her mind filled with him. She wondered where he was and what he was doing all the time. Standing before her now, his face despondent and his eyes distant, she doubted she had occupied his thoughts at all. Placing her hands on the chair in front of her, she waited for him to speak.

He walked to the table. Lowering his gaze, his fingertips gently touched the surface. Looking up, he said, "Andrew Moray was injured at Stirling."

Of all the things she expected him to say, this was not one of them. Her brow furrowed.

"He has asked for you."

She knew what his words meant. She did not want to accept it, but the concerned, disheartened look on Seton's face was too clear to ignore. Her fingers pressed harder into the back of the chair.

"He does not have much time left."

It felt like her body was at war with itself. She wanted to ask Seton why he had not returned, but she was over-whelmed with thoughts of Andrew dying somewhere in the Highlands. Her frustration melded into distress. She felt suddenly warm.

Seton moved towards her.

She stepped back. Unable to look at the pain on his face any longer, she left the hall before he could say anything else.

The wind howled as they rode for Avoch. Smothered beneath the thick wool cloak, she felt nothing. For a week, they travelled in silence. Even Jardine kept his brazen remarks to himself. Passing through the gates of the castle, the winter breeze off the North Sea pricking her skin, the hard wall she had firmly entrenched around her wilted away. She stared up at the tower. The night clouded everything in darkness. She wanted to be anywhere but here. Seeing the others dismount, she reluctantly dropped from her horse.

Seton led her towards the keep. Comyn men watched as she went. She could not imagine what they were thinking – a Bruce within their walls – but as she climbed the stairs, following Seton up to the hall, those thoughts left her mind.

"Wait here."

Seton left her outside the room. Christina leaned against the wall. He was gone for only a moment. Appearing once more, he held the door open. Pushing herself upright, she walked into the hall.

Seton did not follow. The door shut behind her. She found herself alone with a bundled figure resting in front of the fire. Her legs felt stiff and heavy. Taking a breath, she stepped forward towards the man in the chair. She stopped beside him.

Andrew turned his head. He smiled softly. "You came."

The weakness of his voice felt like a punch to the stomach. Gaunt and pale, he looked nothing like the man she knew. She fought to keep the despair from her face. Pulling a chair up next to him, she sat down and leaned into it. The steadiness of the wood comforted her. When she turned to him again, he was staring at her.

"You look the same in my dreams."

Unsure of what to say to the revelation, she remained silent. Sighing, Andrew looked back to the fire.

"I can feel it. My soul leaving my body. I feel less alive each time I wake." He turned to her again. "I wanted to see you before it was too late."

A sudden chill made him shiver. Finding another blanket, she placed it over him. She tucked the fabric under his chin.

"I am sorry," he said.

Her fingers stopped. Staring back at him, she saw the pain written across his face.

"I should not have given up so easily. I should have fought for you."

She felt only sadness. Giving him a small smile, she sat back down. He took her hand. His skin felt cold and clammy.

"Forgive me." Tears filled his eyes. "Please, Christina. Forgive me."

Saying nothing, she placed her hand over his. He leaned back into his chair.

She did not know how long they sat there. When she looked back over to him, he was asleep. His head rested comfortably on the cushion behind him.

Careful not to wake him, she placed more logs on the fire and headed towards the door. Her body craved rest. But as she stepped from the room, pulling the door closed behind her, she saw that she was not going to get it. The Lord of Badenoch waited for her. It felt like she had entered a wolf's lair.

"I respectfully ask that you come with me."

His voice was deeper than she remembered. Staring back at the man in charge of the most powerful kindred in Scotland, she did not answer. She wanted to say no – she had had enough agony for one day. But this was Moray. She was in Comyn land. Stepping forward, she unwillingly followed the Red Comyn's father down the stairs.

He led her out of the castle. Crossing the bailey, he

entered one of the buildings. Voices drifted from the open door. She stopped. She could enter that room and face whoever was waiting, or she could get on her horse and ride for Garioch. Neither option appealed to her. Jardine and Cailean stepped in beside her. Bolstered by their presence, she walked through the door.

Several faces waited inside the armoury. Besides the Lord of Badenoch, the Mormaer of Buchan was also there, his glare greeting her from the other side of the room. The two men surrounding him were Andrew's uncles – the clergyman David Moray and the Lord of Bothwell. They smiled warmly when she looked their way. Leaning up against the workbench not far from the door, she waited for the Lord of Badenoch to tell her why she was there.

"I would have never expected this," he said. "Someone like you, here, in our midst." He paused. "But you have shown your loyalty. You will be a part of this."

The scoff that came from the Mormaer of Buchan's mouth was too loud to ignore.

The Lord of Badenoch looked over at him. The irritation in his expression was clear. It was obvious who held more power in the Comyn kindred. The Lord of Badenoch waited for an explanation from his cousin. The Mormaer of Buchan stepped forward.

"I will not stand silently by and let a Bruce be privy to our discussions." He looked disgusted by her presence. "Anything we say will just be repeated in the English court."

Christina had not seen the mormaer since the tournament in Edinburgh over two years ago. It already felt too soon.

"She cannot be trusted." He practically spat out the words. "She is nothing but a spy and a whore."

Christina could not stop the smile from forming. The insult should not have amused her. Any slander against her virtue, whether it was true or not, could ruin her – both her and her family. All it had to do was take root, and she would be marked forever as a harlot, a slut. Jardine did not take the accusation so lightly. He was halfway to the mormaer before the Lord of Badenoch blocked his path.

"Enough." His voice boomed across the room.

Glaring menacingly at the mormaer, Jardine did not move. The Lord of Badenoch looked expectantly at Christina.

"It is all right," she said.

At the sound of her voice, Jardine backed away. The mormaer's eyes shifted to her.

She held his gaze. "He only speaks of what he knows." She smiled sweetly. "He has spent more time kneeling than all the whores in England."

The mormaer tried to come towards her. His larger cousin shoved him back.

The Lord of Badenoch's face reddened with anger. "You will behave in the manner that is expected of you, or you will leave. Decide."

The mormaer did not even look at the man before him, his gaze only on Christina. She kept the smile on her face. Adjusting his tunic, he stormed out of the room.

"Forgive him," the Lord of Badenoch said. He watched the other man leave in frustration. "On my word as a nobleman and as a lord, such accusations will never leave his lips again."

Christina highly doubted it. The Mormaer of Buchan thought only of himself. He was unable to see past Bruce or Comyn. She nodded anyway. Leaning more of her weight into the table behind her, she wished he would get on with it. She was tired of being there. The Lord of Badenoch clasped his hands behind his back.

"I have gathered you here because we need to decide on a way forward. Wallace and the Mormaer of Carrick are holding the border." He glanced at her. "But it will not be enough to keep the English out. They will return with an army as soon as the roads open in the spring." His eyes found the two Moray men. "We need more than a Guardian. We need a king."

He suddenly had her interest. David Moray turned towards her.

"William Lamberton, the Chancellor of Glasgow Cathedral, has gone to Rome to ask the Pope for help." He hesitated for a moment. "Our aim is to secure King John's release."

She did not dare look away. The information was surprising and substantial. Her mind was calculating what it meant when David continued.

"King John is being held in the Tower of London, along with William Douglas, the Bishop of Glasgow, the Mormaer of Ross and Andrew's father. If the Pope can convince King Edward to release John into the Kirk's care, Scotland's king will return. John Balliol will once again take the throne at Scone."

Her exhaustion no longer mattered. The idea that a king could willingly give up the throne and then change his mind to rule again was preposterous. She wanted a Scotsman on the throne as much as anyone else, but it had to be the right man. There was no point in placing the crown back on John's head if he was just going to cower to Edward once more. The three men waited for her response. Wiping the indignation from her face, she looked to the Lord of Badenoch. "What are you asking?"

"Support our cause to return John to the throne." His face was genuine. "We cannot defeat the English if we are divided from within. We must not think of House Bruce or House Comyn. Let us think only of the land of Scots."

She could not help but find it ironic. The peace offering she had once longed for, the one that would have allowed her to marry Andrew, had come a couple of years too late. But it was of no consequence now. She still had time to correct the mistakes that had been made.

Folding her arms across her chest, she said, "I will not speak for my father. He has made his choice. As for the rest of our House…" She paused to find the right words. Their position needed to be clear. "I cannot promise that we will support John Balliol's return to Scotland. But we will not act against it." She looked at the faces before her. "If John is the king Scotland wants once more, we will not stand in his way."

The Lord of Badenoch smiled. He seemed satisfied with her reply. "We are united then," he said. "From Galloway to Buchan, Caithness to Dunbar. We will face the English as one, as we once did eleven years ago."

His words stayed with her as she left the armoury. She wanted to believe him – that Bruce or Comyn no longer mattered, that the kingdom would act as one. Looking up at the castle looming in the dark, she felt dissatisfied. John's return to the throne was not what she wanted. It was not what she had been fighting for all this time.

"Lady Christina."

She turned at her name. A man a bit younger than Mary

walked towards her. He looked tired and wet, his face splattered with specks of mud. Only when he stopped before her did she realize who he was. From Annandale, he was the oldest son of Morna Kerr. The only son she had left.

"I have been sent to warn you." His words were quick. "Your father has come back to Lochmaben. Englishmen are with him. They await your return."

She stared at the boy in silence, overwhelmed by the message. Her father had every right to be in Lochmaben. He was still the lord of the land. But she did not know what to make of his sudden appearance. Perhaps he had discovered that she was supplying Wallace's army. Maybe it was simply because she had ignored his summons to Writtle. Whatever the reason, the result would be the same. The moment she stepped foot in Annandale, he would drag her to England.

Looking over at Cailean and Jardine, their hardened faces told her just what they thought. Jardine's eyes gleamed with resentment. Cailean sent a wad of spit to the ground. She could not return to Lochmaben, not now. She needed to run. This time, she would go somewhere her father would never dare to follow – to Garmoran and Cairistíona Nic Ruaidhrí.

CHAPTER SIXTEEN

GUSTS OF WIND off the sea pushed strands of hair across her forehead. Standing atop the rocky crag along the western coast, the Small Isles visible in the distance, Christina glanced at the dark-haired woman beside her. Cairistíona nic Ruaidhrí did not move. Her eyes were closed, face lifted towards the sun. Watching her cloak sway in the breeze, long legs peeking out from her skirts, Christina looked to the sea once more.

She had spent the winter here, under the protection of the woman who ruled Garmoran. As the sole legitimate child of the head of the Ruaidhrí kindred, Cairistíona had inherited Garmoran, Moidart, Arisaig, Morar, Knoydart, as well as the isles of Eigg, Rhum, Barra, Uist and St Kilda when her father died. But she gave almost everything, including the right to lead their House, to her two older half-brothers both born out of wedlock. The act did not diminish her stature within her familial lands. In fact, it increased it. Cairistíona honoured blood over Anglo-Saxon norms. She may not have the title, but as Christina walked with the other woman back to the castle, with three buannachann men around them, there was no doubt in her mind that Cairistíona nic Ruaidhrí was the Lady of the Isles.

Castle Tioram jutted out into the loch. The fortress was a stronghold of Clann Ruaidhrí, with access to both the sea and a prominent water route into the Highlands. Cailean met them at the bottom of the rock mound, the castle just up ahead. He handed her a sealed note.

Christina had received two letters during her time in Garmoran. The first was from David Moray. Andrew had died not long after she left Avoch. The second was a warning. Sir Robert Clifford of England was in Annandale searching for Rob. The Englishman's presence at Lochmaben made her return more unlikely. Taking the note from Cailean's hand, the paper dirty and thin, one glance told her who it was from. She broke the wax seal.

Lady Christina Bruce of Annandale and Carrick,

Your presence is requested at council to discuss matters of the community of Scotland held in Selkirk on the eleventh day of March of the year one thousand two hundred and ninety-eight.

William, son of Alan Wallace, guardian of the kingdom of Scotland

It only took her a moment to read it. She considered what it meant. Those active in the Scottish cause would gather together under Wallace. She wondered if he knew about the plans the Comyns had for the kingdom. Her thoughts were cut short by a voice beside her.

"Will you go?" Cairistíona asked.

Christina turned to her older cousin and into the sharp eyes that stared back. Their mothers were sisters, both of Carrick, but they did not look the same. Cairistíona took after her father, Ailéan mac Ruaidhrí. It was the reason why Christina's father had not come for her here. There was no love for him in Garmoran.

"No." Christina folded the letter back up. She took a few steps up the hill towards the castle. When she saw that Cairistíona did not follow, she stopped. She looked into those eyes once more.

They seemed darker, as if a storm was on the horizon. Cairistíona glanced out at the loch for a moment before she spoke. She returned her gaze to Christina. "Come with me."

The birlinn glided soundlessly down the River Shiel. Rock cliffs rose up on their right with rolling hills to their left. Christina sat near the bow, twisting with the bends as they headed south. She watched the trees drift by. She did not know what they were doing or where they were going. The river widened. The landscaped opened as they entered the loch. Without a word, the birlinn jumped forward.

She stood. Wind pressed against her face as the oars moved in perfect unison, three men to each pole. The passageway narrowed before it expanded again, but the rowers did not abate. Fingers of land branched out into the water. Mountains rose in the distance. The loch continued farther than she could see. An island sat in the centre of the water. Spotting the chapel ascending into the sky from the top of the hill, the birlinn slowed beneath her feet. It banked on the shore. Following Cairistíona, she climbed out of the boat and up the slope.

A large cross greeted them as they reached the top. They

would not be here long; none of the men had followed them to shore. Christina gazed at the sanctuary dedicated to Saint Finian. It was small and peaceful. Seeing Cairistíona move past the chapel, she followed her into the burial grounds.

Grass swayed in the breeze as Christina carefully stepped through the graves. Some looked old while others were fresh. She stopped next to Cairistíona. Looking down, she saw the markings on the small stone before them.

"Did you know my husband?"

Christina shook her head. Cairistíona had married Donnchadh, the brother of Domhnall, the Mormaer of Mar, when she was young. Donnchadh had died a few years ago. When Rob took Isabella as his wife, it bonded the Bruce family to Cairistíona's once more.

"When we wed, he was already an old man. No child would grow within me." Cairistíona looked up at the sky. She watched a red kite soar above them. "I believed them when they told me it was my fault, that I had done something to bring a curse upon my family." Her eyes dropped to Christina's face. "But how could I be to blame? I was thirteen-years-old, barely a woman and my husband was older than my father." She stepped away, turning to look out at the water. When she met Christina's gaze once more, the storm in her expression had returned. "You know my son. Tell me. Does he look like he is from Mar?"

Christina did not move under the eyes that held her. The boy's dark features came to mind. She knew what the answer was, having already thought it many times over. But it was one thing to think something and another to say it. Knowing her cousin expected an honest answer, she pushed aside her uncertainty and answered, "No."

Cairistíona smiled. "That is because he is not. My husband was too weak to give me a child. But that did not stop me from continuing my line. It should not stop you either."

Christina looked back at her in confusion.

"You have been invited to council, to speak for your family and your land. And yet you will not go. Why?"

"It is not my place." The words were out of her mouth before she could stop them.

Cairistíona scoffed. "Not your place? The only one who thinks that is you. Why else would he send for you?"

Christina crossed her arms in front of her. "I am certain Rob will be there."

"What does that change?"

She did not have an answer.

"He did not ask for *a* Bruce. He asked for you." Cairistíona took a step towards her. "Do not be limited by the rules of old men who no longer matter. Take what you have earned. Take what is yours." She paused. "For if you do not, there will come a time when you wished you had. And then it will be too late."

Cairistíona's words stayed with her as they travelled back. Christina had not thought of her grandfather in a while, but he was with her now. She wondered if this was what he meant that morning on the hill – when he told her to find a worthy man to follow. He would have liked the outlaw. They had the same determination, the same lust for life. The two men never doubted what needed to be done. A king, Wallace was not. But he was born to lead. Of that, she was certain. As Castle Tioram came into view, she knew what her grandfather would say to her if he were here. She knew what needed to be done. Back on her horse, Cailean and Jardine beside her, they rode for Selkirk and William Wallace, the Guardian of Scotland.

The torches made the forest glow, noblemen and knights filling the spaces between the trees. Every House in Scotland had answered the call.

Sitting with Rob and Neil, the men of Lennox and Atholl beside them, Christina watched as Wallace took his place at the head of the circle. James Stewart and William Lamberton were at his side. The conversations ceased when Stewart stood.

"I would be remiss if I did not acknowledge each of you here," Stewart began. "You came when we asked, and for that, you have our thanks." Pausing, he took a step into the circle. "But my gratitude is not why you have come. Each and every one of you, as mormaers, lords, knights and servicemen of this kingdom, has the right to help determine our future, the future of Scotland." He turned the other way and studied the faces in front of him. "I will not pretend that everyone agrees on the path forward. Some of you are for England, like the Mormaer of Angus and the Lord of Annandale."

The mention of her father made her tense.

James Stewart continued. "That is why, before we go forward, I ask that each of you declare himself before God and countrymen." He looked around. "Speak for your lands and your house. Tell us which kingdom you fight for."

He sat back down. Silence filled the ring. Everyone waited for someone else to begin. It was the only other woman in the circle, Euphemia, Countess of Ross, who stood first. She walked forward.

"It is not my intention to dishonour those here and those who are no longer." She glanced around as she spoke. "I admire the valiant way in which you have fought for our freedom and for our kingdom." She paused. "But that is all I can offer. My husband, William, is still in England, a prisoner of Edward. I will not risk his life and the future of our house." She turned to Wallace. "Ross is not for England, but we will not stand against her either. We will remain impartial."

Wallace did not reply. Stewart nodded, and the countess left. The men of Ross followed her. There was a hole in the circle; they were no longer complete. Seeing Gartnait of Mar stand next, Christina's heart sank. His father had just returned home from England. His health declining in prison, Edward had taken pity on the mormaer and had him released. Watching Gartnait step forward, she knew this would not go the way she wanted.

"I am Gartnait, son of Domhnall, the Mormaer of Mar." His face was flushed and sweaty. He looked like he was about to puke. "We take the same position as Ross. We are not for England, but we will not fight."

Christina glanced at Rob. She did not need to wonder what he thought. His eyes were narrow and the muscles in his face clenched as he listened to Mar abnegate. Perhaps she should have married Gartnait. Then Mar's decision might have been different.

The abstention did not end there. The earldoms of Strathearn and Menteith also voiced their withdrawal. Following the Scots loss at Dunbar two years earlier, both Houses had given Edward two sons as hostages. They would not risk losing their future lords.

Christina watched the mormaers leave, taking with

them the men Scotland needed to win against England. She found it difficult not to be resentful. Every time the English invaded, the Lowlands suffered. Not Ross, Mar, Strathearn or Menteith. All those lands were safely tucked away in the Highlands, far from the warpath Edward carved. It was Dunbar and March, Galloway and Carrick who lost homes, land, men, families. Their refusal to fight was the reason Edward took hostages. It worked.

When all was said and done, six earldoms – Dunbar and March, Carrick, Buchan, Lennox, Atholl and Sutherland – and five lordships – Lochaber, Badenoch, Moray, Stewartry and Galloway – were declared for Scotland. Spotting David Moray sitting with Lamberton, the two men speaking in hushed voices, she thought the arduous part was over. Then the Mormaer of Buchan entered the circle.

"No one here can deny the importance of what we have achieved this past year."

Those that remained looked towards him. The circle fell silent.

"I could not have dreamed of such success." He paused to look around him. "William Wallace and Andrew Moray have led valiantly in our absence. But we cannot falter now. Scotland must be guided by the right men. By men chosen by their king."

The implication that Wallace should no longer lead them exasperated her. She had not thought it possible, but her opinion of the mormaer worsened. She looked to the man sitting at the head.

Wallace did not move. His gaze was on the ground and his arms were folded across his chest. The mormaer's words were insulting, but he gave no indication of what he thought. He simply remained as he was.

Rob stood and walked into the centre. "And who would that be?" He looked at the mormaer. "Would that be you? Are you the one to lead us?"

The mormaer did not answer.

"If memory serves me," Rob continued, "you were in France fighting *for* King Edward while Wallace and Moray were at Stirling." He smirked at him. "You seem quite eager to take credit for a victory you did not earn."

His glare emanated across the circle. Rob stepped closer.

"Were not you also the one behind King John, urging him to invade England, to attack Carlisle without a single siege weapon two short years ago?" Rob's face contained not a drop of humour. "Is that how you would lead Scotland now?"

His reply was not needed. His past was enough to condemn him. Recognizing that he had lost his point, the mormaer changed tactics. He turned to face Rob fully.

"You may not have learned this since your father failed not only his family but his countrymen."

The insult was unnecessary. The tension spiked. Rob took a menacing step closer.

The mormaer was undeterred. "Scotland has been led by noblemen in the king's absence for centuries. That will not change simply because you wish it." He looked around him at the others. "We have a duty, to our subjects and to our king, to lead with integrity and honour. That can only be done through a nobleman, a man appointed by the king."

"Does Wallace not have the qualities you speak of?"

Christina watched Lamberton join the conversation. Rising from his chair, he stepped into the circle.

"Is he not loyal?" Pointing to Wallace, he glanced at the people who had gathered. "Is he not honourable?"

Lamberton's gaze came to rest on the mormaer. The man from Buchan looked at the faces of those seated around him. He was not winning them to his side.

"I do not doubt his loyalty," he answered. "That was never in question. But we all know what happened in England this past fall. We all know what men under Wallace's command have done." He paused for dramatic effect. "Seven hundred villages were burnt, entire towns looted and destroyed. That is not the mark of an honourable man, one who values integrity above all else."

Christina could barely stand the hypocrisy. Wallace had only gone into England because the Gallovidians had crossed the border on their own. They raided the villages and the towns unhindered. Their tactics were brutal and unforgiving. Wallace went there to try to control them. But that was not what infuriated her. The marauders were King John's own people – Comyns – the mormaer's own kin. The only reason why he had a problem with it now was because it suited him, not because it was true.

"Nothing done in England was not done to us first by Edward's men." Rob's comment drew murmurs of agreement from the crowd. "It seems you care more for England than you do for us."

"I care because of what Edward will do." The mormaer had to raise his voice to be heard. The noise faded with his response.

"He will retaliate. That is why a nobleman must lead. We know of these things; we know the king. Even in war, we must keep the integrity of Scotland whole."

"It is difficult to keep integrity from your knees."

She forgot where she was. The words left her mouth

before she had time to consider the consequences. The circle turned to her expectantly. Forcing herself to stand, she stepped forward.

"There is not a single man here who has not bent the knee, save for William Wallace." She looked at the faces around her. "While you were swearing fealty to an English king, giving up your sons as hostages, Wallace was the only one to stay on his feet. He was the only one who refused to accept a foreign king."

Her eyes landed on the Lord of Badenoch. He had been oddly silent from the beginning, showing support for neither Wallace nor his Comyn cousin. He did not look away.

"You may not think him noble because he has no title, no land to prove it." She glanced around her again. Anger filled her voice. "But if Wallace does not have the heart of a nobleman, then neither do any of you."

Furrowed brows stared back at her.

"Keep your titles and your land, I do not care." Her indignation rose. "Just give me a man I can follow."

Silence covered the gathering once more. Having nothing left to say, she made her way back to her seat. She stopped when the Mormaer of Buchan's voice sounded behind her.

"He is not even a knight."

Spinning on her heel, she let her frustration show. "Is that your only complaint? Is that the only criticism you have of the man before you?"

Taken aback by the forcefulness of her response, he did not answer.

She found the whole affair ridiculous. They questioned Wallace unjustly, as if he had not proven himself repeatedly over the past few years. When the mormaer remained silent, Christina turned and looked at her brother.

Rob's hand was already on the hilt of his sword. Stepping forward, he withdrew it and said, "William, son of Alan of Renfrewshire." His voice rang out across the forest. "Kneel and accept the honour you rightly deserve."

She returned to Annandale, but it was not to take residence at Lochmaben. Those days were over. She was going there for only one reason – to scorch the land and burn everything down.

The villagers did not need to be told twice. They packed what they could onto carts and headed north. The English army would come as soon as the snow melted. Burnt earth would be all that waited.

Watching the thatched roofs catch fire, the wells poisoned and the fields black, Christina found it difficult to leave. Memories of days spent walking the land with her grandfather washed over her. He would have made the same choice; she was certain of it. But knowing that did not make it any easier. Unwilling to look upon the destruction any longer, she turned away.

She went to Garioch. A few families from Annandale followed her there, settling in Inverurie. It was a restless spring and an even worse summer. News of what happened in the Lowlands slowly trickled north. Edward had returned from his war in France to deal with the Scottish insurrection himself. Marching across the border, he brought not just Englishmen, but over ten thousand Welsh longbowmen. It did not go as the Scots had planned.

Wallace and his army shadowed Edward as soon as he entered the Lowlands. They kept close, but out of sight, wanting to attack when the English ran out of supplies and began to withdraw. But that never happened. Receiving word that Wallace was in Falkirk, only thirteen miles away, Edward advanced his army to meet him. England went on the offensive.

The Scottish cavalry fled, abandoning the archers and foot soldiers on the field. The Scots lost a third of their army in a single blow. Wallace himself barely escaped, fleeing into Torwood Forest on foot. When Christina heard what had happened, she almost did not believe it. They had prepared their defense, trained their men, and anticipated being heavily outnumbered. And yet none of it mattered. Perhaps her family was cursed after all.

She was summoned to council a second time. The request did not come from Wallace. A Comyn man before her, Christina looked down at the marked letter in his hand. The seal was of Badenoch. The message brief, she rode for Ruthven Castle.

Situated within the Cairngorm Mountains, the seat of Comyn power in Badenoch perched high on a mound near the River Spey. The estuary flooded constantly. Boggy marshland encompassed the fortress. Her horse stepping carefully over the frozen ground, Christina moved through the open gate.

The hall was full. Making her way through the men who had gathered, Christina took note of the faces present. James Stewart was there, as were the mormaers of Lennox and Atholl. William Lamberton stood with David Moray near the table. Lamberton had recently been elected as the new Bishop of St

Andrews, making him the most powerful man in the Kirk of Scotland. Wallace had a hand in it. Lamberton was a staunch ally. Thinking of the outlaw, she glanced around.

She could not find him anywhere. His brother Malcolm was present, as was Alexander Fraser. As soon as she spotted Rob, Wallace left her mind. She rushed towards her brother and wrapped him in a tight embrace.

His relief to find her there was the same. She had not seen him since he had knighted Wallace in Selkirk Forest. Rob was not present at the battle in Falkirk, but Edward came for him nonetheless. After his victory over the Scots, the English king went to Turnberry to try and catch the Mormaer of Carrick. He was too late – the castle was devastated and the village was burned. Someone had warned Rob that the English king was coming. He left nothing for Edward but a blackened and barren keep.

Christina let go. Rob grinned down at her.

"You look well," he said. "Garioch agrees with you."

She smiled. Life there was peaceful. There were no English, no soldiers to raid the villages or destroy the land. She spent almost all her time with Ena. She enjoyed it, but it was not what she was used to. It was not home.

A call to gather made everyone approach the table. Noblemen took their seats, the men who followed them standing behind. Christina had just pulled out a chair, the wooden frame within her grasp when Jardine appeared at her side. He leaned down to whisper in her ear.

"William, the Lord of Douglas, is dead."

His words made her hesitate. She remained standing.

"He was murdered in the Tower of London. Edward continues to search for his son."

She remembered the last time she had seen the warlord. Stood in the grounds of his castle, Andrew Moray entrusted in his care, he had watched her ride out. But she did not have the chance to think further. Jardine was not finished. He had something else to tell her.

"Seton is in England," he said. "Your father has found him a wife."

Christina could not stop herself from turning. The seriousness of Jardine's gaze told her it was not a joke. Her arms felt numb and her chest was tight. She struggled to move. Jardine stepped back.

Everyone else was seated. Silent looks from around the table waited for her to do the same. Reaching out, Rob lightly touched her arm. She lowered herself down into the chair.

The Lord of Badenoch began to speak. She barely heard him, her mind on what was happening south of the border. She doubted her father knew what Seton meant to her. At twenty-years-old, Seton was an honourable and loyal man. He had gained a reputation and a knighthood fighting under Wallace. The people called him Good Sir Crystell. It made perfect sense for him to marry now, but the news did not devastate her any less.

A murmur around the room made her look up. The Lord of Badenoch's hands were raised, appealing for quiet. He waited for the noise to die down.

"I understand your frustration. Wallace's resignation is a surprise to us all." He glanced around the table. "But we must move forward. We have men to train and land to win back. We need to decide who will lead us now."

The hall went silent. It unsettled Christina to know that Wallace was no longer their guardian. People followed him willingly. His intentions were pure. He did not care about the rivalry that divided their land. But the loss at Falkirk had been too much. They had taken heavy casualties. None more so than Wallace's desire to lead them. A chair scraped across the floor. Christina watched the Mormaer of Lennox stand.

"I nominate Robert Bruce, the Mormaer of Carrick." His voice rang through the hall. "He is the man to lead us."

Fists pounded the table in agreement. Christina looked at Rob beside her. His face was stoic and his body was still. The Mormaer of Lennox took his seat. Another man stood.

The Mormaer of Buchan did not waste any time. "I nominate John, the Red Comyn, son of the Lord of Badenoch." He pointed to the man. "He should be guardian."

Christina shifted her eyes to the Red Comyn. He met her gaze.

She had not seen him since he threw her out of Lochmaben. Captured at Dunbar, he had been sent to France to fight for Edward. Christina did not know how he had made it back to Scotland. There was no word of Edward granting his release. All she knew was that he had been at Falkirk with Wallace.

Hands hit the surface once more. Though not as loud, it was almost equal. A man pushing his way through the crowd towards the table silenced the noise.

Alexander Stewart slammed both fists down onto the wooden surface. His voice rang out. "My father is dead! And it is because of that man!"

Christina looked to where his finger pointed. When she saw the Red Comyn at the end of it, his face as still as stone, she instinctively leaned back in her chair.

"He left the field at Falkirk," Alexander continued. "He

took the entire cavalry with him." The anger in his voice grew. "Because of him, thousands of our men are dead!"

His glare radiated across the room. Christina looked at James Stewart. Alexander was his nephew. James' brother, John Stewart of Bonkyll, had led the archers at Falkirk. When the Red Comyn had fled with the cavalry, everyone on the ground was left unprotected. Archers and foot soldiers were cut down by the thousands. Christina could see the concern written all over James' face.

Alexander punched the table once more. "I will not stand here and allow that man to become guardian." His word dripped with scorn. "At worst, he is a traitor. At best, he is a coward." He stared at the Red Comyn, his eyes narrowed. "He has no right to lead us."

The Red Comyn rose to his feet. Half the table stood with him. Not in support, but in concern. The tension in the hall was so thick Christina could taste it. All it would take was one person to remove their blade and it would be over; they would be defeated. England and her threat would no longer matter.

"Please, my lords." Lamberton's voice came from the front of the room. "Restrain yourselves."

The Lord of Badenoch left his seat. Stepping forward, he moved in beside the Red Comyn, breaking the line of sight between the two men. His gaze shifting to his father, the Red Comyn sat back down.

Alexander Stewart remained where he stood. He continued to glare at the Red Comyn as another man stepped through the crowd.

Kin to Alexander and a follower of Wallace, John Menteith stopped beside his cousin. Like the Red Comyn, John had been sent to France to fight for Edward after his capture at Dunbar. He had also made it back to Scotland in time to battle against the English at Falkirk. But unlike the Red Comyn, who had sat in relative safety atop his horse, John had been one of the men abandoned on the field when the Red Comyn fled. His presence at the end of the table did nothing to calm the hostility.

John placed a heavy hand on Alexander's shoulder. For a moment, the other man did not move. Then he shrugged John's hand off. The crowd parted willingly as he turned. The two men left the hall.

Watching them leave, Christina glanced over the men standing near the door. Disgruntled knights stared back at her. It was not Alexander Stewart they were unhappy with.

In the end, both Rob and the Red Comyn were chosen as guardians. They would lead Scotland together, as Wallace and Andrew Moray had done after Stirling. The partnership gave Christina no comfort. The two men had been pitted against one other since they were boys. Riding from Ruthven Castle, her cloak wrapped tightly around her, she hoped they used their tempers against the English and not each other. It did not take long for the Kingdom of Scots to realize just how foolish their decision had been.

CHAPTER SEVENTEEN

PEACE FROM WITHIN was not to be. War had begun, and they were not fighting England.

For more than a year, Rob and the Red Comyn tore Scotland farther apart. They argued over everything. Men chose sides. Daggers and lines were drawn. When the Mormaer of Buchan accused William Lamberton of treason at a council in Peebles, Christina knew it was over. Scotland was united no longer. Rob resigned the guardianship and returned to Carrick.

Summer passed, and with fall came a gift. King Edward agreed to a truce. Beginning in October, it would last until the twenty-first day of May in the year one thousand three hundred and one. But the additional time changed nothing. As soon as the truce expired, Edward's armies returned to the Lowlands. They conquered castles only to be driven from them weeks later. Men died unceasingly, and Scotland still was not free.

Christina was in Garioch when she heard Rob had recaptured Turnberry for the second time. He had chased King Edward's son, the Prince of Wales, all the way to Carlisle. Leaning close to the fire, she wondered what her father thought of it. Half his children had disobeyed him, choosing to fight against him instead. Edward, Thomas, Alexander and Matilda were with him in Writtle, but Christina was certain it was not by choice. She had not seen them in years. She could only imagine what Matilda looked like now. A whistle sounded from outside. Pushing herself up out of her seat, she walked from the keep.

She stopped the moment she saw him ride into the bailey. Her heart jumped into her throat. Halfway down the steps, she was still a considerable distance away, but it did not matter. She would recognize Christopher Seton anywhere.

He slowed as he came into the grounds. Catching sight of her, his face grew grim. She felt her stomach knot.

Four years had passed since she had seen him at Avoch. He looked the same, but she knew he was not. His wife had died in childbirth less than a year after their union. Jardine had been the one to tell her. Staring at the man still seated on his horse, she wondered if his daughter had green eyes like him.

Movement near the gate made her look away from Seton. Rob rode through. Mary was with him, as were Neil, Áed, Randolph, and Hay. Their arrival surprised her. It was almost winter, and Rob did not leave Carrick often. Mary looked miserable. Even the men seemed discontented. Watching her eldest brother dismount, a disheartened smile on his face, uncertainty grew within her. Marjorie ran towards her. Smiling as she caught her five-year-old niece in her arms, Christina led them into the keep.

"I am tired."

Sitting in the hall near the head of the table, Christina looked over at Rob. The evening meal was over. Everyone else had left. Rob slumping back in his chair, she waited for him to tell her why he had come.

"Carrick is suffering." His voice was quiet. "The lands of our family are destitute. I can fight the English no longer."

He looked as he sounded – worn down. His eyes were heavy and his shoulders drooped. He was thinner. Christina did not know what to say. She wanted to tell him to reconsider, but could not. The constant struggle of the past three years had taken its toll.

It was a while before he spoke again. When he did, he sounded wistful. "I want Carrick to be prosperous like it once was." He met her gaze. "I want to watch my daughter grow into a woman surrounded by kin in Turnberry, not hiding in the wilds like an outlaw." His eyes filled with sorrow. "I want her to know her mother. I want her to feel safe in her grandmother's land. I want her to love Carrick, as I do."

The longer he talked, the more worried Christina became. Rob did not sound as if he just wanted a break from the fighting. He spoke as if he was finished, as if he would never take up arms against England again. Though she did not doubt he had considered this for quite some time, it did nothing to alleviate her misery.

"What about the rest of us?" she asked. "What about Scotland?"

He looked at her as if she did not understand. "John Balliol is a free man in France. He has already appointed a new guardian." He shook his head slightly. "Even if I wanted to, even if I had the men and the means to keep fighting, to what end, Christina?" His eyes implored her to answer. "Why should I continue to sacrifice my land and my people for a king who cannot stand on his own? For a king who does not see me?"

She wanted to lie. If she could tell him that King John would be different this time, then maybe he would reconsider. But she could not. Once John sat on that throne again, the kingdom would go back to what it knew best – Bruce against Comyn. It would be detrimental to their House. They would not survive being in the crosshairs of two kings this time. Comyn or English – they would have to pick a side. Rob was choosing England.

"I will surrender to Edward as soon as the new year comes."

It sounded like a death sentence.

"I will take a wife and give my daughter the life she is owed."

Christina found it difficult to look at him. Heartbroken, she kept her eyes on the table.

"I will not insult you by asking you to kneel with me. But, Christina-"

She forced herself to look up.

"You must know." His eyes holding hers, his voice broke as he spoke. "You are exposed. There are holes in your defenses. Your walls will not stand."

She understood what he was trying to tell her. She was twenty-three-years-old and unmarried. She had defied her father in every way, and now her only brother with influence, the only one who carried weight in both Scotland and England, would be against her. Rob did not need to say anything else. He did so anyway.

"Your family will no longer protect you." He spoke as if

the words pained him. "Whatever you do now, you do on your own."

She thought of how her head would look dipped in tar. Jabbed onto a stake, it would most likely be displayed over the gates of Lochmaben. Her death would be quick, of that she was certain. But she was not ready to give up yet. She did not have to swear fealty to John to continue fighting for Scotland. She knew just how to protect herself.

She found Seton by the river. His back towards her, the moonlight shimmered across the water in the dark as she approached the bank. He turned to find her beside him.

She glanced up. His stare bit into her. Though he seemed less angry, there was still a hint of resentment in his eyes. She looked out across the river. Determined to break the tension and see this through, she asked, "What is she like? Your daughter?"

It was the wrong thing to say. His jaw clenched. "I would not know. I have not seen her since the birth."

She felt foolish. Of course his daughter was not with him. Scotland was at war, and he was a knight – not a lord or a mormaer. He could not protect her or give her what she needed here.

"I am sorry," Christina said.

He did not respond.

Strained silence descended upon them once more. Christina struggled to find the words she needed. She considered just blurting it out when he turned his head.

"Why did you leave Avoch without telling me?"

The question caught her off guard. Avoch seemed like a lifetime ago. She had not thought of Andrew in such a long time, it felt odd to remember him now. Seton's unnerving gaze rested heavily on her. She opened her mouth to answer when he spoke again.

"I brought you there because Andrew asked me to. But then you vanished." He looked angry. "I did not know where you were, if the Comyns had taken you, if you were alive or dead." His voice rose in frustration. "You should have told me you were going to Garmoran. I would have come with you. Instead, you left me without a word."

Though she did not find it funny, she could not stop the smile from forming. She looked at him to see if he was joking. The intensity of his eyes told her he was not. She did not bother hiding her irritation. "I left you?"

Knowing the question was sarcastic, Seton did not answer. His mouth set in a hard line.

She turned to face him fully. "You are the one who left after Chester. You joined Wallace, and then followed Andrew north." Her words were pointed, as if she was a monk listing sins. "You avoided me at the council in Selkirk."

He opened his mouth to defend himself. Her anger cut him off.

"I had to hear about your wedding from someone else!" She did not care that she was shouting. She could no longer remain calm. All this time, he had been mad at her for nothing. "You could have come to Garioch. You knew I was here. But you did not."

Seton did not answer.

Folding her arms in front of her, she turned away and pushed the depth of her hurt down. "You let me long before I left you."

Silence filled the space between them once more.

Taking a breath, Christina stared at the trees on the other

side of the bank. Darkened silhouettes covered the field. The quiet dragged on. This was not what she wanted. She did not want things to be difficult – not with him. She tried again.

"Whatever has happened, I-" her voice trailed off.

His head turned. She met his gaze.

"I do not want to fight with you."

He stared back at her. "All right then," he said. "We will not fight."

She smiled, amused that it could be so simple.

Seton seemed to agree. A small smirk pulled at the corners of his mouth. He looked at her like he used to, green eyes on fire.

She asked the question that had brought her to the river in the first place. "Will you go with Rob to surrender to Edward?"

The humour left his face. He took a moment before he answered. "No."

She found his response unsurprising. He was much like Wallace. She doubted Seton would ever bend the knee to Edward again. "Stay with me. Here, in Garioch."

He smiled as if she had told a joke, but his merriment was brief. Irritation returned to his face. "No."

Her brow knotted. "Fine." She sighed and straightened her posture. "Where shall we live then?"

He went still. Uncertain of what she was asking, his forehead dented slightly.

She enjoyed the sight of him unsettled. Staring back at him, she kept her expression serious. "We will need to reside somewhere after we are married."

His eyes searched her face.

She did not blink. "Should we return to the Lowlands, or would you prefer to live farther north?"

He glanced away. For several moments, he did not move, but when he stepped towards her, the motion was quick. His face hovered above hers. She tilted her chin up.

"Is this your way of asking me to marry you?"

A small smile fell across her lips. She hesitated, taking in how near he was and said, "I am not asking."

They were married at Saint Mary's Kirk on a sunny winter's day. The church was small, the nave filled with those who had come to witness Lady Christina Bruce of Carrick and Annandale wed Sir Christopher Seton of Cumberland.

Most of her family was missing. Rob had surrendered to King Edward in January, like he said he would. Christina had received a letter not long after announcing his marriage to Elizabeth de Burgh. It was a good match. Rob's new wife was the daughter of one of the most powerful lords of Ireland. Elizabeth's father also a close friend of the English Crown, Rob could not have placed himself in a better position.

Walking with Seton down the aisle, Christina noted the faces present. There were lords, bishops and men who had fought with Wallace. Spotting Mary at the front, Neil and Áed beside her, she smiled. Their smirks beamed back at her. They were not supposed to be there, but they came nonetheless. Perhaps she was not forsaken after all.

Music and laughter poured from the hall. The celebration was in full swing, drunken mormaers and knights filling the grounds. The irony of where she would spend her wedding night was not lost on her. It was not so long ago that she had fought against marrying a man in Kildrummy Castle. Glancing around the room at all the faces, men and women from different houses and lands sitting side-by-side, she found that this time she did not mind. This time, it was her choice.

"Lady Christina."

She barely heard his voice above the noise. Turning, she found David Moray standing across from her in front of the table. He had been elected as Bishop of Moray by Rob and the Red Comyn. It was one of the few good things they had accomplished as guardians. Noticing the young boy standing with him, she smiled.

"I have someone I want you to meet." He placed his hands on the boy's shoulders. "This is Andrew Moray, Lord of Avoch, Petty and Bothwell."

Her face fell. She kept her eyes on the child for a moment longer before she looked to the bishop for an explanation. He simply held her gaze.

Christina had heard that Andrew's wife had given birth to a son a few years prior. It made her happy, knowing how important it was for Andrew to continue his House. But the thought that she would meet his child had never crossed her mind. Looking at him now, she saw the resemblance. She was just about to greet him when Seton beat her to it.

"You look too young to be a lord," he said. Seton leaned on the table towards the boy. "Are you certain you can lead men?"

He contemplated the question with all the seriousness a four-year-old could muster. His eyes never left Seton's face. Eventually, he nodded. "Yes."

Seton smiled. He reclined back into his chair. "You are like your father then. Good."

As the bishop left, taking the young Lord of Avoch with him, Christina found herself watching her husband. Seton did not seem to notice. He took a drink of the ale before him. Lowering the cup from his mouth, he caught her stare out of the corner of his eye. He set the drink down and turned.

She said nothing, resting her chin in her hand as her eyes roamed every inch of his face. When she decided to marry him, she told herself it was because she needed a husband to protect her. But that was not the whole truth. She needed him, yes, but she wanted him more.

As if he knew what she was thinking, he reached out, his fingers gently wrapping around the exposed skin on her wrist. She kept her face where it was. He ran his thumb against the side of her cheek. Her heartbeat quickened. They were interrupted by the sound of someone clearing their throat.

She refused to look. The smirk on Seton's face grew. He turned to whoever was waiting behind them. Sighing inwardly, she followed his gaze.

Alexander Fraser grinned back at her. "It's time."

The hall erupted the moment they stood. Whistles and shouts of encouragement filled the air. Unbeknownst to everyone else, it was not the bedchamber they were heading towards, but that did nothing to prevent the heat from rising in her cheeks. Her backside burned as they left the hall. Following Fraser up the stairs, she stepped onto the top floor of the keep and opened the door.

The conversation stopped as she entered the room. It was quite cramped, mormaers and lords filling the chairs that lined the walls. Not waiting for an invitation, she walked forward and took an empty seat.

It was not her idea to hold council at her wedding. After Seton had agreed to marry her, she wrote to John Soules, the new Guardian of Scotland, to ask for permission. His reply was quick. Their union was approved. She had already made plans to get married in Garioch when the letters came.

The bishops of Glasgow, Moray and St Andrews would be attending her wedding, as would the mormaers of Lennox, Atholl, Menteith, Mar, Buchan and Badenoch. By the time the buannachann arrived from Garmoran, bearing gifts from Cairistíona nic Ruaidhrí, Christina knew she had wasted her efforts. Even if all these men were coming simply to watch her wed, the Bass could not hold them all.

"I had hoped your brother's surrender would be temporary."

Christina had barely sat down when the Mormaer of Atholl began. Seton took the chair next to her. She looked at the mormaer expectantly. He continued.

"Truth be known, I thought he might be submitting simply to marry Elizabeth de Burgh."

A few heads nodded in agreement.

"But he is not here, even when others from your family are. There is no denying it. He has chosen England."

Hearing the murmur around the room, her mind drifted to Neil and Áed in the hall. She had seen their drunken faces at a table not far from where she had sat moments ago. They seemed to be enjoying themselves immensely, fists pounding in time with the music, voices raised in song. She hoped no trouble came of their presence here.

Faces waiting for her to respond, she looked at the mormaer and asked, "What would you like me to say?"

His brow furrowed. He did not reply.

"Would it make a difference if my brother submitted for love? Would it change anything if he simply had enough of the fighting?" She glanced around the room. "Tell me what you would like to hear, and I will say it."

The room was silent.

She exhaled. "Rob is for England. That is all. Reasons change nothing." She straightened in the chair. "I know it is difficult to accept. But I suggest we focus our attention on matters within our grasp."

It did not take long for the conversation to shift to John Balliol. Everyone knew he was a free man in France. He had been released from papal custody a year earlier, and still, he did not return. Christina had her reservations, but she kept quiet. They needed someone to unite them. As much as she did not want it to be John Balliol, he was the only king they had.

In the end, they decided to send a delegation to Paris. They had the time. Rob's submission pleased the English king enough to offer the Scots a nine-month truce. John Soules, James Stewart, Bishop Lamberton and the Mormaer of Buchan would journey to France. The Red Comyn would act as sole guardian in their absence. The kingdom would be prepared for war.

The meeting finished, Christina rose to leave. The Red Comyn stopped her at the door. She wanted to ignore him and follow Seton, who was already halfway down the stairs. Though she and the Red Comyn were on the same side, she had no desire to help him. His actions over the past few years were selfish and short-sighted. He was equally responsible for the damage his rivalry with Rob caused. Not wanting to repeat the same mistakes, she set her dislike for him aside. She waited for him to speak.

As if he could feel her impatience, he was brief. "We need Norway. We cannot arm ourselves without iron and steel. Norway has what we need."

She knew what he was asking. Though her older sister was no longer the Queen of Norway, Isabel still had power in the Norwegian court and with the merchants. All Christina had to do was ask for assistance. "I will write to her."

He smiled. He opened his mouth to reply but Jardine inserting himself between them interrupted him.

Christina stared up at the man from Annandale. His face exceptionally close to hers, she could smell the mead wafting off him.

He pointed a finger at her. His voice was low. "You will not be Lady Christina Seton until you walk down those stairs and into that bedchamber."

He was bold when he was drunk. Then again, he was the same sober. She could practically hear the grins splitting on the faces around them.

Undaunted by her irritation, Jardine continued. "I suggest you go before that man changes his mind."

She could not be mad. A smile crept over her lips. There was something she had been thinking about doing for a long, long time.

CHAPTER EIGHTEEN

SEATED ATOP HER horse, Christina watched the water. Ships moved slowly by. Their sails open, wooden hulls glided silently on the Firth of Forth. Her eyes caught sight of a large vessel entering the harbour. Spotting the Norwegian flag above it, she turned her horse and descended into the town.

Almost a year had passed since her wedding at Kildrummy. Their truce with England had expired, and her sister Isabel had not let her down. The iron she sent was not as much as Christina had hoped for. Norway's approach to their conflict with England was more hesitant now that Isabel was the queen mother. When her husband died four years prior, Isabel had no son to take the throne. Her husband's brother became king instead, and the new King of Norway was not eager to anger his English counterpart.

Christina met the ship at the docks. Seton was already there. He and other men loaded the crates onto the waiting carts. It was the third shipment her sister had sent. Christina doubted they would receive another. Edward would most likely return in the spring. She calculated what they had. She did not think it would be enough. A horse galloped down the wooden landing towards her. She looked up as the rider dismounted. The crest of Douglas decorated his cloak.

"Lady Christina." He did not hesitate to approach. His face was flushed, as if he had been riding all night. "John Segrave has been spotted crossing the border at Norham." The words rushed out of him. "The English army is with him."

She did not need a moment to understand what it meant. She had guessed wrong – Edward was not waiting to start his campaign. Scotland was not ready. She searched the docks, looking for Alexander Fraser. He had already left with half the shipment. The only one mounted, she pressed her heels into her horse.

She rode as fast as she dared. The path slick with mud, people glared at her as she passed. Reaching the edge of the town, she did not slow as she entered the trees. She caught a glimpse of the carts up ahead. She urged her horse forward.

"Fraser!"

Riding at the front of the train, he barely heard her, but it was enough to make him pause. His head turned as she galloped by the wagons. She pulled to a stop beside him.

"The English army rides for Edinburgh."

She did not need to say anything else. Fraser sprinted down the road, dirt kicking up behind him. Catching her breath, Christina watched him go. She hoped he reached the Red Comyn in time.

She had returned to Garioch when news of the battle at Roslin reached her. With a force of thirty thousand men, John Segrave led the English into the Lowlands, trying to find out what the Scots were doing. The Red Comyn rode all night to meet him. It was a slaughter, and not for the English. Using the cover of darkness and his knowledge of the land, the Red Comyn and his army of eight thousand eliminated the three English divisions one-by-one. They showed no mercy, cutting down all who fled. By the time it was over, bodies strewn across the fields and into the trees, less than two thousand English soldiers still had air in their lungs. Segrave was taken hostage and thrown into a dungeon. Thinking of how Edward would have to pay a large sum to get him back, Christina smiled and set down the letter.

"What do we have here?"

Sitting near the hearth in the Bass, the cold spring day kept them inside. Seton was next to her. His tall frame relaxed in the chair. Hearing the voice behind them, a smile emerged on his face. Christina turned in surprise and stood.

William Wallace walked towards them. His long strides made the room seem small. Coming to a stop, he grinned at her.

"I go to France to gather support for our kingdom, and this is what I come back to." He glanced over at Seton. "The two of you snuggled up like bunnies in a burrow. No wonder we are losing the war."

She smiled, not bothered by his teasing. He could say anything he wanted to her. Gone to France for the past three years, she had stopped waiting for him to return. He looked older but more rested. She hoped this meant he was ready to lead them once again.

He took a chair out from the table. Sitting down in front of them, he got to the point. "I saw John Balliol in France."

The light-heartedness was gone, his face suddenly serious. Christina could not help but notice that he had not called John king.

"The French have entered into treaty negotiations with England. They will stand by us no longer." He extended his legs out in front of him and leaned back into the chair. "John will not return. He will not be King of Scots again."

Christina did not know what to think. On one hand, she was relieved. Scotland would not be led by a feeble king. But the consolation of Wallace's words was fleeting. The throne was empty. There was no king to claim it. She knew just what the Red Comyn would try and do.

❧

The Red Comyn never got the chance to take the crown. Before the ink was dry on the Treaty of Paris, the alliance between France and England complete, Edward invaded.

He conquered the Lowlands easily and continued north. Wallace harassed the soldiers Edward left behind. The outlaw was merely an irritation. It did nothing to deter the English king. Perth fell in July. Montrose, Dundee, Brechin and Aberdeen submitted a month later. Riding undeterred to Badenoch, Edward took young Andrew Moray hostage. The Red Comyn was unable to stop him. By the time he returned to the Lowlands in the fall, the Highlands were vanquished. It was over. The Scottish rebellion was finished. The only one still willing to fight was William Wallace.

Led by the Red Comyn himself, the Scots surrendered to Edward on the ninth day of February in the year one thousand three hundred and four. Taking Rob's advice, Edward allowed the disobedient nobles to keep their lands. They could even get their revoked English estates back for a fine.

But for William Wallace, there would be no surrender. Declaring him an outlaw, Edward demanded the knight from

Renfrewshire be brought to him, sending packs of men north to hunt him down. There was no reasoning with Edward. He was determined to enact his wrath on the one man who always stood in his way. But no matter who or how many men Edward dispatched to find the outlaw, Rob among them, they always came up empty. The Scots would not give up the only man who refused to swear loyalty to an English king.

A fist pounding on the door broke her from her sleep. She felt Seton rise from the bed. The distant murmuring of a quiet conversation reached her. Hearing the door creak shut, she pulled the covers closer to go back to sleep. Seton threw the blankets back.

"Christina, get up."

The uncertainty in his voice woke her faster than the sudden cold. His face was full of anguish. Concerned, she wrapped her shawl around her and followed him down the stairs.

Cailean and Jardine waited for her in the hall. She did not recognize the third man, his back to her as she entered the room. The moment he turned, she stared in surprise at the likeness. He looked exactly like his father.

"Lady Christina."

The last time she had seen James Douglas, he was sailing away to France, trying to escape the English king. He had been a child then. Now, as he stepped towards her, eliminating the space between them, she saw he was a boy no longer. She smiled at the man before her. "James."

The agony in his face disappeared for a moment before it returned. "You remember me."

She smiled again. "How could I forget the Lord of Douglas?"

He did not respond. The despair in his face only deep-ened. He looked away. When his eyes met hers once again, he was calm. "Bishop Lamberton has sent me to tell you something."

He paused again. Her happiness as seeing him dissipated. Every second he did not speak caused her more concern. She wanted to reach out and shake the words from him. Instead, she waited, wrapping her arms around herself. Her fingers dug into her skin.

"William Wallace has been captured."

Each word felt like a slap.

"They have taken him to the Tower."

She stepped back. Seton placed his hand on her neck. The pressure steadied her. It only took her a moment to react. Pushing the distress from her mind, she turned and sprinted from the hall.

She was on her horse and riding for Carrick before sun-light broke through the sky. The journey was silent. She tried not to think of anything as they headed south – not how long ago Wallace had been taken, not how many days Lamberton had waited before sending James to Garioch. But it was no use. Every time she lay her head down for the night, sleep eluded her. She could not stop picturing Wallace imprisoned in the Tower of London. By the time she rode through the gates of Turnberry Castle, dark skies looming above, she did not care if Rob was for England. He would help her with this, whether he wanted to or not.

He was in the hall. His daughter and his new wife sat beside him.

Neil and Randolph stood in surprise as she entered.

Unclasping the cloak from around her neck, she yanked it off her shoulders and threw it onto the table.

"Leave us."

They hesitated for only a moment. The sound of footsteps filled the hall. Elizabeth was still in her seat. Christina watched her look to Rob for instruction. Her husband kept his gaze on his sister before him. Taking Marjorie by the hand, the new Countess of Carrick walked out of the room.

A few moments passed before Christina moved. Her hands shook as she gathered her thoughts. She stepped forward slowly. Her feet stopped when she noticed the redness of Rob's eyes.

"It is too late."

His words rang around the room. The sound echoed in her head. Unable to deny the sorrow in his face, she refused to believe him. "No."

Rob pushed himself from his chair. The closer he came, the tighter her chest felt. It was as if each step he took weighed her down.

He stood before her. "You do not understand." His voice was angry. Taking a letter from his pocket, he placed it firmly in her hand. She barely heard him repeat himself. "It is too late."

Staring at the piece of paper in her grasp, she shook her head. She did not want to read it. She was too afraid of what it might say. But Rob's word would not be enough. Her stomach clenching in fear, she opened the letter.

Though James Stewart's writing was straight and to-the-point, his words painted a vivid picture. Wallace had been delivered to Carlisle at the beginning of August. Eager to show off the man who had plagued the English for longer than any other, John Segrave led Wallace on a seventeen-day journey south to London.

The court proceedings that followed were just for show. Edward denied Wallace rights he had given other Scots at trial. The crimes charged against him were long and varied. It took no time for the court to find him guilty.

The first sentence of death was given for robberies, homicides and felonies. Wallace disputed none of them. The second was for countless depravities committed against God and the Church; again, none of which Wallace denied. But when the third sentence of death was called, for outlawry and treason against his king, he kept quiet no longer. Wallace declared it was not possible for him to be guilty of treason. He had never sworn fealty to the English crown – not for a single moment of his life was he Edward's subject. An outlaw he may be, but a traitor he was not.

It made no difference. Stripped naked, he was tied to a horse and dragged through the city. For over four miles, his body scraped against the road, the streets lined with onlookers as he was brought to his death.

They hung him first. The rope closed off air to his body until he almost asphyxiated. Cutting him down alive, they waited for him to gain consciousness before they severed his genitals. He was ripped open from groin to nape. They took their time removing his innards. They pulled out his intestines, lungs, liver and finally his heart – the vessel that pumped life into Scotland herself.

While Wallace was dead, his soul finally set free, Edward did not stop. Intent on destroying as much of him he could, the king ordered that his organs be burned and his body emptied of everything else. A shell of a man was all that remained. Dragging him up to the block, they chopped off his head.

Rob reached out and gripped her shoulder. Unable to look away from the piece of paper that gave her so much pain, she did not move. Her mind struggled to make sense of it. No Scot would have willingly given Wallace up. How had they found him?

"Christina."

Rob's voice interrupted her spiralling anger. Folding up the letter, she did not acknowledge him. His grasp tightened. She reluctantly raised her head.

"I made a mistake."

She did not understand what he meant.

"I should not have done it." His face was full of contrition. "I should have never surrendered to Edward."

She stepped away then. His hand fell down. She could not believe he was saying this to her. Not now, not after they had lost so much. The letter shook in her clenched fist.

"Forgive me."

She kept her eyes down. She had no desire to look at him. He did not give her a choice when he walked up and cupped her face in his hands.

"I need you." His eyes pleaded with her. "Please, Christina. Help me make this right."

She could not stand there any longer. Prying his fingers from her face, she walked out of the hall and rode for Garioch.

It could have been anyone's leg. Long and broad, it was beginning to yellow as it hung in Stirling square. She was too far away to see the plaque, but she did not need to read what it said. She knew just who that limb belonged to. Her horse slowed to a stop.

She heard Seton say her name somewhere behind her, but she remained where she was, unable to look away from the flesh nailed to the post. English soldiers stood around it. Their hands menacingly held the hilts of their swords as a crowd began to gather. Shouts of anger burst into the air. Christina turned her horse away.

They found his arm in Perth, but they did not slow to look. It would be displayed the same – the dismembered appendage nailed to the post, a sign stating that it belonged to "the Outlaw William Wallace." She wanted to kill the soldiers and burn down the post, give Wallace the burial he deserved. But he was not hers to take. Back within the walls of the Bass, she lowered herself wearily from her horse. A familiar face met her in the hall.

Alexander Fraser stood as she entered. For a moment, she did not move, simply staring in disbelief at the man before her. She strode towards him. Her arms wrapped around him tightly.

"Were you there?"

Letting go of her, Fraser sat back down. He had rejoined Wallace upon the outlaw's return from France. He had been with him at Earnside, the last skirmish Wallace had with the English before the former guardian disappeared. Christina had not been concerned when word reached her that he had vanished. It would take him time to recover and build a new army. But when James Douglas appeared to tell her about Wallace, she had not known who else had been taken. She was relieved Fraser was still free.

"No," he replied. He looked as she felt – tired and worn. "But I know who it was." He stared at her. "I know who betrayed Wallace."

She froze.

"John Menteith."

She took the chair across from him. Slowly sitting down, she could not quite believe it. John Menteith had fought with Wallace against the English many times. He was kin to the Stewarts. His treachery made no sense. He had driven English soldiers from Lennox only two years ago. Her confusion quickly morphed into anger. It did not matter. If she ever saw John Menteith again, she would kill him herself.

"There is something else you should know."

Fraser's voice made her look up.

"When Wallace was taken, he had…" He hesitated. "Certain letters on his person."

Apprehension ran through her. "What do they say?"

"A few are from France, from King Philip and John Balliol. Others are from the Kirk, Lamberton and Wishart in particular. But he also kept some of yours."

He paused to give her a moment to absorb the information. While she had not been so foolish as to sign her name, the details in her letters were enough to identify where they had come from. She did not need Fraser to say it. It would not take long for the self-proclaimed Hammer of the Scots to figure out what she had done.

She glanced back at Seton. The concern on his face was clear. Nodding slowly, she took a breath. There was only one thing left to do.

CHAPTER NINETEEN

SNOW FELL DOWN around her as she entered Lochmaben for the first time in nine years. The land had changed significantly. Her grandfather's castle lay in ruins. King Edward had built a larger, stronger fortress in its place. Directing her horse around the rubble, she cantered through the gate.

She found her family in the hall. Gathered around the table, they quieted as she entered. It was not just Rob, Neil, and Mary who had come. Edward, Thomas, Alexander, and Matilda were present as well. Their father had died two years prior. Matilda was already nineteen. Rob now the head of their kindred, nothing would keep them apart.

Her eyes drifting over the changed faces, Christina smiled. It did not matter how much time had passed. They had come when she called. House Bruce was united once more. Not just as a family, but as Scots. It made all the difference.

Neil and Thomas rode for Dalswinton Castle the following morning. The Comyn stronghold was just west of Lochmaben, not even half a day's ride away. If everything went according to plan, the Red Comyn would meet Rob at

Greyfriars Kirk in Dumfries on the tenth day of February in the year one thousand three hundred and six.

Standing with Fraser and Cailean at the door of the keep, she watched the men mount their horses. The thought of Rob and the Red Comyn being in the same room made her nervous. But as Seton looked back at her, sitting atop his horse next to her brother, she relaxed. Rob would not be going into the church alone. Seton would be with him. She trusted her husband to keep the man who led her family safe and calm.

The day of the meeting arrived. Christina restlessly paced the grounds. She needed this to work. If the two most powerful families in Scotland could not come to an agreement, it was over. They could not survive another rebellion against England if the Comyns were not on their side. Rob's offer was simple – one man would take possession of all Bruce and Comyn lands, and the other would be king. Wealth or power, those were the choices. Walking once more through the bailey, she did not know which one the Red Comyn would pick.

It turned out to be neither. Walking towards the keep, a shout from the wall went up. Áed galloped through the gate. He had left with Rob, and now he was back. Not knowing what it meant, Christina stayed where she was. He jumped off his horse and ran into the tower.

Men poured out moments later. Fraser was among them. They put on their armour as fast as they could. Áed returning, he walked towards her. This time, there was no humour in his face.

"The Red Comyn is dead."

She was not certain she heard correctly.

"He was struck down at the altar." The words poured out of him. "Rob has taken Dumfries and heads for Buittle Castle. Neil and Thomas have returned to Dalswinton to attack it." He paused to glance behind him at the men readying their horses. "We ride for Tibbers."

She felt as if she was outside her body, watching the world crash down around some other poor soul. This was not what they had decided. This was not what they had planned. But as she watched the men follow Áed out of the gate, her brothers Edward and Alexander flanking him, she told herself to move past it. Their plans did not matter now. The Red Comyn was dead and Rob was responsible. Retribution was coming for them all.

Rob and his men seized control of southwest Scotland quickly. The castles of Dunaverty, Ayr and Tibbers fell before the month was over. Rob wrote to King Edward, telling him to recognize him as King of Scots. Edward refused. When word reached Christina that the English had been driven out of Rothesay in Lennox, she gathered the women and just enough men for an armed escort. She was not going to wait at Lochmaben to be taken hostage by Edward or the irate Comyns of Galloway. Charging Jardine with the defense of the castle, they rode for Paisley and the safety of House Stewart.

Christina closed her eyes as she sat in silence. Other than the clergymen, there was no one else inside the church. Candles cast light around the nave. She felt unsettled, her mind and body refusing to rest. The door to the chapel opened behind her. Reluctantly leaving her peaceful state, she turned to look.

Relief washed over her the moment she saw Seton in the

entranceway. Smiling at her, he stepped through. Christina stood to greet her husband. Her happiness disappeared at the sight of Rob behind him.

He came towards her, the sound of each step grating on her nerves. She had not realized how angry she was with him. He stopped in front of her. She glared back.

Rob looked like he had been dragged through the mud. His clothes were dirty and his face was unwashed. The bags under his eyes were darker than hers. Staring at the man who had changed everything, she saw no weariness or regret. Only determination.

"I know this is not what you wanted."

She kept her mouth shut as more men entered the church, Roger Kirkpatrick and Alexander Fraser among them. She did not need to state the obvious.

"But this is where we are." He stared back at her. When he spoke again, his voice was quiet. "The Bishop of Glasgow has absolved me of my sin. I am to be crowned king in ten days. Tell me you are with me."

She felt every pair of eyes in the church turn to her. Not a sound was made, the silence uncomfortable and heavy. She looked only at Rob. She wanted to lash out – to tell him he was a fool. His temper and hatred for the Red Comyn had ruined everything. But as furious as she was with him, they could not go back now. King Edward would not forgive them for what they had done. They either took the throne or died like Wallace. Shoving her anger aside, she stepped forward and cupped his face in her hands. "I am with you, brother. Until the end."

They rode for Scone the next day. The train of people that followed grew longer with each town they passed, men and women flocking to the banner Rob raised in rebellion. Robert Wishart, the Bishop of Glasgow, travelled with them. As soon as Christina saw James Douglas ride up, stopping before Rob on the road, she knew Lamberton had received the message. There was just one more person she was waiting for.

Pacing along the grass, she glanced over at the people already gathered atop Moot Hill. In the whole of Scotland, there was not a place that mattered more. Though not as large or extravagant as Elgin Cathedral, Scone Abbey dominated the landscape, its towers jutting up and over the trees. The spire that adorned the central tower was like a singular point into the heavens. A wide ditch encircled the mound upon which kings were made. Every King of Scots since Iber Scot had been crowned here. John Balliol had been the last, fourteen long years ago. Looking back out at the road, the darkness preventing her from seeing much farther, she prayed Fraser made it back in time.

She had sent him into the Highlands with a message for David Moray. As much as the Comyns were against them, now more than ever, they needed the north. Scotland would not survive a war fighting both themselves and England. The past ten years had proven that. Though David Moray was a Comyn, he was also a man of the Kirk. She hoped his duty to God was strong enough to make him forsake his blood.

"Christina."

She turned at Seton's voice and watched him come towards her.

"It is time."

Her hopes fell. Fraser had assured her he would return in time for Rob's coronation. But it was too late, he was not here and they needed to begin. Disappointed, she walked with her husband back towards the gathering. She stopped as soon as she heard the horses.

Fraser almost rode into her. Pulling to an abrupt halt, he jumped down from his horse.

Christina smiled as soon as she saw David Moray behind him. But when the third rider came into view, blond curls breaking away from the long braid that sat on her shoulder, she looked to Fraser for an explanation.

He grinned knowingly at her. "I brought you a gift."

The young woman dropped from her horse. She straightened her cloak before she stepped forward. Throwing back her hood, Christina stared in disbelief.

It had been a while since Christina had seen Isabella MacDuff of Fife. About Matilda's age, she was married to the Mormaer of Buchan and was now considered to be a Comyn. But that was not why Christina had a hard time believing Isabella was there. For longer than Christina could remember, a Macduff had crowned every King of Scots. With Edward taking Isabella's brother, the young Mormaer of Fife, hostage two years ago, Christina had thought it impossible for the tradition to continue. Someone else would have to place the crown on Rob's head. But as she looked at the Countess, stubborn conviction emanating back, she knew Edward had not accounted for this. There was only one question she needed to ask. "Why are you here?"

Lifting her chin, Isabella smiled. Her face was radiant in the moonlight. "I am here to crown a king."

Mormaers, bishops, lords and knights knelt in revered silence to witness Robert Bruce become King of Scots.

Isabella MacDuff of Fife stood beside him in the middle of the sanctum. Placing a crown on his head, the voice of a Highland seanchaidh called out God's blessing on their new king. Christina would never forget the moment. After ten long years, Scotland had a king once more.

Her happiness was short-lived. Waking the next morning, Seton no longer in the bed beside her, she found him speaking with Rob in the hall. The two men turned as she entered. Rob gave her a strained smile. Her stomach filled with dread. She knew what that look meant.

"I am returning to the Lowlands."

On top of a hill not far from the river, Christina stood with her face turned upwards towards the sun. Her skin felt warm beneath its gaze. Hearing his voice, she lowered her chin to look at her husband.

He watched her intently. "We will secure the castles while the king continues north."

She stared back at him. King Edward would undoubtedly attack the fortresses in Annandale and Carrick first. The thought of Seton trapped in a castle with English soldiers all around did not ease her mind. "I will come with."

He smiled, the slow, light expression she had come to cherish covering his face. "No."

She looked away. Irritation surged through her. She had not gotten married so someone could tell her what to do. Seton placed his hand on the back of her neck. The feeling was warm and comforting. Her anger melted away as she lifted her eyes to his face.

"Now is not the time to be stubborn." He smirked at her. "I cannot have you in the Lowlands when Edward rides north. You need to stay with your brothers." The humour in his expression dropped away. He stared down at her. "If anything happens, go to the Orkneys." His eyes were serious. "Promise me, Christina."

For a while, she did not reply. She simply looked back at him. She was not sure she could do what he wanted. He was asking her to run away, to give up fighting, to leave him and everyone else behind. Unwilling to do that, she shook her head.

He sighed in frustration. He did not like her answer. "Edward has declared that you, the queen, the princess and your sisters are to be treated as outlaws. That means-"

She did not want to hear it. She tried to move away, but the hand around her neck held her still.

He lowered his face towards hers. "It means, Christina," his voice was low, "that any man can do anything they want to you. Without punishment. Without consequence." His gaze never moved from hers. "So when Cailean tells you to go north, you will do as he says."

She pulled back. This time, he did not try to stop her. She was angry – angry with him, angry at Cailean. They had planned and discussed this without her. It was her life. She had not fought this hard and this long for a king simply to be pushed aside and told what to do. She would rip the crown from Rob's head before she let that happen.

She started to turn away before she stopped. Seton remained where he was, giving her the distance she wanted. Meeting his gaze once more, she asked, "How will you find me?"

His quiet smile began again.

"If I go north and you go south, how will you know where I am?"

He stepped towards her slowly. Taking her face in his hands, his fingers lovingly brushed the hair back from her eyes. "Go wherever you want," he said, his voice thick with emotion. "It does not matter. God could not keep me away from you."

Staring up at him, her heart was full. In all the plans she made, she had not prepared for the possibility that they would be apart. She needed him, but it seemed Rob needed him more. She watched the light dance across his green eyes in silence. She hoped he was right.

Seton left before dawn. Stood in the grounds, Christina watched him ride from Scone, his brothers John and Humphrey beside him. She wished she could run after him and tell him not to go, but she remained where she was. He said he would come back. Following his frame as it disappeared from view, she decided that his word was enough. She would hold him to it.

Rob took the army to Perth and then Dundee, both burghs falling in the first week of April. Edward sent Aymer Valence, the Earl of Pembroke and brother-in-law to the murdered Red Comyn, to deal with the rebellious king in the north. They were in Kildrummy Castle when word reached them that Valence had recaptured Perth. Christina watched Rob as he contemplated his decision. They could not avoid the English army forever. Eventually, they would have fight and prove their worth, as Scots and as free men. Now was as good a time as any.

Marching his men south to Methven, Rob left Christina and the ladies of the court behind. For over a month, they waited. Not a single man returned to Kildrummy. When the messenger finally came, everyone ran to meet him at the gate. Rob was in Aberdeen, and he needed them to come now. The horses readied, they rode for the coast.

It was not what Christina expected. Their army was decimated, over four thousand dead. The bishops Lamberton and Wishart had been captured, along with Fraser, Randolph and others still. One look at Rob's embittered face told her all she needed to know. They had no men; they could not fight. The only thing left to do was run.

Sending Matilda north with David Moray, they travelled west to the safety of the isles. But they never reached them. The MacDougalls of Argyll and Lorne, cousins to the Comyns and sworn enemies of House Bruce, stopped them in Dalrigh. Barely able to fight their way out, they escaped into the hills of Atholl. Whatever Rob's plan had been when he had taken the throne, it was in shambles now. As soon as Christina saw Cailean approach, the look of warning in his eyes all too familiar, she knew what it meant. It was time to go to the Orkneys and seek Norway's protection.

They headed north once again. Rob did not come with. Led by Neil and the Mormaer of Atholl, Christina and the other women arrived in Kildrummy in time to hear that Valence and his English army were already in Aberdeen. Neil stayed behind to defend the castle while they fled deeper into the Highlands. They rode through Mar and then Moray, entering Ross as they passed by Loch Ness. If they could make it to Duthac Chapel in Tain and enter the stone boundary around the sanctuary, no one would touch them – not even King Edward himself. Crossing through the line, their cheeks flushed and bodies spent, Christina smiled. They did not have far to go.

The night was quiet as she stood outside. The others were

in the chapel, sitting around a single candle, their only light in the dark. They would stay here until Cailean returned, protected by the sacred sanctuary dedicated to sheltering fugitives. Cailean had already left to meet the ship that would bring them farther north. She could not wait to see Matilda and know that she was safe. All she had to do was survive the next three days.

She slept poorly, the hard bench underneath her sore frame providing no comfort. She could hear the others squirming as they tossed and turned. Unable to take it any longer, she sat up in frustration. Her neck ached. She placed her hand on the back of it. The doors of the chapel burst open.

William, the Mormaer of Ross, stared back at her. He looked around the room. The others rose.

Christina watched in disbelief as men poured into the church.

"Elizabeth de Burgh, Marjorie Bruce, Christina Bruce." The Mormaer of Ross' voice rang out clearly as he named them one-by-one. "Mary Bruce, Isabella MacDuff of Fife and John Strathbogie, Mormaer of Atholl."

The only man with them cut the Mormaer of Ross off. "You are breaking sanctuary!" the Mormaer of Atholl yelled at him.

The Mormaer of Ross continued on undeterred. "I hereby arrest you on the orders of King Edward, rightful ruler of England, Wales, Ireland and Scotland." He paused and glanced over each of them again. "May God have mercy on your souls."

Marched outside, they were placed back onto their horses and promptly led south. They rode through the night, the Mormaer of Ross determined to get them to the English garrison at Urquhart Castle as quickly as he could.

Arriving at the fortress along the loch, Christina was forced off her horse. It was not lost on her that she could see Badenoch from where she stood. It was quite fitting. The land of the Red Comyn stared back as they were handed over to the English. If Wallace were standing here with her, he would laugh.

"Lady Christina."

She turned at the quiet voice. The man who had helped her down stood before her. His head was bent, his fingers moving slowly as he untied the rope around her wrists. When he glanced up at her again, she recognized him. Named Hugh, he was the Mormaer of Ross' seventeen-year-old son. She gave him her undivided attention.

"Your husband, Christopher Seton, was captured at Loch Doon."

For a moment, she forgot to breathe. Then her mind filled with Seton. She wondered if he was all right. Forcing herself to remain calm, she focused on the young man in front of her once more. "When?"

"Two weeks ago."

The ropes broke loose. Her wrists free, she rubbed them fervently, trying to get the feeling of twine off her skin. She needed to figure out where Seton was. Most likely, he had been taken to Dumfries, but she doubted he had remained there long. Edward would not have left him there with Annandale and Carrick so close. Seton was probably in Carlisle or even in London by now, awaiting trial.

An English soldier walked forward. He shackled her wrists in irons.

Christina hardly noticed. All she had to do was get a message to Rob. He would find Seton and figure out a way to free him. Then everything would be all right. She was thinking of where they might stop on their way to England when she noticed that Hugh was still standing in front of her.

The look on his face concerned her. Trying to keep her voice steady, she asked, "Is there something else?"

He nodded. Locking eyes with her once more, he brought her worst fears to life. "They hung him."

He kept talking, but she heard nothing else. The sudden ringing in her ears drowned out his voice. She felt dizzy, as if the ground was spinning beneath her feet. The soldier led her to the carriage. The others already waiting inside, she had no strength left to resist. The only sound she heard, as they were taken south to face judgment for their crimes against God and the English king, was her mouth gasping for air.

AUTHOR'S NOTE

Not much is known about Christina Bruce. Born in 1273 or 1278, historians believe she played an important part in the Scottish Wars of Independence.

But how could she not? The descendant of Celtic and Norman kings, almost every member of her family was spectacular in some way.

Some scholars claim that she did, in fact, marry Gartnait of Mar. Others say it could not have been her. What we do know is this: Christina was born to Marjorie, Countess of Carrick and Robert Bruce, Lord of Annandale, the sixth of his name. She married Sir Christopher Seton sometime between 1301 and 1305, and in 1306, she was captured and sent to England. She would spend the next eight years imprisoned in a nunnery.

I would tell you what happens next, but I don't want to ruin the story.

ACKNOWLEDGEMENTS

First and foremost, this book would not have been completed without Gill Watcham. You, my friend, are a delight and a real gem for driving my demanding arse all over Scotland. I owe the description and the feel of the landscape to you. From tussocks to berries, I have never laughed harder in my life. When I sell the movie rights, we will do it again. But with fancy hats and a butler for the luggage. You know how I overpack.

A special thanks to Skye Andersen and April Jenkins. Your encouragement and feedback kept me going. Even when I wanted to throw the story in the garbage and light it on fire.

The castle illustrations and the always-helpful answers to my never-ending questions are thanks to Joel Feenstra. Would you stop being good at everything? You are making the rest of us look bad.

And to Matt – as always, you were very unhelpful. Try harder next time, would you? Olive juice baby.

ABOUT THE AUTHOR

Raedene Jeannette Melin is a fiction writer and author of the new novel *To Crown A King*. Born in British Columbia, Canada, she holds a BA in History and a Master's in Integrated Studies. Her debut novel, *Las Hermanas*, published in 2018, won the National Indie Excellence Award for adventure fiction and placed as a finalist in the Next Generation Indie Book Awards. Infatuated with trees and fresh mountain air, Raedene lives in Salmon Arm with her husband and two dogs.

Visit Raedene online at www.rjmbooks.ca.
Find Raedene on Facebook and Instagram or follow her on Twitter @RJMBooks.